MORNING IN THE SHADE

After the doctor left the room, I found myself staring at the blank wall across from my hospital bed. The longer I stared at that wall, the surer I became that I could not depend on the stability of my own mind. I felt an irrepressible need to escape the confines of that barren room. I decided to take a walk.

It was mid-morning as I strolled the hospital grounds. Under the shade of a large hemlock tree, I found relief from the hot August sun. Sitting there, I thought that perhaps I would be alright after all. But I was distracted from my reverie by a vision passing before my line of sight. Was I hallucinating again? Having another one of my dreams? There, walking in front of me, was a Lamaist monk, his purple robes flowing in the breeze. As it occurred to me that none of the other patients seemed to notice him, the conviction that I was losing my mind was confirmed. Nevertheless, I decided to follow him. His walk was steady, purposeful, his path straight as an arrow. Suddenly I saw what he was leading me to. I stood behind him in awe—the question of my sanity no longer a concern . . .

The Vanderleigh Legacy

by Betty Caldwell

ZEBRA BOOKS
KENSINGTON PUBLISHING CORP.

ZEBRA BOOKS

are published by

KENSINGTON PUBLISHING CORP.
475 Park Avenue South
New York, N.Y. 10016

Printed in the United States of America

ONE

I stared into the muddy open pit which would become my father's grave. The drizzling rain had made a quagmire of the gravesite and rusty brown water seeped into the freshly laid footprints of the elderly minister and two grave diggers who stood there with me. I knew Dad would want to be buried in this rural New Jersey churchyard, beside my mother, but the circumstances made it seem such a cold and lonely ceremony.

I suddenly realized I had not heard a word Reverend Worthington had said. Standing there tall, thin, and ramrod straight, he was a misty portrait in gray: gray hair, gray suit, even his skin had an ashen tone. I tried to concentrate, to let his words come through, hoping they would be of some comfort, but he only seemed to be mumbling the same combination of indistinct sounds over and over again. He had never met my father and hadn't met me until yesterday. This was only a job to him.

There was a tightness in my throat and a heavy congested feeling around my eyes, as if I had been crying for days—but I had not cried at all. I was still numb from the shock of Dad's death. He couldn't leave me, not this way, not without pulling me under the protective wing of his arm, planting a noisy smacking kiss on the top of my head and saying, "Don't worry, Maggie! Everything's going to be all right."

My eyes misted at my selfish thoughts. Dad had died at forty-eight, much too young for a man of his energy and zest for life. Fate in the form of a senseless automobile accident had snuffed out the life of this vital human being with relentless finality. Here I stood, safe and alive, feeling sorry for myself and thinking only of how lost I will be without him to share my joys and problems. But isn't that the way death always is? The mourned one is beyond suffering; it is the survivor who must find a way to go on alone.

It was impossible for me to return to Cambodia, where I had spent most of my life. When the Khmer Rouge seized control of the government, Americans had no choice but to leave. We went first to Thailand, but then came back to New Jersey when Dad accepted the position as Director of the Asian Section of the University Museum. Until the fall term began, he had been working as a consultant to the wealthy historian Jonathan Vanderleigh on his large estate in southern New Jersey.

The minister's tremulous voice took on an inflection which signaled the end of his formal liturgy. My body stiffened involuntarily, preparing me for the final step of this ritual. The casket was lowered slowly into the grave and released clumsily into its eternal rest. A shovel full of muddy slush thrown upon his coffin grossly emphasized the stark finality. Each splash of mud against polished oak smothered me. I felt a suffocating tightness in my chest as though it refused to expand and draw in enough air to sustain me: as though I too should join my mother and father. We would all be together then, no one of us would ever be alone again. Eternally together.

The world began to spin.

"Miss Driscoll?" Reverend Worthington's gnarled and bony fingers grasped my arm. "Come, Miss Driscoll. You're much too pale. It's better to leave now. Come back again at a calmer time to say your goodbyes."

His unyielding grip on my arm made the world stand still while his words pulled my mind back into the present. I had come face to face with the bitter meaning of the world "final" and was left alone and afraid. I felt like a frightened five year old, lost in a dark and forbidding forest with no sense of where I had been or where I should go.

He released my arm. My body again felt firmly weighted to the earth. "Thank you for helping me bury my father, Reverend." I searched for kindness in his pale gray eyes, but could find no real warmth there, only professional courtesy. Nevertheless, I felt compelled to explain why I mourned my father alone: "He would want to be buried here beside my mother. We left twenty years ago and gradually lost touch with the people we knew."

"I understand, Miss Driscoll. Let me see you to your car."

"Thank you, no." I felt a strong urge to be away, to straighten out my thoughts. "I'll be fine." I immediately felt guilty for my rudeness and tried to soften the bluntness of my words. "I'll drop in to see you when I come back again, Reverend Worthington."

He nodded a patient, "Yes, I understand," as I turned away.

The many old and weathered gravemarkers bore testimony to the fact that I was not the first to lose a loved one. Dizziness and a wave of nausea swept over me as I passed near another newly covered grave and caught the distinctively funereal smell of carnations mixed with the odor of damp earth. Reverend Worthington was right, I should leave. I must learn to face my loneliness and look on it as a part of living, of being responsible for my own life and my own happiness. I must cope alone, almost a stranger in the country I left at the age of four.

I glanced to my right as I turned down the worn muddy path and saw a tall gaunt man draped in a wrinkled black raincoat. Although I hadn't noticed him earlier, I realized he must have been standing there during the graveside service. He stepped toward me.

"Miss Driscoll?" His haggard face, wet from the drizzling rain, was deeply etched with lines of tension and unhappiness.

"Yes?" My reply was hesitant, puzzled.

"Jonathan Vanderleigh. I don't mean to intrude on your grief, but I wanted to express my sympathy. Your father was a friend of mine."

"Mr. Vanderleigh!" I was surprised to see that he

seemed so much older than my Dad. It struck me as strange that he had stood so quietly in the background and had not introduced himself earlier. "If I'd known you were here I would have introduced you to Reverend Worthington."

"No need. I was late arriving and the service had begun. Come, I'll walk with you."

We walked in silence through the tree-studded graveyard of this small rural church. The damp fog seemed to close around us, walling us apart from the rest of the world. I did not feel at ease with this tense man. I was so turned inward with my grief I just couldn't focus on anything to say.

He finally spoke, relieving me of the responsibility. "I don't know what your plans are, Miss Driscoll, but I know how lonely you must be, having just returned to the States after all these years. You're welcome to spend some time with us until you feel more adjusted. You could even come today if you like."

"Thank you. You're very kind and thoughtful, but my world's in such a turmoil right now that I can only decide what to do for the next half hour: go back to our apartment. Beyond that short span of time, I have no plans and just don't want the pressure of making any until I've had some time to think."

"It's good to keep it that way for a while, I guess. Just take one step at a time. Would you like for me to come home with you now?"

"No. Thank you for thinking of it, but frankly I want to be alone."

"I understand. Come down when you can; just

consider it an open invitation. There's no need to call, just stop in where you're near Bleekston. Someone is always home. Oh yes, there are some things of your father's still there in his room. If it's okay with you, we'll pack them up and store them until you visit."

"Yes, that will be fine. I'll try to come soon, Mr. Vanderleigh."

"Well, I'll leave now. It's a long trip back home."

I looked around and could see no car. "May I take you somewhere, Mr. Vanderleigh?"

"Oh, no. I'm parked on a side street around the corner."

"I see." He held the car door for me and watched in silence as I pulled away. I looked in my rear view mirror and saw him turn to leave.

The foglike mist seemed to follow me as I maneuvered my small blue Toyota from the cemetery and drove along the narrow winding country roads towards the quiet little university town where I was born. I had only gone a few miles when my car suddenly coughed a few times, then gave a short gasp and died just as I pulled it onto the shoulder of the road. I started it up and drove a few more feet before it stopped again, this time for good.

My first reaction was fear. The fog, although not as heavy as it had been earlier at the church, was still around in isolated pockets. My car had carefully chosen one of those pockets in which to gasp and die. It's not very smart to stop in a fog; that's how multi-car pileups occur. I switched on my emergency blinkers and hoped it wouldn't be long before help came.

After about twenty minutes, I realized that no help would be offered by any of those cars passing me by; they too knew better than to stop in a fog. It was equally dangerous, but I felt I had no choice but to get out and find a phone. I hadn't walked fifteen feet beyond my car when a gaily decorated low-slung sports car pulled in front of me. I didn't know what to expect from someone who would drive around in a car like that.

"Can I be of any help, Miss?"

I hadn't known what to expect, but a guardian angel was what I got. "You certainly can! My car—it just quit on me. I have no idea what's wrong with it."

"Well, let me take a look. If I can't figure it out, I'll go on to the station about three miles farther down the road and send someone back to take care of it for you."

"Oh thanks. Thank you very much."

He pulled a rubberized yellow poncho from the back seat of his car, threw it around his shoulders and climbed out. A tall guardian angel at that, I thought, as I looked at the over six feet of blond-haired, blue-eyed teenager who was gallantly coming to my rescue.

"If you'll give me your keys, I'll take a look."

"Oh yes! Here they are." I fumbled in my bag and pulled out the bunch of keys.

He stood there for a moment shuffling through the keys on the ring.

"Oh, I'm sorry!" I blushed as I suddenly realized

that I had not selected the ignition key from the jumbled bunch of about ten keys I had handed him.

He unlocked the car, slid behind the wheel, and turned the key to start the ignition. "Hey, you're out of gas."

I hadn't even thought to check that. "But that's impossible! I just filled it this morning and I've driven less than thirty miles since then."

"Uhmm. Do you have a flashlight? Maybe you have a leak in the tank."

"It's in the glove compartment." He looked at the tank. No leak.

"What could have happened?" I asked in confusion. I had filled the tank just before I left the university this morning on my way to the church.

"Well, you know how it is these days, with the price of gas and all. Someone probably borrowed your gas. Siphoned it out. It happens. I have a gas can in my trunk. Why don't you wait here in your car, and I'll fill it up at the station and come right back."

"Thanks," I handed him a five dollar bill. "Just a couple of gallons. I'll stop by the station and get the tank filled."

"Be right back."

I tried to console myself that I was actually lucky. Something really drastic could have happened to the car, and I didn't want to face a major problem like that right now. I decided to have the station check to make sure there was no leak. It was hard to imagine anyone just stealing the gas right out of my tank—near a church, no less! Oh well, maybe I have a lot to learn about America.

The young man was back in less than fifteen minutes. I thanked him profusely, to his obvious embarrassment, and after a stop at the station, I was soon on my way. The whole delay was a little more than three-quarters of an hour. It could have been worse without my guardian angel.

A blinding downpour came in on the heels of the fog and turned what should have been a leisurely half-hour trip into a tense two-hour battle through bumper to bumper traffic and flooded roads. The muscles in my back finally relaxed a bit when I reached the outskirts of the university.

As soon as Dad and I returned to the States, he had gone on to the Vanderleigh estate while I stayed here and set up our new apartment near the university museum. I was just finishing the necessary paperwork to continue my studies in Eastern philosophy when I was called about Dad's death. My thoughts dwelled on him as I drove through the streets my parents must have walked, hand in hand, many years ago.

The earliest recollection I have is that my mother was very ill for a long time before her death. I remember Dad's concern and worry, and then his sadness when she died, but I can't really say I remember her. I only have a hazy memory of a pretty, but very pale, lady in a bed I was just tall enough to look into. I'm sure it must have been her, but I can remember nothing more.

Dad had never remarried. Since I was his only family, he had sheltered and protected me shamelessly, disregarding every word of warning given him by those well-meaning people who took it upon themselves to interfere in our lives and play surrogate mother. All his self-appointed advisors felt I should be sent to England or America to a boarding school. Thank goodness he never listened! Thailand was his choice for me and, compared to the alternatives, that didn't seem very far away at all.

I relished every minute we had together. He was a brilliant scholar, but also a warm and loving human being who knew by instinct how to fill the dual-parent role in a way that was best for us both. He never set his own feelings aside, but let them show, seeing no reason to make me believe he was an emotionless rock of authority with nerves of steel. He was real and wanted me to know him just the way he was.

So I knew him, and loved him, and still thought he was the most wonderful person who ever lived. He was always uncomfortable with my exalted view of him. "I'm just an ordinary man, Maggie, with a lot to learn in this exciting world." He was so enthusiastic about life; fascinated with its ancient mysteries and future promise. I may be unsure of the future and my ability to make it on my own, but I know one thing: Dad was an important part of my life and would always be a guiding and calming influence on me, whether he was physically there or not.

It wouldn't be easy for me. We had lost practically everything when we left Cambodia. Dad's reputation as an outstanding scholar and historian was his only remaining treasure, but there were many people with much less of an educational background than mine who managed to support themselves, even families. If anybody could do it, I told myself, Maggie Driscoll, or rather Margaret Ann Driscoll, daughter of Professor Matthew and Belinda Driscoll, could too: all five feet, eight inches, one hundred twenty-six pounds, and nine hundred ninety-nine freckles of me!

I was very tired when I finally pulled into the driveway of our apartment house that evening, but I felt a warm sense of security when I saw the old house again. It had once been a truly elegant home, but was now only an ornate shell covering four spacious apartments. We were lucky enough to get the best of the four, though, and I looked forward to curling up on our comfortable new couch with a hot cup of spicy tea.

I inched beneath the ancient sugar maple spreading over the driveway to avoid hitting a large black motorcycle parked near its trunk. Anyone should know better than to park so close to the drive! It was hard to see that black machine in the dark. I hoped it didn't belong to one of the students who just rented the upstairs apartment; I'd hate to put up with that all year!

As I pulled into my waiting garage space, I was tempted to stay in the car until the rain let up a bit. I quickly realized I was much too restless to sit still in such a confined space and gathered my bag, some books and miscellaneous papers from the car. Bundling my things close in my arms to keep them as dry as possible, I closed the garage door with a squeaking, grinding thud, then made a dash over the puddled gravel driveway toward the porch.

I was soaked through in the short time it took to

reach the front door. My shoes squished with a sound that told me their life had been severely shortened. I must look a sight, I thought, wiping the water from my dripping face. It was a good thing my long reddish brown hair is straight anyway, since it now hung in limp wet ropes around my shoulders. If anything could make me overcome my aversion to umbrellas and raincoats, it would be another day like this one.

I opened the door and flicked the foyer light switch. Nothing happened. "Oh, I just changed that bulb! It couldn't have burnt out again!" I threw my books and purse to the floor with a frustrated moan and kicked off my wet shoes. I knew this apartment well enough by now to make it to the lamp in the living room without risking too many shin bruises.

I had only taken two steps from the foyer when I tripped and fell. "Ouch! What the . . .?" My bare toes throbbed with pain. "There shouldn't be anything there!" When I tried to stand, I was shoved back down with a tremendous force and held hard against the floor. I started to scream, but someone shoved a dry rough cloth deep into my mouth and a blindfold was stretched over my eyes. Panic seized my mind and I kicked and struggled to pull loose, but it was no use; I was held fast by the weight of his body. My cheek painfully scraped the uncarpeted wood floor as he turned me over and pushed my head down, crushing my hands as he tied them behind my back. Strong fingers grasped my legs and I moaned in frustration and pain as he tightly bound my ankles together.

Blinded, I was held frozen by the sound of his

heavy breathing. I sensed his footsteps moving away, then heard the sound of rustling papers. The familiar jingle of my key chain confirmed he was searching my handbag. Anger flowed through me. All this for the few dollars I had. Take it, you gargantuan brute! Just take it and go! I heard him toss my bag aside, then begin to leaf through my books and papers. What could he want with those? Oh I don't care, take anything, anything you want, just leave!

The dry rough fabric had soaked up all the moisture in my mouth and my throat was becoming dry and sore. I gagged with nausea. Every nerve in my spine went tight as I sensed him step toward me again. A muffled scream ripped from me as I felt his hands grasp my back. I kicked my bound legs with all the strength I could muster and with a sickening jolt struck flesh and bone with the full force of my heel. Certainly that had hurt him, but he said nothing, made no sound at all, just seemed to breathe a little harder. He grabbed at my waist and tore my skirt from my body. I screamed again, the jagged waves of muted sound scraping my throat raw. I ineffectually writhed in snakelike movements to keep away from him. It was useless. I knew I could not stop him, but I was too frightened to quit trying; my body continued to struggle independently of my mind's control. He used his weight to hold me down again, then loosened my blouse, running his fingers over each seam and pleat of the fabric. He then ripped it free of my body, seeming to discard it as though it no longer held interest for him. His hands began to move slowly over my body, covering every mound and fold of flesh. My face burned with humiliation. I was glad now that I could not see his face. I arched my back in a final thrust of anger as his rough hands moved over my waist and grasped my thighs. Frightened bitter sobs broke through my terror.

He stopped abruptly as heavy footsteps sounded on the wooden porch. "Cut it to the left, farther; now straighten it up! Right on! Okay, let's get that stuff unloaded."

The upstairs tenants must be moving in!

He shifted his weight and lay down beside me, motionless, that heavy breathing drowning all other sounds from my mind. Suddenly he moved away and a moment later I knew that he had gone. A gentle breeze fluttered soothingly over my body. The back door must be ajar.

When I was absolutely certain that he was no longer here, my body slowly began to relax and I cried, starting tentatively with frightened whimpers and increasing finally to hard heaving sobs. I cried for my dead father and for my own vulnerability.

I had been frightened beyond anything I would ever have imagined. All my life I had felt strong and tall, but in those brutal hands my strength had been as effective as a limp rag doll. How sheltered my life had been! I had never even come close to danger, but now I knew the smell of fear; that salty, sweaty, almost musty odor emanated from every pore of me.

Now that the threat was gone, I tried to tell myself that he had not injured my body in any lasting way, but I knew I'd never forget it. The horror he caused me to suffer was a rape of my soul;

I'd do anything to prevent having to face that wrenching fear again. My body shuddered involuntarily at the memory of his brutal touch.

I had to face it; I must understand my reaction to those hands. They had been rough and unrelenting, yet totally impersonal. There was no recognition of me as a living being, as an individual. I was treated as an object—that was the frightening thing.

He had not spoken, only breathed—slowly, heavily, horribly . . . like an animal. I heard the sound again and my heartbeat quickened; it had risen from my imagination. I realized it would lurk there forever, just like the pressure of those hands I would always feel on my body.

TWO

Still blinded and bound, I lay there for what must have been hours, wallowing in my fear, feeling each nuance of its texture. This was where my sheltered life had let me down: terror was an unknown. Those who had led harsher lives than I would be marveling at how lucky they were to have escaped unhurt, but I was peeled to the core with fear and horror over what might have happened and wringing every possible ounce of self-pity from my experience.

There would be no one to help me. I had to get up by myself; I had to do it alone.

I began to squirm in my snakelike fashion toward the direction of that cooling breeze. The back door opened off the kitchen and it was there I would find a tool to slice these bindings. My head hit the base of the door frame and I felt the slick cool tile of the kitchen floor against my forehead. These small victories!

Unable to see and working behind my back, it took an excruciating length of time to cut through the ropes binding my arms. My first reaction on freeing my hands was to rip that nauseating gag from my mouth. My throat would be a long time recovering from the strain of those ineffectual screams. Next, the blindfold: my vision was blurred from the pressure of the binding. I stooped to slash the bindings from my ankles, then stumbled toward the sink to turn on the cold water. Water would lessen the pain; it is a healer. I splashed my face, then cooled my eyes and filled my sore and swollen mouth.

I wanted to swim in a lake, a cool fresh lake to remove the touch of those hands, or a secluded lagoon where I could float endlessly, soaking the fear and filth away.

I glanced toward the living room as I reached for a cloth to blot my dripping face. What I saw there added another dimension to my nightmare. The room was a total shambles, every upholstered cushion was slashed and every drawer and cabinet emptied. The few possessions we had were strewn irreverently over the uncarpeted floor.

I wanted to scream in outraged protest, but could only emit insignificant gasps and moans as I looked at the rampant destruction. I staggered through to my bedroom; the bed was ripped apart and the mattress and covered box springs slashed open. What few clothes I had lay in a tumbled heap on the floor. My photograph albums were torn apart, the photos scattered haphazardly through the wreckage. Dad's room was the same. Toiletry items and medicines had been dumped into the bathroom lavatory, leaving the empty bottles strewn on the vanity and the medicine chest open and bare.

What kind of madman could have done this? Why? There was no reason! We had no valuables, and what little we did have had just been senselessly destroyed. There seemed to be something insane about this, insane and quite frightening.

I grabbed my robe from the crumpled pile, called the police, then huddled in the middle of the devastation to wait for their arrival. I was shaking violently. I wasn't sure whether it was rage, fear, or shock, but my teeth chattered and I shivered as though I was freezing.

Calm down. Just calm down, Maggie. I kept trying to convince myself it was all over, that no one was here anymore, but my mind could only ask, "Why? Why us? Why me?" The anger and revulsion I felt at some mindless stranger coming here to my apartment, threatening me physically and senselessly destroying my things was entirely new to me; it was a violation of my warm, secure place, my home. Is this part of growing up and being on my own? Is this the jungle of life?

My frantic thoughts were interrupted by an authoritative knock on the outer door. Two young uniformed policemen stood on the lighted porch, their rain parkas dripping little shiny beads of water onto the gray-painted wooden floor.

The taller one spoke: "Miss Driscoll?" I nodded, afraid to trust my voice not to quaver. "I'm Lieutenant James Davis and this is Patrolman Burt Adams. May we come in please?" They removed their dripping parkas and left them on the porch near the door.

I moved aside to let them pass into the living

room and wordlessly waved toward the destruction. They seemed a little self conscious, unsure where to start. As soon as I thought about it, I realized they were concerned about me, my mental stability. I certainly looked a mess: bruised and tear-stained face. I could feel the set of my features and knew my expression was tense and wary.

I found my voice. "My house was ransacked while I was away for the day. He was still here when I got back. He tied me up and frightened me badly, but did not really hurt me. I have no idea why, absolutely none." I started to offer them a seat, then realized none remained.

Lieutenant Davis paused at the archway and glanced slowly around the room. "Have you been able to determine whether anything is missing?"

I went over to my handbag, shuffled through its contents now scattered over the floor, and shook my head. "Everything's such a mess, I can't tell. My money, just thirty dollars, is still here in my wallet. There was really nothing to take. We have no valuables."

They went from room to room while I remained in the kitchen leaning against the counter. I could hear the steady drone of their voices as they talked to one another but I was unable to distinguish words. I was just beginning to prepare a pot of tea when they returned to the kitchen.

"Would you care for some tea?" I asked. I was moving like an automaton in a dream world, trying to maintain an appearance of control.

"No, thank you," answered Lieutenant Davis.

I began to pour my cup. My hand shook so hard I

felt ridiculous and stopped when it was only half full.

"Miss Driscoll, I know you are upset about what has happened and you certainly have reason to be, but we must ask you a few questions. Will you describe exactly what happened when you entered your apartment earlier this evening?"

My knees were so weak I just had to sit down. I righted a breakfast chair, ignoring its slashed cover, and sat. I began my account with the failure of the foyer light fixture and ended with the sounds of the neighbors scaring the man away.

"It seems to me that whoever threatened you and did this damage was looking for something specific. I believe you were not the victim of a sexual attack but of a systematic body search." He motioned me silent as I started to repeat that we had nothing of value. "A common thief wouldn't have taken the time to ruin the furniture, and vandals would have made an even more outlandishly destructive display. They would have torn down drapes, knocked holes in the walls and spilled messy liquids like catsup or syrup over the floors and furniture. We believe that whoever did this was looking for something so small it could have conceivably been hidden beneath a photograph, in a medicine bottle, even in your clothes or on your body." Patrolman Adams nodded in agreement. "We're also certain that he did not find what he came for, since there is not one corner of this apartment left intact. He went through the whole house, and even felt it necessary to search you. Now think, Miss Driscoll, what could he have been looking for?"

I was crying now. "But don't you see, we have nothing! We lost everything in Southeast Asia. We have absolutely nothing anyone would want to steal, not even the usual things like a television or a stereo tape deck. He must have made a mistake, picked the wrong house or something."

"Who shares this apartment with you, Miss Driscoll?"

"My father. At least he did. He died in an automobile accident several days ago. I was attending his burial today."

A look of concern passed over Lieutenant Davis's face, and he took a deep quick breath. "I'm sorry." He stood quietly for a moment, his eyes fixed on the floor, then continued, "We can do nothing more here tonight, but I'd rather not leave you alone. Is there someone you can call to stay with you?"

"No, no . . . Don't worry. I'll be fine. Really I will. I doubt he'll come back again, don't you?"

"You can't be sure, Miss Driscoll. He didn't get what he came for. If I were you, I'd go to a hotel."

I shook my head negatively.

"Well, I'd appreciate it if you would come to the station tomorrow to help finish our report. Make a note of anything you find missing and be sure to mention it then. Oh, by the way, was the time of your father's funeral announced?"

"No. Why do you ask?"

"Wedding and funeral announcements alert thieves that a house will be unoccupied."

This is a jungle, crawling with predators.

After they left, I remained sitting at the breakfast table staring unseeingly into space. I felt shattered, defeated, and alone. It wasn't the destruction of my things; nothing ruined was really irreplaceable. It was the recognition of the fact that some mindless creature could senselessly frighten me and destroy everything I owned. My body shuddered involuntarily, trying to release the tension within it.

Was someone watching me now? I rose to close the kitchen curtains, automatically glancing out the window. "Dummy! You can't see into the dark from a lighted room!" I quickly shoved the curtains closed when I also recalled that anyone in the dark could see into this lighted room very clearly. Could someone be watching my every move?

What a frightening thought! I must gain control of my imagination or it will defeat me.

What could I have that anyone would want? What could they believe I had? I didn't know, I just didn't know. I shook my head slowly from side to side as the tears began to flow again. The policemen must be wrong. The whole thing was so senseless!

I began slowly and methodically to pick up, straighten, and clean the apartment. An upholsterer would have to repair and recover the furniture, and I'd probably need to replace the mattress and box spring. Other than that, it was merely a matter of putting everything back in its place and discarding what had been ruined. I knew I wouldn't be able to sleep. It was better to spend the time cleaning than sitting around worrying about why this had happened to me.

I stopped for a moment, shoving my hands into my pockets like a general planning an attack. The jarring ring of the phone frightened me and my hands clenched into tight fists. Who could that be? Control, Maggie; get under control. You're all you've got now; there's no one to serve as your buffer from life. Deep breath. Pause.

"Hello."

"Miss Margaret Driscoll, please."

"Speaking." This deep masculine voice was unfamiliar to me.

"You don't know me, Margaret. This is Martin Ingram, an old friend of your father's. I just learned of his death. I want to express my sympathy and offer any help you may need."

"Why, thank you, Mr. Ingram." My mind was racing. I couldn't remember ever having heard his name. "I don't recall my father speaking of you. Did you know him a long time ago when he lived here in the States?"

He seemed to hestitate, then continued pleasantly, "We were members of the same group, the Silver Circle, and have known each other since school days. I want very much to see you. Would you let me know when you could come into Manhattan?" I didn't answer immediately, then, just as I started to reply, he interrupted with, "On second thought, how about tomorrow evening? Take the train in and I'll meet you at Penn Station."

I felt confused. I didn't want to agree to meet a total stranger, but it would mean so much to talk with an old friend of Dad's now. His voice sounded so strong and distinguished, and I needed to know *somebody* in this strange and frightening country. I'd have to take his word that he was Dad's friend; there was no way I could check that out tonight. I made no excuses; I decided to go.

"The train would be a good idea. I can walk to the station and catch it there. I'll meet you at Penn Station around seven-thirty tomorrow evening. Is that a good time for you?"

"It certainly is!" He seemed relieved. "I'm glad you can make it. I'll wait at the Thirty-third Street and Eighth Avenue entrance. By the way, so you'll recognize me, I'll be wearing a light blue sport coat."

I thought of my clothes in their heap on the floor. "Oh, brother! I haven't the vaguest idea what I'll find to wear, but I have long brown hair, green eyes, and a thousand freckles. There aren't many people who could match that description, especially the freckles."

"Sounds good to me," he laughed. "I'm looking forward to meeting you, Margaret. Goodbye until then."

I hung up the phone and looked around the room again. I felt better. The room seemed less strange. Well, no use putting it off any longer, it won't clean itself!

As I worked, my mind drifted to Mr. Ingram. Dad had never mentioned him, I was sure of that, but he had always carried a beautiful silver medallion on his key chain. He called it his good-luck charm, his silver circle.

His key chain? Where was it? He hadn't been carrying it when he died; his personal items had all been returned to me. I mentally catalogued everything I had picked up in his room. No, not there. He always carried it with him. So it must still be at the Vanderleighs'; I'd probably find it when I visited them.

By one-thirty in the morning, the apartment was back in a semblance of order and I felt more mentally organized. I was much too tired to work any more, but I still had trouble falling asleep. Every little sound alarmed me. I knew I should go to a hotel, but I was even afraid of driving alone through dark streets. I tried to convince myself there was nothing to worry about; all the doors and windows were locked and the new tenants were upstairs. But words meant nothing. My body remained tense and stiff, unable to forget those rough, grasping, hands, while heavy breathing still echoed around the dark corners of the room.

Some time after the clock struck four, I must have drifted off, but it was a fitful sleep, not at all restful. I awoke with a start when the paper hit the front porch around eight the next morning, no more rested than I had been when I crawled into bed the night before.

After a long cool shower, I dressed quickly and walked into town. A toasted English with marmalade and some spiced tea at the Sweet Shoppe helped me face the task of choosing a new fabric for the couch and chairs. I found one almost identical to the original and arranged for the upholsterer to pick up the furniture after lunch. I knew my actions were mechanical, but it gave me some feeling of control.

I decided to try Dad's old advice to smile and use my happy face muscles to make me feel better all over; my fears were not going to make me miserable. This sunny, beautiful day was perfect for dinner in the city and my blue-gauze plaid shirtdress and white high-heeled sandals made me feel very pretty and feminine. I bought a pair of large round white button earrings and three matching bangle bracelets at the drugstore near the police station. Five dollars' worth of "summer white sale" jewelry was all it took to make me feel complete.

My obligatory visit with Lieutenant Davis was uneventful. I had found nothing missing, other than Dad's medallion, and could think of no reason why I had been physically threatened and my apartment ransacked. I thanked him for responding so rapidly to my call, signed the formal complaint form, and left. By six o'clock, I was on the train for New York City. I had not been there since we first returned to the States.

Although I knew I wouldn't want the congestion of big-city life all the time, the buzzing pace of Manhattan always set my pulse racing with excitement. It made me feel alive and at the center of the universe. There's no other place like New York; you feel important just being there.

I walked with the crowd toward the Thirty-third Street entrance, but didn't see anyone who could be Mr. Ingram. I hoped he wouldn't be late—I hate standing around alone in a strange place. A man with gray hair at the temples looked about my Dad's age, but he had on a brown suit, not a blue sport coat. I stood near the doors and watched the cars and people moving on the street. Strains of Gershwin's "Concerto in F" ran through my mind as I began to feel the beat of the city.

Someone touched my arm. "Margaret Driscoll?"

I turned. "Yes."

"Martin Ingram."

I looked up into sky blue eyes and a well-tanned angular face. The face and voice were pleasant, but I could only feel anger.

"You aren't Martin Ingram."

"I'm sorry?" He had a confused questioning look.

"You're not Mr. Ingram. You're too young to be an old school friend of my father's!" I almost began to cry in frustration; everything I had held in since last night burst out. "Who are you? Why are you doing this to me?"

"Wait! Hold it! Calm down, Margaret." He tried to touch my arm, but I moved away.

"I don't know what your game is, but I can tell you that I'm in no way impressed or amused."

He stood there wordlessly for a moment. His perplexed look slowly became a smouldering glare. "Look, there's been a misunderstanding. Let's go. I'll explain over dinner."

I stepped another step back from him. "I'm not going anywhere with you. There's no misunderstanding. I understood perfectly. You said you were a friend of my father's. You said you were in school together and members of the Silver Circle. I'm recalling correctly so far, right? How could there be a misunderstanding about that? How could a man who would be stretching it to say he was a day over thirty-five have been in school with someone who was nearly fifty?"

His eyes shot icicles. "Yes, you are recalling correctly, and you're close on the ages. I'm thirty-four and Mat Driscoll was forty-eight. Now, come on!" He grabbed my arm roughly. "I don't like arguing in the middle of Penn Station and furthermore, I'm hungry! Are you going to have dinner with me or am I going to eat without you?"

His jaw looked set in stone and his eyes locked into mine. I was too angry to be embarrassed, although we were certainly attracting a lot of amused attention. I had been through a lot of things I didn't understand lately, and the last thing I wanted was to add another item to that list. But I was hungry, and curious about who this overpowering male animal was and what possible connection he could have had with my father. I breathed a resigned sigh. "All right. Where do we eat?"

Several amused spectators applauded lightly and then went on to find another show to watch.

"That's better," said Ingram. He relaxed and slightly loosened his grip on my arm, still holding on firmly, however. "We'll take a cab to a very tiny French restaurant I know, called Le Bouton. I'm sure you'll like it. Since they only serve one meal, you won't have to make any more difficult decisions. You just relax and eat the delicious food they put in front of you."

THREE

Martin Ingram was greeted at Le Bouton like an old friend. After a warm welcome and my introduction to the owners, Charles Bracquemond and his wife, Nina, we were served a delicious meal. The congenial atmosphere of this small family restaurant made me feel ashamed of my earlier rudeness.

Any woman could be proud to be seen with Martin. His dark chestnut hair was styled in the soft and fashionable shorter look, and his clothes, more than merely creating his strikingly handsome appearance, were themselves enhanced by his tall, slim frame. His projected image was both classic and current at the same time. Intelligence and a warm personality radiated from his slightly tanned, clean-shaven face, yet the sharp angles of his cheekbones, jawline, and chin were a message to the world that he would be tough to deal with if given just cause.

Since Martin had insisted that there be no serious talk during dinner, he entertained me by explaining the intricacies of high-rise living in unionized New York City. "There's always at least one group of workers on a strike which affects some vital aspect of your daily life. You must try to have a job that requires little travel to save you from being inconvenienced when either the trains or the airlines aren't running. To avoid being stranded when the bus, subway and/or the taxicab drivers stop work, you should live within walking distance of your office. Take an apartment on one of the lower floors of the building so you can walk up and down easily when there's an elevator-operator's job action. Of course, this will also be safer in case the firemen go out on strike.

"It's important to be adept at repairing things, such as a leaky kitchen faucet or a noisy toilet, if your building maintenance men don't show up for days at a time; and you should have a trash compactor, plus nasal blockage and/or a strong stomach for those hot summer days when the garbage collectors choose not to collect. Finally, when the policemen decide to have the blue flu, you should have a black belt in karate or be very good at just plain street fighting. Once you get all that, New York is a great place to live *if*—and this is a biggie—*if* you can afford it!"

At the end of this monologue, I realized I was really laughing for the first time in many weeks. I was well fed, comfortable, pampered and entertained; just what any doctor would have ordered after the turmoil of the last few days.

As the coffee was served, Martin's mood became more serious. "I know this is going to be a rough time for you, Margaret. Your life has been turned upside down and all foundations jerked from under you." He looked down at the table, avoiding my eyes. It was obvious Dad's death had deeply affected him.

My own tears began to surface and I talked to push them back. "Martin, how did you know my Dad? You're so much younger than he was. I don't understand how you were in school together."

"I did overdo that a bit, didn't I?"

I knew my flushed face showed how angry and perplexed I was at this remark. "Overdo it? What are you talking about? What exactly do you mean?"

He explained hastily. "I met Mat Driscoll in Cambodia twelve years ago, when we were working with the Central Intelligence Agency. Then later, when you were both living in Thailand, he helped me train for some work I'm now doing with Interpol. By 'overdo' it, I only meant that I wanted very much to talk to you and the old school tie was the first thing I thought of to make sure you would see me."

"My father worked with the CIA and Interpol? I don't believe you! Dad was not a violent man."

"Only as a consultant, not as an operative. He knew more about the Siamese and Khmer cultures than anybody on our side. His advice helped us to understand and gain the confidence of the local people."

"I see." That I could understand. My father did have a unique understanding of and respect for the Khmer culture. He would have wanted to help others feel that same respect.

"Once Mat and I worked on a project with a Cambodian silversmith. That's where we got the silver-circle medallions. The silversmith gave them to us as a way of saying thanks. I've always kept mine as a reminder of my friendship with Mat and have come to think of it as sort of a good-luck charm."

"That's what Dad told me his was, a lucky piece. I don't understand what happened to his medallion, though, it wasn't with his things."

"I have it. Yesterday when I returned to my office after a week long trip to the West Coast, I found it in my mail with a note from Mat asking that I call him at the Vanderleigh estate. When I called, the maid told me of his accident and death several days earlier. She gave me your number and you know the rest."

He handed me the medallion. "This is yours now. The rights pass from generation to generation. You are a member of a protected and exclusive group of two, and you're to call on me when you need a friend. Deal?"

I was speechless with gratitude. It was such a thoughtful gesture. "It's a deal. Thank you, Mr. Ingram."

"I prefer the way you say *Martin*. I'm not that old, remember?"

"Martin." No, he didn't look old at all.

I took the small engraved medallion and studied it closely. The circle was formed by intertwined dragons writhing around the edge of the disk. Cambodians are known for the intricacy of their silver work and this was a good example. I turned it over in my hands as my thoughts focused on my father again. "Did Dad often call you?"

"No. In fact, I hadn't heard from him since we

had lunch several weeks ago, right after you got back to the States."

"Why would he have sent you his medallion?"

"I don't know anything except that I feel he needed my help. I am sure of one thing: It was important. He sent the medallion to emphasize that."

"Well, I guess we'll never know now."

"I thought you might be able to shed some light on it for me."

"If there's one thing I have learned in the last few days, it's that my Dad didn't burden me with his problems. I'm in the dark about so many things now. Dad prepared me pretty well for ordinary living, but he didn't train me for his death, or for what's happened since he died."

"Like what, for instance? *What* has happened? Martin's face was wary, poised for my answer.

I was suddenly embarrassed, unsure of myself. "Oh, I guess I could be overreacting, but I have to admit that I'm scared. I returned to my apartment last night after the funeral to find that it had been completely torn apart. The man was still there when I got home and although he badly frightened me, he didn't really injure me. I have no idea what he wanted; he never spoke a word, and I never even saw his face. The police feel he didn't find what he was looking for. I try to tell myself that it's all a mistake, that he got the wrong apartment, but they don't agree."

"What do they think?"

"That whoever it was had a definite object in mind, and that the object is small enough to fit into a medicine bottle. Many of our small jars and bottles were opened and emptied when the apartment was torn apart. The whole thing has left me feeling pretty miserable and incompetent to cope in this urban jungle. I'm becoming a little paranoid about it, and convinced that someone is watching every more I make."

Martin's smile seemed reassuring, but his eyes remained cold and serious. "You do have a lot to learn about this part of the country, Margaret. Experiences such as yours are the common fare these days."

"If you're trying to make me feel better, Martin Ingram, you're not doing a very good job of it. I'm scared! I can't think of one reason in this world why anyone would want to search my apartment. I'm beginning to see villains in every shadow."

"That's a natural reaction, and one that will pass with time. Maybe you should leave your apartment for a while. Is there anywhere you can go?"

"No, not really. I have to start school in a few weeks. I've been invited to visit the Vanderleighs, but I don't know them. I just met Jonathan Vanderleigh at Dad's funeral."

"What is he like? I've heard so little about him."

"He was nice enough, but somewhat strange. By that I only mean he seemed very tense and pressured, or at least he was the day I met him. He was certainly kind to me though, and thoughtful."

"Then why not visit for a few days?" urged Martin. "Perhaps you shouldn't stay alone until you get over your fright."

"I might. I just don't want to commit myself to

anything at all right now."

"Have you made any plans?"

"Well, I know I'll have to find some kind of a job to help me through school. I'm working on my doctorate in Eastern philosophy and religious thought."

Martin smiled. "I'm impressed."

"Don't be. I'm going to have to figure out some way to make money with it. I hope to teach at the university level, but the world is full of teachers these days." There I go again, sounding like I'm feeling sorry for myself.

"There's always room for excellence, Margaret. It's mediocrity that the world is saturated with. Become one of the best in your field and you'll get what you want." He rose and reached for my hand. "Let's see some of the city before you have to catch that train back to the boondocks."

"Boondocks?"

"Provinces."

"Oh, you snob!"

We walked around the upper Fifties between Madison, Park, and Lexington Avenues, looking in the shop windows at expensive antiques and designer items we'd never be able to afford. We ended our exploration gazing up at the golden beauty of the Seagram Building as we sat on the edge of its brilliantly lighted courtyard fountain.

In spite of all that had happened, I felt good just being here. "This is certainly a long way from Cambodia, in every way you can compare it."

"Do you miss Cambodia, Margaret?"

"I miss the way it was years ago. It's a grim place

now, though. Do you ever hear anything official about what's really happening there?"

"Not much, and nothing good at all. Before the Vietnamese takeover, it had become an isolated society. All reports are from escaped refugees, and they paint a depressing picture of a totally regimented society where punishment, even for minor rule infractions, is brutal. Families are totally scattered; men, women, and children are divided into separate work forces. The people are treated like the lowest work animals. Food is practically nonexistent and disease is rampant." He shook his head as if to deny the visions his words were creating. "No goal is worth that price in human suffering. Nothing can justify it. What men can do to one another in the name of nationalism or ideology is an outrage."

I shuddered at what he was telling me. "Most of our friends left when we did, or earlier, but a few chose to stay behind rather than leave their homeland. At the time I understood. Who would have expected such a brutally inhuman dictatorship among those gentle people? Will it ever end?"

"The Cambodian people, or what's left of them, are starving. They're so weak and oppressed there is no way they can revolt. Everyone is cautious. Food aid is trickling in, but no one wants to step into a quagmire like Vietnam again."

"I guess the historians will see it as just another chapter in the agony of the Indochinese, but I can't really feel that removed. I liked those people. It seems so incongruous to be looking at the skyscrapers of this magnificent city while discussing the inhuman treatment Cambodians have suffered at the hands of their own leaders. It should be something that happened back in the dark ages, not something that could happen in the same time frame as these buildings and this country."

"As much as we'd all like to believe otherwise, Margaret, civilization is a tenuous thing that has been achieved with great difficulty and can be lost with frightening ease."

"We've certainly learned how easily it can be lost," I agreed. "In no time at all, Cambodia lost more than half its population and stepped back several hundred years."

"Not just Cambodia, Margaret. How civilized did you feel this country was when you came home to your apartment last night? How advanced is this society when a lonely elderly woman must wait until morning to buy necessary food or medication? She's learned not to go out after dark, and to be on guard even in the daytime against thieves who find the aged easy prey."

"It's like the hair's breadth between sane and insane."

"Yes, it can easily slip away."

"Oh, I don't want to think about it anymore! Let's talk about something else." I shook my head, trying to banish my conjured fears.

Martin looked at me thoughtfully, then glanced down at his watch. "Hey, it's getting late. You're going to miss the last train." He grabbed my arm and practically dragged me down the steps leading from the fountain to the street, hailing a cab at the same time. We made it to Penn Station without a moment to spare, and I was tossed on the train after promising to call regularly to let him know how I was doing.

Once in my seat, when I had caught my breath, I realized that I had enjoyed this evening very much. To think I had almost refused his invitation!

We had just entered the tunnel leaving Manhattan when the train came to a jolting, screeching halt. After a moment's pause, it began to back up very slowly until we were out of the tunnel again. The passengers turned toward each other in confusion, then looked back in unison as the conductor entered from the rear of the car. "Everybody off the train. Quickly, please." I grabbed my bag and stepped into the aisle, letting an elderly lady move in front of me.

"What do you think it is?" she asked, her eyes wide with fear.

I tried to comfort her, "I don't know, but I'm sure it's something minor. They probably need to do some work on the train and can't do it with the passengers on board. The conductor didn't look very worried, just rushed. He'll explain as soon as we get off, I'm sure. Here, let me help you." I took her pale and wrinkled arm to guide her down the steep steps to the ground. The conductor led us across several sets of tracks to a point well away from the train. As he did so, about twenty men swarmed over the empty train flashing lights in every crevice and corner.

"What in blazes is this all about?" asked an angry and haggard middle-aged man.

The conductor replied in an even voice, "We've had an anonymous tip that there's a bomb hidden aboard the train, and it was set to explode while we were in the tunnel under the river." A shocked silence fell over the crowd. "This kind of thing happens so often we're sure it's just a crank call, but as you can appreciate, we can't take the risk of actually acting on that assumption and ignoring the threat."

"How long do you think it will take?" the man asked, obviously impatient at the delay. "I'm in a pretty big hurry."

"No less than an hour. The risk is too large to miss checking a single possible hiding place. We're sorry for the inconvenience, but I think you'll agree it can't be helped. This is the kind of thing society must cope with these days. There just doesn't seem to be any end to it all."

"Is there any way I can get out of here? I can't afford the hour."

"No, I'm afraid not. The only way is over these tracks straight back into the station, but I can't let you do that, it's too dangerous."

His voice took on a combative tone, "There's no way you can stop me, buddy!"

"No, but those men can." The conductor pointed to a group of policemen standing several yards to the rear of the train.

"Police state!"

The conductor's patience was stretched to the limit. "Oh, for heaven's sake, Mac, calm down. By the time you got back and found another way out of the city, we would be on our way." The irritable man gave a disgusted sigh and walked along the tracks toward the group of policemen.

A pale young man with the look and pallor of a

hard working student spoke up, "New Yorkers! I love the city, but I hate the people. They haven't the vaguest idea of cooperation. No wonder society is ripping its seams. The greatest city in the world is populated with rabblerousers to whom rudeness is a way of life. In my best dreams I see myself sitting alone in an arena watching a group of these fast talkers insult each other to a bloody pulp." The passengers laughed knowingly at his remarks as he lit his pipe with a flourish and resumed reading a book by the light of the conductor's lantern.

The train was proved clear of a bomb and we were soon on our way, although I for one didn't really breathe easily until we were completely through the tunnel. A pleasant camaraderie had been established among the passengers by the incident and it continued for the duration of my trip. I enjoyed it; perhaps I should spend more time around people now. I resolved to visit the Vanderleighs on Monday, then sat back to watch the lights pass by, each one briefly illuminating small patches of the dark landscape reeling past my window.

University Station was deserted when I arrived shortly after midnight. The brief sense of security I had enjoyed during the past few hours with Martin Ingram abruptly left me as I walked toward the questionable safety of my apartment. Next time I would drive my car and leave it at the station. I should have realized that even this short walk alone, and late at night, was not a smart thing to do. Would I ever learn?

Dim streetlights cast eerie moving shadows across

my path as wind gusts rocked the twisted branches of nearby trees and shrubbery. Words my father often used in convincing me not to fear the dark floated through my mind. "There's nothing in the dark that isn't there in the daylight, Maggie."

"But I can see it better when it's light, Daddy. I can see it *so* much better!" I laughed and relaxed a bit when I realized that I had spoken those words aloud.

As I turned the key to my apartment door, some sound or movement caused me to glance toward the garage. The light was dim, but I could see that my garage door was not completely closed; it was open to about a foot or so off the ground. I wouldn't have left it that way! I quickly relocked my apartment door and ran toward the garage, throwing the door fully open with much more force than was needed. When I flicked on the overhead light, I almost screamed at the sight of my car. There was no doubt in my mind that the person who had just searched it was the same one who had torn his way through my apartment last night. The car seats were cut open and the carpet ripped up. The glove compartment was gutted, its contents spilled and scattered all over the floor of the car. The two large boxes I had stored on the overhead racks had been emptied and their contents strewn around the garage.

I began to straighten out the car as much as I could, but my vision was hampered with tears of rage and frustration. I didn't want to go back into my apartment, but I had nowhere else to go. There was no doubt in my mind now that I was the target and that someone was definitely looking for something I was supposed to have. Whatever it was, it couldn't be as valuable to me as a new mattress and box springs, new upholstery for my furniture and now a complete recovering of the interior of my car. I felt like putting signs on all my remaining possessions, "Do Not Destroy! Just ask, I'll give you whatever you want."

I ran back to the apartment more angry now than frightened. It was just the way I had left it earlier; no new visitors had come during the evening. That should have helped me feel a little more at ease, but it didn't. I sat at the kitchen table, my legs curled tightly under me, and slowly sipped a cup of hot tea. Martin Ingram was right; it was better not to live alone right now. The kitchen walls, normally a cheery bright white, seemed a cold and icy gray. It helped a little to leave the radio on; the late-night music seemed to take my mind off my vulnerability by making me feel less alone. What had been a cozy and comfortable apartment had become an alien shell. I could not relax.

Why was this happening to me? There were certainly no family jewels hidden in my car. I was sure now that I would get another visit; if total destruction meant anything, he certainly didn't find what he was looking for this time either.

I suddenly realized that I just couldn't take it anymore. I hurriedly threw as many clothes as I could into my bag and left to find a hotel room. Luckily my phantom searcher hadn't felt the need to tear the engine apart in his hunt. The car started right up and I breathed a little easier as I pulled from the driveway onto the street. I'd let the police in on the latest search-and-destroy mission in the morning and then I'd go on to the Vanderleigh Estate in the afternoon. Enough is enough, and I had reached my limit.

FOUR

I took the heavily traveled turnpike down to the Edwinsberg exit, then left it to make my way through rural New Jersey's bumpy back roads to the Vanderleigh estate near the small village of Bleekston.

As I rode through the heavily wooded hills, I realized that the driving I had done during the past few days had slowly changed my opinion of New Jersey. First impressions can be misleading. My initial introduction to the state, via the turnpike from Manhattan's Lincoln Tunnel to the university, had left me with the unpleasant impression of ugly sprawling refineries and factories spewing forth their health-threatening vapors into the air I had to breathe. Multi-laned highways set high on concrete arches charged through decaying cities and neglected neighborhoods giving no thought to the air and noise pollution their oppressive presence contributed to the area around them.

I was slowly learning that, once away from the congested highways and deteriorating cities, the far larger part of New Jersey was a picturesque state, the equal of any of the other forty-nine in the beauty of its deciduous forests, lakes, rivers, and farmlands.

Bleekston was a prosperous farm community and the villagers seemed to be making every effort to insure that it retained a Colonial hometown feeling. The brick sidewalks, cobblestone streets, and closely grouped wood-frame buildings, their windows flanked by colorful shutters, created a picturebook air. Storefronts proudly displayed signs bearing quaint names like "The Cranberry Scoop," "Ye Olde Cobbler Shoppe," and "The Calico Cat." I was sure that prices would be at least ten per cent higher here than in the normal five and dimes, or the Joe's Shoe Repair shops you find on the main streets of most towns, but it was nostalgic and charming and they certainly had achieved the atmosphere they set out to create.

I pulled my car into an empty parking space in front of an idyllic little Colonial cottage called the Butternut Inn. As I entered the lobby, a small bell tinkled, and the enticing smell of freshly made bread led me to the dining room. The crisp blue-and-white decorating scheme, combined with beautifully shaped and carefully tended live green hanging plants, looked cool and refreshing. A clean white tablecloth and a freshly cut daisy, set in a sprig of its own feathery green leaves, said "Welcome."

I chose a table near the sunny front window and was glad to see that there were only two other customers, local businessmen discussing town politics over coffee. An attractive blonde woman in her middle thirties came to my table. "Hi. How about some coffee while you look at the menu?" Her fresh white uniform was almost hidden by a frilly blue gingham checked pinafore apron. A matching gingham ribbon held her golden hair back from her face. She looked so cheerful it was easy to smile back.

"Thank you, but I'll just have some tea and a warm sweet roll with butter. You certainly have a lovely inn here, but it looks so small. Do you really have guest rooms?"

"Yes," she laughed. "Four. They're small too, but cozy and homelike. Everyone who has stayed here has seemed pleased."

I played a hunch: "Does the inn belong to you?"

She nodded affirmatively and smiled a warm smile that made little laughlines in the corners of her clear blue eyes. "Yes, I'm Lizbeth Keaton."

"And I'm Margaret Driscoll." I extended my hand to meet hers. I felt instantly relaxed and at ease with Lizbeth. As she walked back to the kitchen, a shaft of sunlight caught her bouncing hair and intensified its golden sheen. She seemed so happy and carefree.

Would I ever be like that again? Could I forget the touch of those obscene hands, that roar of measured breathing in my ear?

I had little chance to dredge up my fears for she returned immediately with the roll, tea, and a newspaper. "Since you're alone, I thought you might like to read the morning paper. I don't know how you feel about it, but I hate to sit by myself in a restaurant with nothing to read."

"How thoughtful. Thank you. I would also appreciate it if you would help me find the Vanderleigh estate on my county map." I unfolded the map and held it out toward her. "I'm not sure how to get there from here, but I don't believe it's very far away."

Her arms remained at her sides and all warmth vanished from her face, as though she had switched from the Greek theatrical mask of Thalia to one of Melpomene. "I won't need to look at the map." Her voice had turned cold, "Just take Route 641, that's the main street, south from here about five miles. You'll come to a high stone fence with an iron gate at the entry way. As you go down the long private drive, you'll see the house through the trees on top of the hill."

"Thank you, I appreciate your help." I smiled, trying to rekindle her vanished warmth. She looked at me, her face still cold, as though she wanted to say more; but seeming to think better of it, she turned quickly and walked away. I wished for a moment that I could be as bold as some people and ask what had upset her, but I couldn't. Since I knew I was in no way at fault, I didn't feel free to pry about something so obviously personal and upsetting.

I finished my tea, then left the money to cover the bill, plus a tip, on the table. As I drove away, I noticed her face at the window. I smiled and waved, but she did not respond. I liked Lizbeth and her quaint little inn, and was sorry that I had in some way triggered an unhappy memory.

The bright midday sun gave way to a gray overcast sky as I started down the narrow black-topped road. A summer shower was definitely headed my way. The brief pleasure I had experienced in the cozy little inn vanished with the sun and I felt the weight of my problems pulling my face into a tense, strained frown. I remembered Dad teasing that tense look away by calling it my pouting face. I felt the loss of him again. A deep sense of despair hit me so quickly it was as though I could physically feel the pain.

Blinding sheets of rain began to fall in one of those heavy afternoon thunderstorms that clean the streets and wash the gum wrappers away. The windshield wipers had trouble coping with the deluge, and I was forced to drive at a crawling pace. I had just decided to give up and pull over for a few minutes, when the rain stopped as suddenly as it had come, and the sun edged out from behind the clouds again. The pavement, baked hot from the earlier noontime heat, began to dry quickly and sent up eerie wisps of steam.

Through the foggy mist, I saw the fence: a greenish brown hand-hewn stone wall at least eight feet high at its lowest point. Massive columns of the same dark stone were placed about ten feet apart. The connecting fence, topped with sharp-pointed rocks, dipped as it left one column, then rose to meet the next one: wave after wave, as far as I could see. The fence, although beautiful in a rustic way, immediately offended me. In this peaceful, quiet, countryside it seemed out of place and an affront to the good nature of everyone who passed by.

I remembered the cold expression of the woman at the inn, Lizbeth Keaton. Surely her reaction was more than local resentment; she had to have a deeper reason for such strong negative feelings.

The huge iron gate loomed before me. Two engraved brass plates, one reading "Vanderleigh," the other, "Jaeger's Nest," were set into the stone columns flanking each side of the closed gate. The jaeger . . . a bird . . . a predator. I wanted to kick the gate when I saw that it was locked, and realized I had probably made this long trip for nothing. As I turned to go, I noticed a box near the left column. I opened it.

"Jaeger's Nest. State your business, please." droned an officious voice at the other end.

"This is Mag . . . Margaret Driscoll . . . Er . . . uh . . . I've come to pick up my father's things." I get so mad at myself when I can't be direct and forceful. I feel so awkward and stumbling, never poised and in control.

"Just a moment, please." It was obvious the voice was checking to see if I should be allowed to enter. "The gates will open now. Follow the road directly to the main house. You will be met there."

I could visualize a stiff, authoritative body, with a face to match that voice, meeting me at the front entrance, handing me Dad's things, and then quickly ushering me out again. Well, that would be just fine with me. I had no desire to stay in a fortress, not even for one afternoon.

The gates slowly began to open. I must admit, there is something royal about big tall gates opening that way, as if trumpets should blare because you're being permitted to enter the land of enchantment. I had expected a grand formal drive lined with spreading lindens or some equally impressive tree, but it was only a narrow, gravel-covered dirt driveway, cut through a virgin wood. A high bank lined one side of the narrow drive, a deep drainage ditch, the other. The dense shade prohibited the growth of sufficient ground cover, causing the banks to slowly erode. Gnarled roots of huge trees grasped for purchase as the life-sustaining earth seeped from under them. The warm rain had left the tree leaves wet and glistening, reminding me of Cambodia's lush jungles. I half expected to see the magnificent splendor of Angkor Wat beyond the next bend in the road.

I did, in a way, for I saw Jaeger's Nest, the Vanderleigh home, for the first time. It was an eerie, breathtaking sight. The house was built of brown rough-hewn stones, like those of the fence but larger. Its trim was wood and copper long since aged green from oxidation. On any other landscape it would have been imposing in its size and beauty, but here it was dwarfed by its wild natural setting. Huge beeches and towering tulip trees, their trunks obscured by an undergrowth of dogwood, cherry, birch and viburnum lent a fairytale air to the magnificent scene. Their leafy spreading limbs created a dark and somber woodland where little or no sunlight penetrated to the ground below. I found the scene hauntingly beautiful, but nevertheless disturbing in its overwhelming dominance of me as a human being.

I parked the car under a magnificent specimen of copper beech near what must once have been the carriage house but now served as a garage. The grounds were neat but informally landscaped. I had already learned that the cost of labor needed to keep a large house and formal gardens was prohibitive these days and even if one could afford to pay, finding a truly devoted and capable groundskeeper would probably be difficult this far away from a large suburban area. It was so different in the Orient, where labor was plentiful and cheap; but, then, there were very few people there who would be able to afford a home as grand as this one.

"Miss Driscoll?"

I started involuntarily and turned to see who called my name. A tall man stood nearby, his face in shadow. I strained to see; again I felt intimidated and defensive.

"Yes . . . I'm Margaret Driscoll. I've come for my father's things."

He stepped into the light. "Sorry if I alarmed you. Welcome to Jaeger's Nest, Miss Driscoll."

I was immediately relieved. "Oh, Mr. Vanderleigh, I couldn't see your face. I hope I didn't come at an incovenient time." While his body had looked young and lean in the shadow, his drawn face and sparse graying hair made him seem much older, even ill. His voice and smile were very pleasant, though, and I welcomed his handshake.

"Not inconvenient at all. May I call you Maggie? Your father always used that name when he spoke of you and I must say, with all those freckles and that burnished brown hair, it fits you very well."

"Certainly, Maggie it is."

As we walked toward the house, Mr. Vanderleigh called out, "Hello, Lillian," to a thin, harsh-featured woman standing impatiently at the entry. "Come meet Maggie Driscoll. My sister, Lillian Vanderleigh, Maggie."

"Hello, Miss Driscoll." As I suspected when I saw her face, hers was the voice of the gate box. "If you'll come this way, I'll show you to your father's room." I knew it, meet me at the door then send me on my way.

As we turned to enter the house, Jonathan called out, "Please join us for dinner, Maggie. We won't be having anything fancy, but it would be nice if you could stay. I want you to meet Catherine, Mrs. Vanderleigh, and I'd like to talk with you for a while."

"Thank you, I'd like that too, very much." I glanced at Lillian; she seemed perplexed and slightly annoyed, but smiled in a grimacing sort of way when she realized I was watching her. She turned to go inside, wordlessly making it clear that I was expected to follow.

I resolved to be as little bother to her as possible and avoid my usual tendency to chatter when I'm nervous. But when we entered the door, I immediately forgot my resolution and marveled aloud at the beauty of the entry hall. The floor was laid with large glazed ivory-toned ceramic tiles which, although beautiful, yielded to the magnificence of the turned-oak balusters of the stairs and the massive dark-oak moldings. The off-white grasscloth wall covering served as a perfect background for an outstanding pair of Chinese silk paintings on the foyer wall.

This was definitely a man's house. Oak and

leather set the theme accompanied by rough woven fabrics like casement cloth, linen, hopsacking and grasscloth. Wood, brass, and carved-stone accessories completed the integrated feeling of the rooms. I liked it. It was a comfortable look, large and overwhelmingly masculine in tone, but its dominant message was casual elegance. Jonathan's wife must certainly appreciate her husband's decorating tastes, as there was no trace of a frilly feminine touch in any room I saw; not one bit of chintz.

Lillian seemed to enjoy the pleasure I took in seeing the rooms. As if she had been reading my thoughts, she said, "The Jaeger's Nest has a personality of its own and will not absorb anything alien. If something doesn't fit, it stands out as such an eyesore you can't feel at rest until it's been eliminated." Her features softened as she continued to talk about the house. It was clearly a source of pride to her. We climbed the stairs and walked down a wide hall.

"Did you do the decorating, Miss Vanderleigh?" I asked, trying to learn more of this softer side of her nature.

"As much as the house would let me. There's really very little to do. I just look for something similar to replace whatever is showing wear. The original selections were made by my father almost fifty years ago. I try to keep it as much like he planned it as I can." She paused at an opened door. "Here is the room Dr. Driscoll used when he was here. I've packed almost everything and could easily finish if you'd like."

"Thank you, no. I really want to do it." I was

surprised when she seemed to understand.

"Dinner will be at five this afternoon. We're eating early today because Bruce, Jonathan's son, must catch an early evening plane."

My face must have shown my surprise. "I didn't know he had a son. Does he attend the university?"

"He did, but he's finished now. He has his Ph.D. in archeology." She suddenly seemed ill at ease, glancing around the room and avoiding my eyes as she talked. "Well, I must go. I have so much to do. I'll leave you now and see you again at dinner." The plush carpet muffled her footsteps as she walked down the long hallway.

This guest room was in character with the rest of the house, masculine and comfortable. I walked from one piece of furniture to another, touching things Dad must have touched, opening the already packed suitcases and riffling through his clothes. I was so lost in the memories of times I had seen him wear each garment that I drew a quick breath when I realized someone had been watching me from the open door. It was an elderly woman, tall and stout, with wispy gray hair and a sad, sweet face.

Her voice was little more than a soft whisper, "I didn't mean to alarm you, Miss Driscoll. I'm Nellie Morgan, the housekeeper. I wanted to give you these." She handed me a stack of several clean white shirts, neatly ironed and folded. "I had done them up for your father." She was obviously shy and found it difficult to talk with a stranger. I was beginning to discover that visitors were a rarity at Jaeger's Nest. "Your father, Dr. Driscoll, was certainly a wonderful person, kind and good to everybody. I'm so sorry he's gone, but I'm thankful I had the opportunity to know him." She looked at me, then down at the floor, her fingers twisting a corner of her stiffly starched white apron.

My heart went out to her in appreciation of how hard this must be for her. A lump caught in my throat and I fought the tears back. "Why thank you, Mrs. Morgan, for being so thoughtful. I know so few people here. I really need and appreciate your kindness."

She smiled and left quickly, closing the door behind her. Her honest and well-meaning words meant a lot to me. She was right about my dad, he had a totally benevolent outlook and always thought the best of everyone until shown differently.

I packed the few remaining things, Dad's camera and some miscellaneous toiletry items, then stopped for a moment when I saw his favorite corduroy sports coat thrown over the back of the leather wing chair near the fireplace. It looked so perfect here in this room. I picked it up and hugged it close to my face. The smell of his aromatic tobacco still permeated the fabric. As I closed my eyes I could see him, pipe in mouth, looking at me as sympathetically as he always did when I explained my latest problem. Poor Dad, who did he ever have to take his problems to? I sat in the chair still holding the coat in my arms.

I don't know how long I sat there staring at that open fireplace and dreaming of times past, but I was abruptly brought back to the present by a knock on the door. For a second I was confused and didn't remember where I was. I hesitated, then called,

"Come in." I felt uncomfortable giving entry instructions to a room I had very little right to be in myself.

The door opened and a man about my age, perhaps a little older, paused wordlessly at the entry. I wasn't sure whether he had come to the wrong room or whether I wasn't the person he expected to see. I'd guess his age at twenty-eight or less, tall and slim, with golden brown hair and warm brown eyes.

His silence made me uneasy. "Hello, I'm Margaret Driscoll. I've just stopped by to pick up some things that belonged to my father. If you wanted to use the room, I'm almost ready to go." There I go, chattering again! I rose from the chair.

He laughed warmly, "Oh no, not at all. I was looking for you. I'm Bruce, Bruce Vanderleigh." His voice was rich and deep. I felt like such an awkward school girl, I stood rooted in place, afraid to take a step toward him for fear I would trip or do something equally gauche.

"I was just enjoying the comfort of the room. I almost wish it were cold enough to light a fire so I could fully appreciate it." He still stood there, looking at me, saying nothing, so I felt compelled to fill up the spaces. "You see, Dad never really spent any time in our apartment near the university. He came to work with Mr. Vanderleigh right after we got back to the States, so he was here in this room more than any other place on this side of the world." I could feel the tightness starting in my throat again and my eyes filling with tears. I was talking too much, as usual. I dropped my gaze to my watch while I recovered my composure. I often find that when I'm running my mouth out of nervousness, the world seems to spin much faster and I begin to feel dizzy. "It's nearly four o'clock. Your father asked me to stay for dinner. Would you mind showing me around a little before then? This is such a beautiful home."

"Certainly. Later. First I have something for you. Your father had given me a letter to mail the morning of his accident. He usually left his mail in the mail box on the highway for the postman to pick up, but that morning we were all out of stamps. I hadn't left for Bleekston when I learned of his death, so since it was addressed to you, I decided to deliver it in person. Why don't you read it now, and I'll meet you later in the library?"

I reached out hungrily for the letter and dropped to the chair, staring at Dad's handwriting on the envelope. I carefully opened it, and began to read, barely noticing Bruce's departure from the room.

Dear Maggie,

Please deposit these two checks in the bank for me. I sold a couple of magazine articles on Cambodia. Three thousand dollars isn't bad pocket money for a start, eh? I'm also working on a book on Angkor Wat for which I'm to receive an advance soon. I've finished the first draft and I'm putting it in final form now. (I bet you thought I had been spending my free time in utter luxury!) I'm using a lot of those slides we made over the years. I wasn't able to bring many material things out of Cambodia, but no one can destroy my wonderful memories or take those years of study and observation from me. My notes and pictures are enormously important now that the ruins may be damaged or destroyed in the political upheaval. That's why the publisher is so excited about the detailed photographs in my book.

Jaeger's Nest is a great place to work. The solitude and peace offered by the magnificent trees is invaluable. We'll have to build a house some day right in the middle of a thick woods.

I borrowed a car and drove around the local area yesterday. I came across something you must see. I won't spoil it for you by talking about it first. I'll just show it to you when you come down to pick me up two weeks from this Friday. (About three o'clock?) Well, I guess it's only fair to give you a small clue: there's a little bit of Tibet right here in New Jersey.

I'll call you this weekend.

Love,
Dad

I had never gotten his call. I would have loved to tell him how proud I was of his articles and his book.

Tibet—here? I wondered what he meant.

I could almost feel his big bear hug and hear the smack on the top of my head. "Everything's going to be all right, Maggie. I've seen to it."

Oh, Dad, I miss you so.

FIVE

I was totally overwhelmed when I opened the heavy oak doors and entered the library of Jaeger's Nest. It was a huge room, at least twenty by forty feet with fourteen-foot-high ceilings, and was lined from top to bottom, and along every available square inch of wall space, with book-filled, dark wood shelves. A conference-sized intricately carved oak table with six equally exquisite carved chairs stood at one end of the room. Beyond it was a boxed-out bay, its leaded windows fitted with dark-stained louvered shutters half open now to admit the dwindling light. A massive stone fireplace, fronted by an Oriental area rug and flanked by two couches and several comfortable chairs, perfectly finished the other end of the room. I turned around slowly, looking up from the intricate parquet floor to the molded ceiling and stared in awe at the domed skylight with its stained-glass border.

I was suddenly aware of Bruce silently watching me from a leather wing chair near the fireplace. I stammered an awkward, "Hello," and felt my face blush red when I realized he was amused with my open-mouthed gaping at this magnificent room.

He laughed and rose to greet me. "Don't be embarrassed. I'd feel cheated if you weren't impressed. The books are a collection of several life-times, started by my great-grandfather Adam Vanderleigh." His arms swept the room. "This represents the Jaeger's Nest's greatest store of riches. While other seagoing men thought of treasure in the traditional sense, Adam Vanderleigh thought only of the wealth of art and ideas."

"It's truly fantastic. But he must have touched some traditional treasure along the way. Didn't he build this house?"

"Part of it, and named it after the Jaeger, a fierce and piratical sea bird which steals its food from other birds and comes to land only to nest. Then his son, Matthew Vanderleigh, my grandfather, enlarged the main house and added this library and the two wings. Grandfather Matthew was the one who made the real money of the family by investing heavily in a few well-chosen industries. Of course that was when fortunes could be made without turning over the bulk of the gains to the government. People who make that kind of money these days aren't allowed to keep very much of it."

"Is that why you decided to be an archeologist?" I chided.

He smiled, a warm smile which put me completely at ease. "You're right. I certainly won't have to worry about the complications of large personal finances as an archeologist." He reached for my arm, "Come, let's look at the grounds while there's still a little light. There's not enough time to go down to the river, and there's little more to see than acres and acres of woods. We Vanderleighs use land and trees only as insulation from the outside world; our interests dwell more on interior and introspective things. We do have one point of interest nearby, though, Mother had Dad put a natural stone floor beneath a group of beeches. It makes a nice place to relax. Come on, I'll show you."

We walked into the hall and toward the back of the house. "I haven't met your mother. Mr. Vanderleigh asked me to join you for dinner. I look forward to meeting her then."

Bruce visibly winced. "My mother is dead. Catherine is Dad's second wife."

I was embarrassed. "I'm so sorry. I misunderstood."

Bruce opened a pair of French doors onto a large terrace. Trunks of huge trees ringed the terrace and their overhanging limbs almost touched the rough-hewn masonry walls of the house. We followed a winding stone pathway for quite some distance through a grove of silver-trunked beeches to the spot where a flagstone floor had been carefully placed under their protective sweeping limbs. "This was my mother's favorite place. She loved to read and would sit here for hours on end." He paused, then added, "It's rarely used anymore."

"It is peaceful here." Several pieces of heavy cast-metal furniture were the only evidence of a human's touch. The stone floor, softened by the green tinge of moss, seemed perfectly natural under the trees. I turned to make another comment to Bruce about this peaceful retreat but stopped when I saw him staring at a lounge chair and table set apart from the other groups. I could understand his pain. I was certain his mother often sat there.

He turned abruptly toward the house. "It's five o'clock. Let's go in to dinner."

I wanted to see more of the woods, but I knew dinner would be waiting. It wouldn't be like Lillian to be late. As we walked back to the house, Bruce slid his arm over my shoulder and pulled me closer. Somehow his gesture seemed more protective than romantic and I realized he was just being kind and comforting because of my father's death. "I'll only be away at this conference for a few days. I want to see you when I get back, and show you more of our part of the world."

"I won't be that far away. I'm still working on my doctorate, so I'll be at the university for years yet." It seemed natural to put my arm around his waist, but I didn't. I just walked on beside him feeling slightly awkward and a little self-conscious.

"Your dad said you were studying the religions of the East. That certainly meshed well with his field. Is that why you chose it?"

"Well, I guess I'd have to admit that his enthusiasm for his work did sway me. He was certainly my favorite tutor. By the way, I want to thank you for bringing me his letter. It was almost like having a chance to talk with him again."

"I felt it would be. I badly wanted something like that of my mother's when I lost her. I was only fourteen when she died and since we'd never really been apart, I had no letters at all."

Jonathan called out and waved as we neared the terrace. "I see you've met Bruce, Maggie. Has he been showing you around?"

"Yes, and it's absolutely beautiful here." I sat on one of the pretty cast-iron chairs near Lillian. "Dad talked about the trees, but he had never really described them as being so overpowering. It's the closest thing I've seen to the Cambodian jungles since I came back to the United States."

Jonathan laughed loudly, "Well, we're not quite a jungle yet, but the trees are getting close in. I'm afraid they'll have to be cut back some this year. We must, after all, show them who's boss, right?" He gestured toward the door. "Let's go on in to dinner. Catherine seems to be a little delayed, but she may join us later."

"Yes, we certainly shouldn't have to wait any longer," said Lillian stiffly as she rose from her chair. I had a feeling that there was little love between Lillian and her sister-in-law.

Jonathan opened the French doors to the dining room and took my arm as we walked in. I found myself contrasting the sociability of the men in this family with Lillian's gruff and officious exterior. I looked forward to meeting Catherine and wondered what she would be like.

As Mrs. Morgan began to serve the main course of sole, Jonathan looked at her in irritation. "Where is Mrs. Vanderleigh, Nellie? I had expected her to join us."

Nellie's mouth dropped open in undeniable surprise. "Why, Mr. Vanderleigh!" She glanced at me and then recovered herself slightly. "She's not feeling well. I'm sorry, I forgot to mention it, but earlier she asked me to extend her apologies. She hopes to be up and around tomorrow and will meet Miss Driscoll then. I just forgot to pass the message on, Mr. Vanderleigh. I guess it's old age creeping up on me. Scatterbrained. Forgetful. Don't know what I'm coming to."

Nellie was trying to smile at me but I was puzzled by the beads of perspiration which had appeared on her forehead and upper lip. She was nervous, no denying that. Why? Mr. Vanderleigh didn't strike me as a difficult employer. Quite the contrary, he seemed most gracious.

The sole had a slight touch of lemon and a delicately browned batter. "Delicious, Lillian. I've never had such a magnificiently prepared sole."

She was obviously pleased and I realized then that her tenseness kept people from seeing her as she really was. Although she seemed stiff and unresponsive, she just didn't know how to relax in social situations. As they discussed Bruce's trip, I found myself wondering if she had ever been in love. It was hard to visualize Lillian as a happy and carefree young girl.

I continued to drift mentally and stopped when I found myself staring straight at Bruce. His perfect mouth . . . I felt a strong urge to touch it—to feel those finely chiseled lips under my fingers. I had wanted to be a sculptress once, and was occasionally bitten by the bug again when I saw an interesting face or a perfect physical feature.

He glanced toward me as he talked to Jonathan across the table. I quickly dropped my eyes to my plate. Did I imagine it? Was there warmth there for me? Would he laugh at me if he knew my thoughts? Would he understand? There I went again; such a dreamer! I brought myself back to reality just as Jonathan returned his attention to me.

"Well, Maggie. Pardon us for ignoring you for a moment. Tell me, what do you plan to do now?"

I wasn't sure whether he was genuinely interested in me or just making polite conversation. "I haven't had much time to think yet, but I don't want to make any substantial changes for a while. I'll continue my graduate courses for the time being. Hopefully I'll be able to find a job teaching or working in some way with the university to help me with expenses."

A smile crossed Jonathan's face as he poured my after-dinner liqueur. "Your father had practically finished his work with me, but I could certainly use some help in organizing my notes and getting the actual writing done. I'd very much like to have you work here with me until the fall term begins and then continue working on weekends during the school year."

I slowly sipped the highly flavored liqueur. He was handing me the perfect job, tailored to my interests and abilities, but I hesitated. I held back as though I couldn't reach to grasp the gift he was presenting me. Why was I hesitating? Was I afraid of my attraction to Bruce? Afraid that he would not share my feelings? Before I allowed myself to think any further, I replied, "Thank you, Mr. Vanderleigh. I'd really like to accept right away, but my life has taken such an abrupt turn that I need time to think things out before I commit myself. It's kind of you to offer." I hope my voice revealed none of my inner confusion.

As if he read my thoughts, Bruce turned to me and smiled. "He really does need you, you know. He's not doing it solely for your benefit. Organization is Dad's weak point, and he could never hope to get anyone more qualified than you to help him." His warm voice and intuitive remarks helped put me at ease.

I looked at Lillian for a clue to her thinking but her face was noncommittal; it was as if she was consciously making her expression a total blank, not wanting to encourage or discourage my coming.

Jonathan quickly interjected, "Oh, don't feel you have to say yes right now, Maggie. Stay with us for a few days, then make your decision. I understand what you're feeling, but Bruce is right: I really do need the help and will be hiring somebody in any event. Your background would qualify you for the job far ahead of any other applicant I could hope to interview."

"Thank you for the invitation, and I'd love to stay over tonight. These few hours were not enough to really see your beautiful home. I also want to thank you for asking me to share so delicious a dinner."

"Our pleasure, Maggie. Your father spoke so much of you we felt we knew you even before you came."

I was basking in Bruce's confirming smile when we were jolted by a heavy clap of thunder. I cried aloud, "Oh, not another rainstorm!"

"Yes, it certainly looks that way. Bruce, you'd better get on the road if you're going to catch that plane. This rain will slow you down."

As I rose to join the others in seeing Bruce off, I staggered slightly and nearly fell. Bruce reached to support me. "Careful there!" I felt a blush spread over my face and my awkwardness came rushing to the surface.

"Thank you. I guess I got up too quickly."

His eyes seemed to cast an enveloping warmth around me. "Take care, Maggie. If you're not here when I get back, I'll call you."

Well, Miss Maggie of the infinite imagination. Just how much can you make of that remark? Oh, why did he make me feel so aware of myself? Would I be feeling this way if he felt nothing in return? Of course, I told myself. Your emotions are vulnerable now, and furthermore you are as inexperienced as a high-school freshman at this game. You're just infatuated with him because he's being nice to you. Wake up, little girl!

Bruce drove away just as the rain began to fall. I stood on the portico with Jonathan for a few minutes watching his car vanish down the drive.

"Let's have some coffee, Maggie," said Jonathan as he turned to go back inside. "I'll ask Nellie to bring in a tray and join you in the library."

I walked on in and sank deeply into one of the fully upholstered couches flanking the fireplace. I was very tired; that was to be expected, I guess, since I hadn't gotten much sleep at all the two preceding nights. The pendulum of the grandfather clock near the door rocked back and forth in its never varying rhythm as my mind drifted dreamlike over the events of the last few days. They seemed less frightening and a little unreal now as I sat here curled up in softness and looked around at this opulent room, the pride of Jonathan Vanderleigh's grand estate. My eyelids were heavy almost beyond my control when Jonathan entered the library with Lillian. I tried to keep my eyes open as they stood there looking down at me. I moved to stand up. "Mr. Vanderleigh. I know it's very rude, but I'm so tired and sleepy I'm afraid I won't be very good company this evening. It's a good thing you offered to let me stay the night—I don't believe I could have driven home. It's been a tense few days, and now it looks like my body has just given up on me."

"Think nothing of it, Maggie. Lillian will be glad to take you on up now. You're sure you're only tired; you're not ill or anything?"

"No, just exhausted and a little embarrassed."

Lillian reached to support me. "Don't be silly, Maggie. There's no reason at all to feel ashamed. I'll take you upstairs. Nellie put fresh linens in the room your father used, so there's no reason at all you can't go right on to bed." She gently guided me up the grand circular staircase and opened the door to Dad's room. "This room has its own bath. You'll find towels and anything else you might need in the linen cabinet opposite the lavatory. And don't worry about getting up early in the morning either. Sleep just as long as you need to."

I smiled a thank you as she closed the door behind her, then immediately shed my clothes down to my slip. I won't wash my face, or brush my teeth, or even brush my hair, I resolved, in defiance of my mandatory bedtime ritual. I was simply too exhausted.

A jarring sound at the window diverted my attention from the welcoming bed and I walked unsteadily toward the drawn drape. I pushed the heavy linen drape aside and tried to see what had caused the noise. It must have been a wind-tossed limb brushing against the outside wall. At first it sounded like a bird scratching to get in, but the wind was an easy guess; the fury of this violent storm was tossing the tree tops back and forth as if they were mere roadside saplings. I dropped the drape and turned toward the bed again.

Was that someone crying or moaning softly? I couldn't trust my own ears; the sound had so quickly come and gone. I shook my head in disgust. Silly! It must be just the wind howling around the corners of this old house. I disregarded my childish worries and fell into the soft, welcoming bed. I'd never been this sleepy in my life. The last thing I remembered was trying to reach a small lamp on the nearby table to turn it off. I'll never know whether I made it or not.

SIX

I never dream: neither sad tales nor happy ones, no dreams at all, and certainly no nightmares. People try to tell me that I really do have dreams, every night, and it's just that I forget them when I wake up. I'd rather they wouldn't make such positive statements about the inner workings of my psyche; I'm helpless to disprove them. It doesn't really matter, I guess, let them express their theories. As far as I'm concerned, though, I just don't dream. At least I never did until that first night at the Vanderleigh estate. Once was enough; I hope I never dream again.

I was in a dark empty place, a nothingness, a void. I could see a pale wisp of a figure, draped in white, leaning over me. Its eyes were large and swollen from hours of tears. My tears? The frightened eyes looked at me with unconcealed curiosity, then, at some sharp noise I couldn't identify, the figure vanished off the edge of my dream. A red glow burned around the edges of my perception; a pulsating incandescence slowly crept over my world.

As the glow oozed closer, I began to see faces in the darkness; agonized and pain-filled faces, tortured, starving souls suffering the terrors of the damned.

In horror I covered my eyes, blotting out the vision, then turned and ran through the eerie red darkness toward a blue light. There was life there in the distance, I could see a haze of green. Vegetation. Sunlight. I was in a field. Birds and insects sang their mating songs and my fears began to fade. A healing warmth spread through my body. Peace.

Suddenly this dream world grew deathly still: no birds, no sounds at all. An unnatural quiet settled over the pastoral land. A feeling of self-consciousness came over me and I realized I was being watched. I could feel a presence. The sound of measured breathing broke through the wall of silence: it was an animal. He came crashing through the brush destroying all in his path. I tried to see him, to visually grasp and understand this stalking, terrorizing force that caused me to react from fear rather than actively control my own life, but I could only hear the sounds of his destruction, he was not visible to me.

I began to run, stumbling, falling. I couldn't let him touch me; his touch meant death. The ground beneath my feet become a congealed, undulating swamp and my steps came harder and slower as I sank into the muck. Floating faces encircled me, their bodiless heads rose from the swamp and darted about me like swarming insects; vegetation clinging to their long flowing hair. Their open screaming mouths revealed toothless bleeding gums. "He's coming," they chirped in unison. "He's coming!"

I still could not see him, but I could feel he was closer, gaining, reaching toward me. My legs were locked in the swamp. "Don't touch me! Don't touch—oh no! No! Don't touch me!" I screamed again and again, the sound echoing around me as though I were in a pit or a cave. His presence seemed to fade into the walls of the enclosure.

The faces began to question me, seeking answers to the meaning of life. I tried to tell them I had not lived long enough to know the answers to such a profound enigma. It was a mystery I could not solve; I was too inexperienced. The faces became angry; they were sure I knew the way, that I was just holding back.

"No," I told them. "If I knew, do you think I would be here trying to learn? I would be a great teacher if I knew the answers you seek!" I began to laugh derisively at their foolishness, obviously irritating the head inquisitor, whose sharp-featured face was suspended before me and surrounded with a glistening silver cloud.

The faces stared at me with huge questioning eyes, their silence overpowering. Then their eyes took on the beat of the swamp, pulsating to a measured rhythm. The beast was returning, oozing from the walls of the cave. I screamed again and again into the soundlessness, but no one heard. . . .

I awoke perspiring heavily, feeling chilled and exhausted. My damp hair clung to my clammy face and neck like a mask. The dreams had drained my strength. I slowly became aware of an unusually sharp and irritating odor. I sat straight up in bed, alarmed and totally confused. There was so little light in the room. I was no longer wearing my satin slip; a rough cotton fabric surrounded my body. This was not the Vanderleigh's guest room, but a strange small cubicle sparsely furnished with a high metal bed, one straight chair, and a three-drawer chest. A heavy drape was tightly drawn over the one narrow window.

Am I awake? Could this be another dream? That pungent odor, is it an antiseptic? Is this a hospital? I slid from the bed to the floor, my bare feet touching the cool, smooth tiles. I tried to stand unsupported but felt dizzy and confused. My hands tightly clutched the foot of the bed. Still holding the foot-rail, then the wall for support, I inched slowly toward the door. It was open just a crack and admitted the only illumination in the room, a three-inch-wide beam of light. I opened the door its full width and stepped into the brilliantly lighted hallway, shielding my eyes from the painful glare.

The walls seemed to wave and curve, nothing appeared solid. Farther down the long hall I saw a dark wood desk. A large person dressed in white sat behind it. Was she a nurse? She looked my way, then picked up the phone and stared straight at me as she talked into the mouthpiece.

Then the tall, heavy-set woman, her white nurse's hat covering most of her cropped red hair, marched toward me as though stepping to a military band. I was still partially blinded from the glare of the light and could not bring her face into strong focus.

"Where am I, please? How did I get here?"

"You must be feeling better now, to be up and around like that. You just jump right back in that bed and I'll order you something to eat. I'll bet you're famished."

Food was the farthest thing from my mind. "Why am I here? Answer me please! Is something wrong with me?"

"Don't worry about it, you're just fine now. Mr. Vanderleigh has been here with you practically every minute since he brought you in. I called him as soon as I saw that you were awake."

"How long have I been here?"

"Well, I'm not exactly sure—to the minute, that is. You were asleep in this bed when I came in yesterday morning, so I assume you came in during the night." She thrust her hand toward me, "Edna Abbott, head nurse, that's me. And you are Margaret Ann Driscoll." She grasped my shoulders and turned me around slowly. "Well, Miss Driscoll, let's move out of the hall and back into our room."

"Would you ask Mr. Vanderleigh to give me a few minutes to wash my face before he comes in, please?"

"Certainly, honey." She opened the drawer of the bedside table. "This kit has some things in it you may want: a comb, toothpaste and brush, things like that. All new, just for you."

"Thank you. I'll need them all."

As she went out the door, she pointed to the closet. "Your clothes are in there when you want to get dressed. It's a little early for that now, though; I think you'd better plan to stay in bed a while longer." She closed the door behind her.

Alone again, I walked to the window, shoving the drape aside to let in some light. I looked out upon a sunlit green lawn filled with feathery evergreens and colorful summer flowers. The world outside looked fine, the trouble was in my foggy mind.

When I switched on the light in the bathroom, I was shocked to see my reflection in the mirror. I was much too pale, even my freckles were barely visible. Red watery eyes stared back at me from deep, dark pits. I turned on the cold water, catching the fast-running stream in my tightly cupped hands and soaking my face and eyes. Perhaps washing my face would also help clear my muddled brain. A few minutes later, hair combed and teeth brushed, I felt a little better. I had just climbed back into bed when I heard a male voice in the hall outside my door.

Mr. Vanderleigh entered, his eyes full of concern and worry. "Maggie, my dear. I'm so glad to see you looking better."

"Better! I must have looked like death before, if I look better now. What happened, Mr. Vanderleigh? Why am I here?"

"You needed help, Maggie. The stress of the past week has been too much for you and you just couldn't take it any longer. Perhaps sleeping in a strange place triggered your reaction. You had horrible nightmares and when we couldn't awaken you, I felt you should be brought to the hospital."

"I'm sorry to have caused you so much trouble, Mr. Vanderleigh. I don't understand it; this isn't like me at all. I've never even dreamed before, much less had nightmares."

"Don't give it a thought, Maggie. It's over. I'm sure it's a once-in-a-lifetime occurrence. As the doctor says, the young mind is also a resilient mind;

within a few days it will be as though nothing happened."

"When can I leave here?"

"Tomorrow. They want you to spend one more night just to make sure everything's okay. You will, of course, stay with us until we're certain you're fully recovered."

"Thank you. When I went to bed the other night, I certainly didn't expect to wake up here like this."

"Well, now that you're finally awake and obviously recovering, I think I should be getting back. I'll pick you up around noon tomorrow. Nurse Abbott is having a meal sent up and I'm sure you'll feel even better after that. Rest well, Maggie; tomorrow it will all be over."

After he left and closed the door behind him, I found myself staring at the blank wall across from my bed. The scenes of the last few days replayed there as though it was a theater screen. My father was gone; I could no longer lean on him. The destruction of my car and my apartment had shown me how little I could count on the outside world. Now the final support had been knocked from under me: I could not depend on the stability of my own mind.

I ate very little from the dinner tray Mrs. Abbott had ordered. This time sleep was a gentle healer as well as an escape from my problems, and I awoke feeling much better mentally and physically. I was still weak, but steadier on my feet. My mind seemed clearer, and a mirror check showed that my eyes had lost most of their tortured look. I tried Dad's happy-face cure-all, but the false smile in my mirrored reflection quickly turned to a tense frown; I just wasn't feeling that good yet.

Around midmorning, I dressed and decided to walk around outside until it was time for Mr. Vanderleigh to come. After a full tour of the carefully landscaped grounds, I plopped down on a wooden bench shaded from the hot August sun by a large hemlock tree. This was infinitely preferable to that small and dreary bedroom cubicle.

A small lonely figure trudged straight across the green rolling lawn of the hospital grounds, distracting me from my melancholy reverie. Surely I had been transported to another world! Was I hallucinating, having another dream? There walking in front of me was a Lamaist monk, his purple robes flowing in the hot August breeze. I couldn't believe it. Was I also unable to trust my vision? I looked again at the small brown-skinned man. His eyes squinted in the bright sun, further deepening the well-set wrinkles around them. This was not a dream; it was real.

I rose from the bench and began to follow him. His walk was steady, purposeful, and his path as straight as an arrow, ignoring the sidewalks. Other people did not seem to notice him or think of him as anything out of the ordinary. Again I felt a twinge of self doubt: were they really seeing him, or was he merely a figment of my imagination?

Suddenly I saw where he was going and again I blinked my eyes, unsure of my sanity. A delicately beautiful Buddhist temple sat in the middle of a clearing. Majestic pines served as its background and a cool green lawn as its base. Its highly peaked pagoda-type roof had been left a natural wood color and topped with a shiny golden ornament, while its base was primarily orange with green and white trim. The architecture was in the Tibetan style, broad below and narrowing toward the top. More golden ornaments were hung over the double front doors. I walked closer to see them more clearly.

I could almost feel Dad walking beside me, sharing my pleasure as he showed me something he knew I would want to see: a little bit of Tibet in New Jersey.

The monk had vanished into a cottage to the left of the temple. As I stood there in awe of the beautiful little building, I turned to find him standing quietly beside me.

"Would you like to see our temple, Miss . . ."

"Driscoll. Yes, very much."

He first showed me the exterior of the building, explaining the symbols incorporated into the design, then opened the door for me to enter. My eyes were immediately drawn to the brightly colored symbolic paintings adorning the walls and ceiling. To my right were a partridge, a rabbit, a monkey, and an elephant, standing one atop the other, symbolizing friendship. To my left, an old man sat meditating under a tree, symbolizing the tranquility of age. The symbolic guardians of the temple stared down at me from the ceiling; a dragon, a tiger, a lion and a half-man–half-bird garuda.

At the altar was the gleaming brass figure of Gautama Buddha, the enlightened one, the great Indian religious teacher who lived in the sixth century B.C. The monk stood aside and let the splendor of his tiny temple speak for itself. I could feel the history symbolized by this building. Since Buddhism is the major philosophical force in the East, my studies were concentrated heavily in that area of thought.

I noticed the throne reserved for the Dalai Lama. It is a feature of every Tibetan Buddhist temple. "Did the Dalai Lama visit your temple when he came to this country?"

"Oh yes. It meant so much to have him come. Now the children really know. They feel proud of their history and constantly refer to his words. 'If you can, help others. If you cannot help others, at least do not harm them.' It is simple and so true." As we walked back outside, he asked, "Tell me please, you said that your name was Driscoll. Do you know a Matthew Driscoll?"

"Why yes, my father."

He smiled broadly, "Tell him you saw me and that I asked of him."

I drew a deep breath. I had to get used to this, as it would surely happen again. I could feel the tears rising to the surface. "My father died last week. He was killed in an automobile accident, not very far from here."

A barely discernible look of concern crossed his face. "I'm sorry to learn that. You have my sympathy. It is not easy to be alone so suddenly."

"You knew my father, then?"

"I only met him a few weeks ago. He stopped by one day, just as you have done, to visit the temple. He was a very learned man, your father. He knew much of the history my people, and he knew how much the temple means to us. He was going to try to help us."

"Help you? How?"

"Some very old and precious objects were taken from us almost four months ago. He felt that he might find some way to help us recover them."

"I don't know what I could do to help, but perhaps if you would tell me about them, I might find a way."

"Our most valued possession was a silver Wheel of the Law, a centuries-old piece carried over Europe and finally donated to us by one of our most respected members. An ancient prayer wheel was also taken. They can never be replaced, of course; I only hope that the person who took them knew of their value. It is the only way they will be protected. Hopefully some day they will be returned to us. The pieces survived so much during the centuries before they became ours, and here, where we felt secure and free, they were stolen."

I could identify with his feelings; it was more than the loss, it was a betrayal of civilization, a step back toward the savage jungle; a realization of the fragility of that thin veneer of peace and order man has achieved over the barbarians.

I could not shake the depression I felt as I walked back toward the hospital grounds. I agreed with him. I hoped the person who took his pieces knew their value. How much of the world's treasure of antiquities has been destroyed in recent years? I had been outraged as a child when I learned of the destruction the Vandals had wrought in Rome. How different is that from the modern-day destruction of

Angkor Wat and of Tibet? Or the willful bashing of Michelangelo's Pieta? Will man never find a way to control the valueless beasts among us?

Jonathan was waiting at the door of the hospital when I got back. As soon as he saw me, he came straight toward me, barely able to contain his anger. "Where have you been, young lady?"

I was shocked. "Why, Mr. Vanderleigh, I just took a walk around the grounds."

"I've been over every inch of grass on the hospital property, and you were not there."

"I'm sorry, Mr. Vanderleigh. I let the time get away from me and I apologize for any concern I may have caused you."

"Where did you go?"

Rebellion was swelling up in me. By what right was he questioning me so demandingly? "You have no right to be so angry. You may think of me as a child, Mr. Vanderleigh, but I am twenty-four years old and perfectly capable of walking up and down the street without parental supervision."

He did not seem to have heard me. "I feel responsible for you, Maggie Driscoll. You're not to do anything like that again!"

I started to blast forth with another angry retort, when I suddenly realized that he was only acting this way because he was concerned with my welfare. Admittedly he was overreacting, but at least there was someone left in this world who cared for me. I forced a smile. "Thank you for your concern, but please don't be mad at me. I followed a monk to a beautiful little Buddhist temple. I found out he knew my father. Dad had been there no more than a month ago."

"The temple? You were at the temple?" He momentarily had a confused, perplexed look, then regained control. "Well, after the way you acted the other night, I was imagining all sorts of things happening to you. I was afraid you might have wandered off somewhere and no one would know who you were."

Again I shuddered at the thought I had been that out of control. I must be able to depend on myself; I'm all I've got now. I took his arm as we walked toward the car. "I thought I was dreaming again when I saw the monk walking across the hospital grounds. I really could not stop myself, I had to follow him."

"Sorry I was so rough on you, Maggie. I just became more and more upset as I worried about what might have happened."

On our ride back to the estate, Jonathan satisfied my curiosity about the Tibetan Temple. "Lamaist Buddhism came to New Jersey with the Kalmuck Mongols, descendants of Genghis Kahn, who left Siberia after the Russian Revolution. Mongols study Buddhism in the Tibetan language and they pray in Tibetan so it was natural that they would welcome the Tibetans who migrated here after the Chinese takeover of Tibet in 1959. When the Dalai Lama paid his unprecedented visit to New Jersey, he pointed out that there are close ties between the Tibetan and Mongol peoples. The name "Dalai" was even bestowed by a Mongol chieftain." Jonathan turned toward me as we neared the estate, "Are you interested in Tibet, Maggie?"

"Oh yes, but I know so little about it; it's like a mystery."

"Most people feel that way, which is why I'm devoting so much time to Tibet in my current project. If you work for me, you'll learn everything I know."

"You couldn't say anything that would tempt me more."

The gates of Jaeger's Nest were a welcome sight this time: the sturdy bulwark signified protection and refuge, not rejection. After the stress of the past week, I craved the security and insulation offered by that massive fence and those thick, beautiful woods.

Before we left the carriage house, Jonathan said, "Once more let me apologize for my anger at the hospital."

"Oh, Mr. Vanderleigh, it's forgotten."

"I'll always take care of you, Maggie, depend on it."

I was surprised that Jonathan would say something like that. Perhaps he had been a closer friend of my Dad's than I had known.

SEVEN

The guest room looked as comfortable as it had when I first saw it only two days . . . a *lifetime* ago. The leather wing chair near the fireplace seemed to be waiting for my return. I stroked the leather, sensing its luxury, then flopped onto the soft bed. How fantastic it felt! So much better than the one I had at the hospital. The unpacking could wait; a short nap seemed much more important. Almost at once I drifted off to sleep.

It was not long before the screams began.

The hideous sounds seemed to be coming from the hall, right outside my room. I staggered dizzily from the bed and reached the door just in time to hear the deadbolt click. Did I imagine that? I grabbed the doorknob and twisted one full turn; the door would not open. I pulled the knob with one hand and beat on the molded panel with the other as the sound of the tortured screams continued to tear through my mind. "Please let me out," I sobbed. "What's happening? Please unlock this door!" The screams went on and on. My God, what torment!

Was this real? Was it really happening, or would I wake up in the hospital again? My hands began to tremble and soon my whole body was shaking from the unbearable emotion wrenched up by those horrible cries.

I fled to the bed and covered my head with a pillow. Tears mingled with the sweat of fear and soaked the pillow through. "Help her," I pleaded. "Oh God, please help her!" The sound of my own screams obliterated hers and when I finally stopped crying I realized no sound was coming from the hall. I turned on my side and stared at the locked door. A few moments later I heard the deadbolt click for the second time. This is a surrealistic dream, I thought. It can't be happening. I must be sick again.

I jumped from the bed and threw open the door. The hallway was empty and the rugs and furnishings were in perfect order. No one was in sight. I slowly walked back into my room and sat down on the bed, staring dully ahead. What was happening to me?

"Hello, Miss Driscoll. It's good to see you back again. Are you feeling better?" Nellie was standing in the door, smiling that sad, sweet smile.

I stared at her uncomprehendingly for a moment. "I don't know, Nellie. I have to admit that I honestly don't know how I am. Did you just hear those screams out in the hall?"

She looked at me with alarm, then stepped back and glanced hurriedly up and down the hall. "Why, no; I didn't hear anything. There's no one here."

"You heard nothing?"

"Not at all." Was she deliberately avoiding my eyes?

"Why don't you lie down and get some rest, Miss Driscoll. It must have been a bad dream. Perhaps you tried to come home too soon."

There was no way I could argue with the logic of that statement and I wouldn't try, but I knew that sleep was one thing I wanted to avoid right now. There was no peace for me there. I followed Nellie into the hall and watched her go on her way. My legs were still shaking from the abrupt and violent awakening. I dropped to an upholstered bench near the stairs and rested my head on the stair rail. No, sleep would be impossible. I need to be up and around for a while, even away. Soon there'll be no more running; I'll hit a brick wall and have to turn and face my problems.

I resolved to shake myself out of this mental muddle and went back to the room to brush my hair and freshen my makeup. A drive would be good; I'd like to see more of the countryside around the estate.

I was adjusting the blanket I used to hide the damaged car seats when Lillian came into the garage. "Maggie, I'm glad I caught you. Nellie said she thought you were on your way out. You'll need this transmitter. Just keep it in your purse all the time and push the button to open the gates."

Brilliant me had forgotten about the gates. "How clever. Is this like a garage-door opener?"

"Well, I'm told the signal is more complicated, so no one will discover how to duplicate the code. My goodness, Maggie, what happened to your car?"

"It was vandalized. A university town doesn't seem to be the place to try to keep things fresh and new. I'm going to get it fixed later, when I find out who's good at this sort of job."

"What a nasty thing for someone to do—I just can't imagine! Bruce will know who to recommend for the repair, I'm sure. He'll be back tomorrow."

"I'll talk to him about it. Thanks for the gate signal, Lillian. I plan to drive around the neighborhood for a little while; I'll be back in an hour or two."

As I started to climb into the car, she reached toward me in a tentative gesture, "I'm glad you're back, Maggie."

I was surprised. Lillian had let her guard down. "Thank you, Lillian. So am I. Hospitals are no fun. By the way, I'm sure I frightened you the other night when Mr. Vanderleigh had to take me to the hospital."

"Oh, no. Well, to be quite honest, I didn't even hear you, I was sleeping so heavily. Jonathan says he became alarmed when he couldn't wake you from your nightmares and took you in without telling me about it. It's all over now, thank goodness."

She smiled and blushed self-consciously when I gave her a quick hug. "You go on now." She pushed me away with a laugh and a pat on the shoulder. "We'll talk more at dinner. Would you like to dress up this evening, Maggie? Just for fun? We don't usually, you know. Jonathan thinks it's pretentious in this day and age."

"That's a nice idea, Lillian. Let's do it." I was glad I had thought to pack my long black evening skirt.

"We won't be eating until around seven, so don't

feel you have to rush back if you find something interesting to do."

"Oh, I'll be back well before seven. Thanks again for thinking to give me the transmitter."

As I left the estate, I turned in a southwesterly direction. The road wound through rolling fields green with corn, soybeans, and other vegetable crops I couldn't identify from the car. I was surprised to see what I later learned was a sod farm, about ten miles from the estate. Acres and acres of parklike grass stretched as far back from the road as the eye could see. Occasionally the ground was bare where the turf had been lifted like squares of green shag carpet and taken elsewhere to grace a suburban lawn.

I slowly became conscious of a noticeable change in the trees along the roadside. Compared to the tall and majestic beech, tulip, and red maples I had been admiring in the countryside around the Vanderleigh estate, these trees were dramatically smaller and seemed to be mainly scrub oak and pine, plus a few sassafrass. I must be nearing the Pine Barrens, that large area of New Jersey noted for its sandy soil and stunted vegetation. I had just read that there's a dwarf forest in the Pine Barrens where fully mature trees reach only three feet high.

Several farms along the highway had vegetables for sale. The hand-lettered signs and bountiful display of one stand, "Molly's Fresh Vegetables," attracted my attention and I pulled in to see what was available. Perhaps I could now identify some of those crops I had been seeing from the road. A heavyset lady opened the door to the nearby farmhouse. "Be out in a minute. Pick out what you want and I'll be right there." She slammed the door and vanished back inside. The stand was a small aluminum trailer with walls which collapsed to form a counter. A colorful array of fresh vegetables were on display: juicy red tomatoes, corn, bell peppers, eggplants, and zucchini. A few bunches of basil were stuck in a jar of water to keep them fresh. I was holding and studying a rounded white vegetable when she entered the trailer from the back and appeared smiling behind the counter.

"Time for Molly MacGregor to get down to business. I should have known better than to try to do some canning when I'm supposed to be manning the store—or should I say 'personning' the store?" She giggled uninhibitedly, enjoying her own remark. Her cheeks and the corners of her eyes were lined with the pleasant laugh lines of a happy woman. "I bet you don't know what that vegetable is." She pointed to the shiny white ball, blushed with lilac, I held in my hand.

"Well, no. I was wondering about it. The top and stem remind me of eggplant."

"Right! Some people like the white variety better than the dark purple ones. These are considered white eggplant, but as you can see, they've been a little too chummy and cross-pollinated with the purple variety. That's what this little bit of light purple here means."

"It's beautiful."

"When you take the time to look at them I guess they are pretty. I just think of them as a crop myself." A motorcycle sped by, momentarily drowning out our conversation. "Damn those things!" she said with surprising bitterness. "Uh-oh! Pardon my language. I'm really down on cyclists these days. The kids think nothing of riding through my fields and tearing up my crops, just for fun. It would suit me fine if those machines were outlawed—not that there's any chance of that happening, of course."

"Motorcycles do seem popular these days," I agreed. "They scare me. I always tense up when I find myself sharing the road with one, and if there's more than one, I get even more nervous. I think it's because I consider them unpredictable and perhaps I, unfairly, judge their riders as unreliable and even irrational."

"That sounds like a nice way of putting it. What I consider them would be couched in much less polite terms."

I decided to take Nellie some fresh tomatoes and a bunch of basil. The eggplant with the lilac blush I bought for me. "Good luck with your canning," I called out as I started my car. I felt better from having talked to her. She seemed so real and happily planted in her world.

"Thank you for stopping by. Come back again." Molly turned toward the house then remembered to wave goodby just before she opened the door and went back inside.

I was very near the Vanderleigh estate when I noticed a black motorcycle up ahead, parked on the shoulder of the road about a hundred yards in front of me. Its rider was nowhere to be seen. As I drove by the parked vehicle, a large man dressed in dark clothes and wearing a protective helmet, came out of the woods and walked toward it. I felt, rather than saw, his stare as I passed by. Something seemed familiar about that partially obscured face; familiar, but out of context.

"Oh, Maggie!" I laughed as I pulled into the entrance of the estate, "You of the infinite imagination! It is highly unlikely that one of the few people you know in this whole hemisphere would be walking out of the woods just as you drove by. I glanced into my rearview mirror as he started to pull past me. The tinted shield of his helmet now fully covered his face. No, I saw nothing recognizable about him, but it was easy to see that he was too old to be tearing up crops and fields for fun.

I pushed the button on my transmitter and once more enjoyed that ego lifting thrill of both tall gates opening majestically as I passed through. Again I felt safe when they closed and locked securely behind me.

I had only gotten half way down the gravelled drive when some movement to the right diverted my attention. I quickly stopped the car and turned around in my seat, hoping to see it again. Nothing was there. As I began to move the car forward, I briefly glimpsed a wisp of white, like the flutter of a large bird's wing. Then, I'd swear I saw a strikingly pale face with large dark eyes. My dream! I stopped the car, scrambled out and ran toward the bank. I had to find that face! My foot slipped on the clay of the wet bank and, with my usual grace, I tumbled onto the rough gravel of the drive. By the time I got up and climbed the bank again, whatever I had seen was gone. I walked back to the car, a little ruffled and muddy but otherwise unhurt.

That face was real, I know it was! Ah yes, Maggie old girl, just like the screams you heard earlier this afternoon were real. I sighed with disgust and slid under the wheel. I have to get my mind off these things and begin to get well. I cannot lose my grip again.

It was only six o'clock. I had plenty of time for a mind-soothing hot soaking bath before dinner. I had to find a way to pull out of this self-destructing behavior. I have no one to lean on any more; I must be strong and in control for my own sake.

At dinner Jonathan, although pleasant and polite, seemed preoccupied with his own thoughts. He listened with only half an ear as Lillian and I took advantage of this opportunity to become better acquainted. She wore a burgundy full length sheath with a softly draped neckline. It had obviously been an elegant gown at one time, but was a little faded now. Her graying brown hair was tightly pulled back into an awkward chignon.

She talked of bygone days too, particularly of her father, Matthew Vanderleigh. "He was a real man, Maggie, a natural leader. His opinions were respected by important people and his advice was sought by leaders in both business and government. There are only a few like him in a generation. Of course, we have him to thank for this beautiful home; he turned it from grandfather's private woodland retreat into an estate and a showplace."

Jonathan interrupted as Nellie entered with the first course. "Lillian has made some of her jellied madrilene. If you've never had it, Maggie, you're in for a real treat."

Until we returned to the States, I had eaten little western food. We'd been back on a few short visits when I was still a small child, but since I don't remember the food, it must have been unimportant to me then. Now it seemed every meal presented a new learning situation. I didn't know the type of taste to expect from this interesting dish. The shimmering gelatin was set in a bed of fresh garden lettuce. It looked as though it might be sweet, but I was pleasantly surprised at the delicately seasoned flavor. Not sweet at all. "Lillian, I love it!"

She smiled broadly, reveling in praise. I marvelled at the change in Lillian from when I had first met her a few days ago. Her features no longer had their hard edge and her eyes showed less tension. "Oh Maggie, if you had only known my father! He would have liked you so much. He was such a mountain of a man, big and burly. Always happy and exuberant—so different from the rest of us I don't know where he came from! He wasn't at all like his father, Adam."

"That's one I want to hear more about! Tell me all you can remember about Adam. What was he like?"

"Grandfather was quiet: strong willed all right, but quiet-spoken and reserved. I was a little afraid of him, if you want to know the truth. He never had much use for me at all; he was Jonathan's friend. Our father never saw much of Grandfather either. Adam was always away at sea when he was growing up. My father really only knew Adam when he was an old man and they were never close; too different I'd guess. Father was outgoing, loved to socialize and enjoyed being around people all the time; Grandfather was the opposite, a loner, impatient with his fellow human beings. Jonathan, you tell Maggie about Grandfather. You and he used to share secrets all the time."

"What?" Jonathan looked startled as though pulled from his own reverie. "Oh, yes. Well, that was so long ago, Lillian, I really don't remember anything Maggie would be interested in hearing. He would just tell me tales of the sea and of the lands he had seen. I was the only one who wanted to hear his stories and he always seemed to have the time to listen to my childish questions. Nothing unusual about that. It's to him I owe my interest in history; I'll always be grateful to him for that."

Lillian was impatient to get back to her story. "Father loved to have big parties. After dinner he and the other men would sit around a glowing fire in the library for drinks, cigars and conversation. When Jonathan was old enough he was invited to join them."

Jonathan laughed. "I really knew I had come of age the first time I was invited to the library after dinner. I think Father was disappointed in me though; I wasn't much of a talker then. I always preferred to read."

"It was very different in those days. We even had dances. Maggie! Everything was decorated so beautifully. When I was too young to go I would stay up late and watch from a hidden corner. Then, when I grew up, everytime Father had a party he would bring me a new dress as a surprise. This was the last one he brought me."

Jonathan tossed off a scornful, "It looks it."

Surprisingly Lillian didn't bristle at his remark but blushed and lovingly touched the fabric of her sleeve. "Oh, I know it's old, but I thought, with only the three of us here, that I would wear it again, just for tonight."

My vision of Lillian as she must have looked in that dress long ago was interrupted by the sound of hesitant foot steps in the tiled foyer.

I looked up as someone walked in and could only hope my face didn't reveal the depth of my shock. This must be Catherine! Her bleached blond hair was frizzed into the so-called curly look. She had obviously tried to brush it into a more elegant style, but several strands hadn't stayed in place. Her dress, a delicate rose chiffon, was of excellent quality, but at least one size too small. Although she was not really fat, she must have gained several pounds since she bought it. The narrow shoulder strap had slipped and lay untidily on her upper arm. Her eyes, their puffy lids covered with thickly applied green shadow, darted nervously around the room.

She spoke breathlessly, "I'm sorry to be late, Jonathan. I tried so to hurry."

Lillian interrupted her apology. "This is Margaret, Dr. Driscoll's daughter, Catherine."

"Dr. Driscoll? Dr. Driscoll is . . . is . . . is gone."

"Yes, now sit down, my dear," said Jonathan. "We've barely started. We're enjoying Lillian's jellied madrilene."

She laughed, a drunk's raucous laughter.

"Lillian's madrilene . . . jellied . . . that is . . . jellied Lillian's madrilene."

I shot a glance at Lillian. This was painful for her. She turned in her chair as if to leave, but when she realized I was watching, she seemed to decide against it.

Catherine sensed Lillian's rejection. Her hands stretched toward her in a pleading gesture, then dropped to her sides at Lillian's refusal to look her way. She turned toward her husband. "Jonathan," her voice was but a whimper, "I'm really not feeling well. If you don't mind, I think I'll have Nellie bring my dinner to my room."

"Whatever you say, my dear. I'm sure Nellie will be glad to be of help. If you're feeling better later, we'd like to have you join us again." His manner, strictly correct and overly polite under these bizarre circumstances, was somehow disturbing to me. Catherine stared at him for a moment as though to apologize again. She then thought better of it and left with Nellie helping to steady her.

The pall she had settled on the evening during her short scene remained with me long after she had gone. She reminded me of a wounded bird; a small delicate bird totally out of place in the Jaeger's Nest.

We continued to eat in silence as Lillian, in Nellie's absence, served the remainder of the dinner. The tense look had returned to her eyes; the brief glimpse I had seen of her girlhood had turned inward again and the harsh, unyielding Lillian had returned.

Nellie appeared at the door of the dining room.

"Miss Driscoll, there's a call for you, a Mr. Ingram."

"Oh, yes. I'll take it now. Excuse me." I could feel both Lillian and Jonathan's questioning eyes follow me as I left the room. As we entered the foyer, Nellie whispered. "I think he called once before, when you were in the hospital, but he didn't leave his name or number. The voice sounds the same though."

"Thank you, Nellie." I put the receiver to my ear. "Margaret Driscoll here. Hello, Mr. Ingram."

"Well, I must say, you're a hard one to track down! I needed all my special training. I tried your apartment, but there was no answer. Thanks to Mrs. Morgan, I learned you were hospitalized. She left it to you to tell me what happened, though, muttering something to the effect that a person's medical problems are their own and not for the likes of her to tell the likes of me."

I laughed. "Well to be honest, I don't really know what happened. Mr. Vanderleigh says I began having nightmares and then, when they couldn't wake me up, they had me admitted to the hospital. Some sort of stress reaction, I guess. Anyway I feel much better now."

"Good enough to join me for lunch tomorrow?"

"Oh, I really don't want to make another trip into Manhattan just now!"

"I should have mentioned, I have to be down that way on personal business for a few days. We could have lunch in Bleekston."

"Will you be staying at the Butternut Inn?"

"Is that a good place?"

"It's the only one I know about. I like the woman who runs it, her name is Lizbeth Keaton. It's right on the main road and shouldn't be too crowded. I could be there by one-thirty."

"Sounds good."

I gave him full directions to Bleekston. "Goodbye until tomorrow, Martin."

I returned to the dining room just as Lillian and Jonathan were ending an animated discussion. The talking had stopped but the anger still remained in their faces as I entered the room. "Just a friend of Dad's. I'm meeting him for lunch tomorrow. No problem." As I took my seat, I realized that their reactions to my returning explanation were odd; Lillian relaxed slightly, but Jonathan became more tense. Oh, some imagination I have! It is sure to get me in trouble some day. They were probably discussing their own personal matters, like Catherine's behavior, while I was on the phone, and my abrupt return caught them by surprise.

A dessert of warm apple crisp with a small dip of vanilla ice cream had been served while I was away. My serving sat waiting with a steaming cup of coffee. The contrast of the sweet crumbled pastry, warm spicy apples, and the cold vanilla ice cream was delicious. "What a perfect ending to a wonderful dinner, Lillian. I enjoyed every bite of it." Her pleasure at the compliment was a little harder to detect this time, but it was there. "Now, if you two don't mind, I'm going to turn in early tonight. I'm still feeling a little tired and weak."

Lillian spoke up immediately, "Oh, Maggie! Feel free to treat this as your own home. I don't want you to feel restrained in any way."

Jonathan also seemed relieved the dinner was at an end. "Yes, Maggie. We'd like to have you enjoy your time here. Don't feel you must have our permission, just do as you wish." His look was a little sheepish; he'd found another way to apologize for his anger at my wandering from the hospital grounds.

As I left the dining room and walked through the foyer, I admitted to myself that I hadn't been exactly truthful with Jonathan and Lillian. I wasn't really all that tired, but I felt that Catherine's short visit had put a damper on the evening. I suspected that Jonathan, and certainly Lillian, did not feel like socializing right now. I stopped off at the library to choose a book to take up with me and read before I went to sleep.

Again I was impressed with the magnificence of this room. I slowly turned and stared at the rows upon rows of books. The shelves were so high that a library ladder, made of oak to match the shelves, was fitted into a track so that you could move the ladder around the room and use it to climb higher for the books on the top shelves.

Just like the grass is always greener on the other side, the books on the higher shelves seemed more interesting. Their bindings certainly were older and more worn. Perhaps Bruce's great grandfather, Adam Vanderleigh, had held those books in his hands. I tried to envision an old, really old, Jonathan. Maybe Adam had looked like that.

I climbed the ladder and turned on an overhead light to illuminate that section of the shelves I wanted to inspect more closely. Just as the light came on, I heard a frantic scratching and flutter above me. I turned in panic toward the strange sound, nearly losing my balance on the ladder. I was astonished to see the claws and fluttering wings of birds overhead at the skylight. Reason left me and I screamed.

I held tightly to the ladder trying to regain a more secure footing. Was it real? I had to know, was the bird real? I looked again toward the skylight. No bird. In its place, further in the distance as though floating in the sky above, I again saw the face with the large dark eyes. My screams were no longer under my control. They seemed to come from the depths of my being, over and over, totally beyond restraint.

"Maggie! What is it? What's wrong?" Jonathan and Lillian came running into the library and found me clinging to the ladder with all my might.

"Help her down, Jonathan," directed Lillian. "Help her down before she falls."

I sobbed as I desperately tried to gain control; I did not want Jonathan to take me to the hospital again. I forced myself to breathe deeply and slowly. I had to convince him that I was all right. "Oh, Jonathan, I'm sorry." I tried to laugh but half sobbed instead. "I'm so sorry that I alarmed you both. I just came in to borrow a book. As I turned on the light and climbed the ladder to reach for a book, a bird fluttered at the skylight and frightened me so badly that I lost my footing. I'm ashamed to admit that's all it was. I can see how upset you both are."

"Was that all! For goodness sake, Maggie!" laughed Lillian. "Well, I guess I'm glad to know it was nothing more serious."

"You really gave me a fright young lady!" joined in Jonathan, obviously relieved. "I came in prepared to fight to the death. My adrenalin is pumping furiously." He began to climb the ladder. "Here let me help you down from there."

The trembling had lessened and I was able, with Jonathan's help, to maneuver down the ladder.

Later, alone once more and ready for bed, I reached to turn out the light and recalled that the last time I had done that I woke up in the hospital. That cannot happen again. What I need is sleep, a dreamless healing sleep, free of screams and faces.

In the dark I could hear the creaking sounds of the old house. It was easy to imagine that I was drifting on an old wooden ship, heaving slowly on a gently rolling sea. This was the first time I had felt the spirit of Adam Vanderleigh. Lillian had succeeded in emphasizing her father Matthew's influence on the house, but in the night, when the tastefully elegant decorating could not be seen, the spirit of the seagoing Vanderleigh permeated every pore of the old wooden frame. Would he cast me adrift?

EIGHT

From my sun drenched table by the window of the dining room, I saw Martin arrive and park his small white sports car in an empty place across the street. He looked so confident and self-assured standing there on the curb waiting for the traffic to clear. A strong gust of wind molded his clothes tight against his body, disclosing muscular thighs and a slim waist, then tossed his hair as he turned to make sure the street was clear of traffic before sprinting across. In a uniquely masculine gesture, he unconsciously raked his wind blown hair into place with strong lean fingers as he approached the entrance to the inn.

As I had expected, Lizbeth's dining room was not crowded at this time of day. Only half of the fifteen or so tables were taken, but all heads turned when Martin entered. Although dressed casually in a cream linen sports suit and a pastel plaid shirt, his presence was commanding. He saw me immediately and smiled broadly as he made his way across the dining room. I had to admit that I enjoyed having people look my way to see who this attractive man was coming to meet. They didn't have to know he was my father's friend, not mine.

"Is that your car or did you just rent it for today's trip?" I asked as he adjusted a chair to sit down. I wanted to say more, something like: I'm so glad you came because I need a strong shoulder, but the words caught in my throat as he looked over at me.

"All mine. Most city dwellers don't bother to own cars since the public transportation around the Big Apple is usually reliable. Garage space is pretty expensive too. But in spite of all the arguments against it, I do own a car, and even a motorcycle, because I feel trapped without my own wheels."

"And I feel deprived because I didn't get to ride in that flashy car the other night."

He laughed. "I rarely use it just to move around the City, parking places are so hard to find. Enough about that though, let's talk about you. I was surprised that you decided to visit the Vanderleighs so soon."

I laughed bitterly, "Oh yes, so much has happened since then, I almost forgot." I started to say more but paused when Lizbeth stopped at our table. I knew she must recognize me, but her greeting and smile were curiously impersonal as she asked for our order. We quickly decided on soup and sandwiches, then resumed our conversation as she walked away. "When I got back to my apartment Saturday night, after our dinner in Manhattan, someone had searched my car. In the process of looking for whatever it is that I'm supposed to have, they almost completely destroyed it; ripped the interior all apart: slashed the seats, ripped loose the upholstered door panels, and pulled up the carpet. There is absolutely nothing I could have that anyone would want this badly! To top it off, my train from Manhattan was stopped because of an anonymous call saying there was a bomb aboard set to explode when the train was in the tunnel under the river. It was a hoax, of course, but still very frightening."

"Did you leave for the Vanderleigh's that night?"

"No, the next day. It was so late I went to a hotel. Then Sunday night I went to sleep in the Vanderleigh's guest room and woke up in the hospital. I can't even depend on myself not to fall apart any more!"

I knew I sounded juvenile and was feeling sorry for myself again. I wanted a comforting hug; I wanted someone to fix my car and make it well. I wanted to wake up from this bad dream to find my dad alive and everything all brand new and untouched. I felt like such an impotent child.

His voice was gentle, "Hang on Margaret. I don't know why all this is happening to you, but since it is, you have to learn to handle it one step at a time."

He was trying to prop me up to face the world when what I wanted was protection from it. I tried to hide my frustration and anger but it finally slipped through. "Well, did you come all the way down here just to tell me to keep my chin up?" He looked at me for an uncomfortably long time, his eyes cold and remote. I deserved to be embarrassed. What in the world did I expect? I'm sure Martin Ingram had a full life before I ever came along; he might even be engaged or even married for all I knew! He probably feels the last thing he needed was to have Mat Driscoll's daughter dropped in his lap! I just never seem to do anything right where he's concerned.

He finally spoke, "Tell me about the Vanderleighs. What did you think of them?" I was thankful he was ignoring my rudeness.

"They're a little stilted, but very nice, and their home is breathtakingly beautiful! I've never even dreamed of anything like it; it's almost like a museum! Jonathan and Bruce, his son, are friendly and gracious, but Lillian, his sister, is less outgoing. It may be that she's just shy." I told him all about the magnificent estate and Bruce. "Bruce's mother died some time ago and Jonathan has remarried."

"And this second Mrs. Vanderleigh, what is she like?"

I was beginning to feel uncomfortable with his curiosity about the Vanderleighs, but then realized that he was probably only trying to divert my mind from my recent frightening experiences. "I really don't know what to think of her; I haven't had a chance to talk with her alone, but she does appear to drink pretty heavily." I stopped suddenly, feeling disloyal. Here I was spreading gossip about the family of a man who had been a friend to my Dad, and to me. I changed the subject. "Jonathan offered me a part time job while I'm in school. He's working on an oriental history project and feels I could be of help to him. I haven't decided whether to accept or not."

"Will you need to work?"

"Oh yes," I laughed, "That much I do know."

"Then why are you hesitating?"

"I'm not sure. I guess things have been happening so fast I just want to rein in and not make any changes or decisions until I have to."

"If you worked for Vanderleigh would you live at the estate?"

"Just until school starts in mid-September. After that, I'd just spend weekends there."

"If the work interests you, take it. It might be better if you didn't live alone right now anyway."

I felt that he was pushing me; I just wasn't ready to make this decision yet. "But I wanted to wait a little while before I decided. I feel like I'm caught up in a whirlwind since Dad died and since I don't have to accept the job right now, I don't intend to."

"Why? Where could you possibly get a job better suited to your interests and abilities? You know and like the people. There's such a thing as taking your time to make a well-considered decision, Margaret, then another thing called being afraid to commit oneself to that decision. I think the second one fits you. You're afraid to commit yourself."

I went hot with an anger I had never felt before and I knew from the way my face burned that I was showing it. I spat the words, "You're not my father, you know."

Martin looked straight at me, his eyes cold and his jaw set, saying nothing. Then, in a voice unnaturally controlled, he retorted, "You're right. I'm not your father and have no desire to be."

An embarrassing silence hung heavy between us as

his words echoed in my mind. My eyes dropped to his hands, resting on the table in front of him, relaxed and controlled. The soft bronze glow of his lightly tanned skin highlighted the physical perfection of those lean sinewy hands. Oh why had I said such a thing? I had acted like a rebellious child again. I finally had to admit he was right. "All right," I conceded in a subdued voice, "I'll tell Jonathan today."

"Good. Nothing comes easy, Margaret. The only way to learn the game of life is to play it. It's too bad that you have to grow up overnight, but it's time that you admitted you must, and grasped control of your own life."

"Obviously. Pardon me if I'm not overjoyed at what that seems to mean." There I go again!

A grim look came over his face. "I guess I'm pushing you a little hard. That's probably the last thing you need today, I'm sorry. Did you call the police about your car?"

I was relieved to change the subject. "Yes, but there was really nothing more they could do than add it to their earlier report. I know it was the same person who searched the apartment; he's very thorough. Why can't he just tell me what he wants? Nothing could possibly equal the cost of the repairs I'll have to make to my car and my apartment!"

"I doubt Mat had renter's insurance on the furnishings, but I feel sure your automobile policy will cover some of the cost to repair the damage to your car."

I was disappointed at his unsympathetic and business-like reaction. I snapped a reply, "Dad always handled all that." Why was he being so cold and distant? Why didn't he offer to help me?

"Well, I'm afraid it's something you're going to have to learn, Margaret. It's not difficult." His voice was unruffled and firm. "I'm sure you'll find your policy in Mat's papers if it's not in the car. Just ask your agent to explain what you need to do to file a claim. It's their business to help you."

I felt he was directing me again, pushing me to act before I was ready, but this time I held my tongue. I had said enough.

"I guess I'm really interested less in what happened, than in why it happened, Margaret. Do you have any idea at all of what could be the reason for all this? It's obviously something someone wants very badly, or maybe it's something they just don't want you to have."

"I know nothing, Martin. The only thing I'm sure of is that Dad was working as a consultant to Jonathan Vanderleigh on an oriental history project. I have no idea what my phantom searcher is looking for. Other than the Vanderleighs, the only other person I know Dad has talked to since we returned to the States is a Tibetan Buddhist monk."

"A monk!" He looked at me so strangely I had to laugh. The world suddenly seemed brighter as he laughed with me. Unsmiling he seemed cold and forbidding, but when he smiled, his face and eyes seemed to glow with pure pleasure.

"I was walking around the hospital grounds yesterday and saw a Buddhist monk; I followed him to a beautiful little temple. When I introduced myself as Margaret Driscoll, he asked if I knew a

Matthew Driscoll and told me Dad had been trying to find some things that had been stolen from them."

"What things?" The cold and wary look returned to Martin's eyes.

I almost stuttered in my effort to reply hastily. I didn't want that cold look again. "A very old silver Wheel of the Law and an antique prayer wheel. They were carefully protected all over Europe for decades. Then, when their temple was built, it seemed a safe enough haven. Unfortunately, it was not."

"Those items were just stolen? There was no damage or defacement to the temple?"

"I don't believe so, he didn't mention it."

"Do they have any suspicion of who may have been responsible?"

"No. I feel so sorry for them. So little remains of their heritage and now even these things have been taken. Do you know someone who can help them, Martin? Dad was going to try, but I don't know what he planned to do."

"I think you may have hit on something, Margaret!"

"What do you mean?"

"This may be the reason Mat was trying to contact me. We had discussed my work with Interpol over lunch several weeks ago. I trace stolen art works and in the past few years I have had a progressively busy job. The value of most art has skyrocketed during the past decade. During that same time, the reported number of art thefts has increased at an even more rapid rate."

"Oh, Martin! It would mean so much to them if you could help. Those beautiful things can never be replaced; they're priceless."

"I'll try, Margaret, but I must warn you that the chance of recovery is small. I'll stop by the temple before I leave to at least give them the feeling that something is being done. Tell me how to get there."

"I'll draw a map." I quickly sketched out the way on my note pad. As I handed the map to Martin, a familiar face passed by the window. "Here comes Bruce Vanderleigh!"

Bruce did not notice us as he entered the inn. He walked directly to the back and noisily greeted Lizbeth with a hearty bear hug. She laughed happily and casually returned his embrace. I tried to cover my confusion by animatedly talking with Martin about the food, the weather, or anything that was distracting, but it was no use; I could think of nothing other than the obvious fact that Bruce Vanderleigh and Lizabeth Keaton were very close friends. She must have mentioned that we were here because he turned to look, then smiled and waved. She walked away from him to serve a newly arriving foursome and Bruce came directly to our table.

"Join us, Bruce, we're just having lunch."

"Exactly what I had in mind."

"This is Martin Ingram, a friend of my Dad's. Bruce Vanderleigh, Martin." Bruce extended his hand to meet Martin's, then, instead of sitting down, he stood behind my chair, his hands resting possessively on my shoulders. "When did you get back?" I asked, leaning my head back to look up at him. He smiled down at me, his tanned face was slightly flushed. He looked wonderful.

"Just drove in. I didn't expect you to return to Bleekston so soon, Maggie. Are you just passing through or are you back to stay for a while?" His strong hands began to gently massage my shoulders.

"Actually, I didn't leave." I glanced at Martin, "I've just decided to accept your father's job offer." I began to feel uncomfortable with Bruce's hands on my shoulders, but I didn't want to embarrass him by saying anything. Martin leaned back in his chair, his arms casually crossed over his chest; his icy eyes coolly appraised and slightly challenged Bruce.

"That was a quick decision! What happened?" Bruce's hands had moved closer to my neck, still gently kneading my tense muscles. I could take it no longer and moved to shake his hands away. "You really should do something to loosen up there, Maggie. You're very tight across your shoulders."

Martin pushed out a chair for Bruce. "Have a seat, Vanderleigh, and order lunch or we'll be through eating before you take your first bite." Martin's tone sounded a lot like an order.

Bruce reached toward Lizbeth's arm as she walked by "Aunt Lizbeth, roast beef on rye and coffee, when you have a minute."

"Aunt Lizbeth?" My voice left no doubt I was surprised.

"Yes." Bruce took the chair. "Lizbeth is my mother's younger sister. She's also my favorite relative. Since her husband was killed in Vietnam and my mother died, we've stuck together. She and Dad don't get along at all, so I usually drop by to see her when I'm in town."

I had to admit I was relieved to learn Lizbeth and Bruce were related. Although I knew I had no right, I had felt a pang or two of jealousy at their relaxed familiarity.

"So, Maggie, why did you decide to stay?"

"Well, I haven't had much luck with Northeastern hospitality. My car and apartment were vandalized, and—"

"Vandalized?"

"Destroyed is a better word for it. Then, the night you left, I ended up in the hospital—a stress reaction the doctor says. I've decided that I don't want to live alone right now, so your Father's offer of a job is a godsend."

When Lizbeth brought our sandwiches, Bruce introduced us. "Aunt Lizbeth. I'd like you to meet Maggie Driscoll, Dad's new assistant, and Martin Ingram, a friend of Mat Driscoll, Maggie's father."

"I'm glad to see you again, Maggie, and I'm sorry about your father. Bruce had mentioned him often." Her eyes made a quick appraisal of Martin and her smile registered pleasure with what she saw. "Welcome to Bleekston, Mr. Ingram; we're not quite the nation's oldest city, but we are one of its more pretentious ones. I assure you it's not as provincial around here as our quaint little town would lead you to believe."

"I can see that," said Martin, smiling broadly at her flirtatious manner. The attraction seemed mutual and Martin's eyes followed her approvingly as she walked away. He turned back to Bruce, "Margaret tells me you're an archeologist,

Vanderleigh, are you working on a specific project now?"

"It's been mainly academic work so far, but I plan to go into active field work within the next six months. Mat Driscoll had a lot to do with that decision," Bruce looked at me as he credited my father. "He helped me understand how important it is to do what I really want to do. Are you in Mat's field, Ingram?"

"No, I'm with the government. Treasury. I met Mat when I was in the service." I wondered about Martin's indirect answer, but said nothing. It was correct, after all; Treasury and Justice share as the United States bureaus designated to serve as our link with Interpol.

Martin had eaten hurriedly and was finished with his meal. "Well, Margaret, I should get going. You'll take care of your car?"

"What needs to be done, Maggie? Maybe I can help," Bruce offered.

My eyes lit up. "I have to talk with my insurance agent about filing a claim for the damage done to the interior, then arrange to have it repaired."

"Oh, I can take care of that! I know a good shop here, owned by a friend of mine. He does nice work. We'll leave it there for an estimate and I'll drive you home. We can call your insurance company later." I looked up at Martin with what I could feel was a smug look on my face as Bruce said, "Don't worry Ingram, I can take care of it."

Martin looked irritated by Bruce's take charge manner. His jaw became set in a hard line. I couldn't let him leave that way. "Martin thank you so much for coming down. I appreciate it, really. Call me when you can."

"Sure Margaret." Martin gave me a wry smile. "I'll leave you in Bruce's hands." He walked straight for the door, pausing briefly to talk with Lizbeth. Whatever he said to her made her feel wonderful; she literally seemed to glow as he left. He was, after all, more her age.

Once out on the sidewalk, Martin turned toward the window to wave and smile at us again. It was a strange smile, sarcastic, knowing. I couldn't define why it seemed to irritate me so.

NINE

As we rode back toward the estate, I sank deeply into the softly embracing seat of Bruce's red Mercedes roadster. The moneyed masculine smell of well cared for, aged leather and the intricately grained burl wood trim of his dashboard let any passenger of this car know that they were travelling in an out of the ordinary way. The FM radio station began to play the Bruch Violin Concerto Number One, one of my very favorites, and my dreamlike world became complete. I felt so much like a fairy princess that I was sure the warm glow inside me must be creating a visible aura for all the world to see: all pampered, pedestalled and protected by someone who looked very much like the prince charming romantic young women often dream about.

Bruce had taken care of all the intricate details involved in repairing my car. He contacted the insurance company from the repair shop and then arranged to have the interior redone as soon as an insurance inspector had looked it over. Martin was right, I could have done it, but it was nice to have Bruce take over and handle it so easily. As the Bruch Concerto ended, I shifted forward in my seat and reached out to touch the warm wood of the dashboard. "This car is a really beautiful machine, Bruce. How long have you had it?"

"I've only owned it for four years, but it's an old one. I enjoy keeping it in top shape. They just don't make them like this one any more. It belonged to a little old lady who had her old world master mechanic cum chauffeur drive her into town once a week for shopping and then take her directly back home again. At least that's what the antique auto salesman said."

I laughed at his joke. "I guess auto salesmen are the same no matter what they're selling, but this is a truly unique car. By the way, I've been meaning to ask how your meeting went?"

"Well, let's just say it's good to be home again. Believe it or not, it was an extremely dull conference, but then I guess a lot of things seem dull to me lately. I'm anxious to get started on some active work. The academic end of this business has become too tame for me right now. I'm not one to risk his neck fighting off the natives for a few shards of pottery, but endless talking about something someone else has done, instead of getting out and doing it myself, is not the way I want to live my life."

"What do you plan to do?"

"By hook or crook, I want to work on the Elba ruins in Syria."

"Of course! I should have guessed that! I've heard a little about them, but not as much as I'd like to."

"The discovery was only announced in seventy-six. The dig started in the early sixties but it wasn't until the middle seventies that they found the archives, with its hoard of inscribed clay tablets, and knew the magnitude of their find."

"What have they learned so far?"

"Of course they aren't ready to announce all their findings, but evidence indicates the area may have been occupied as long ago as fifty-five hundred years. A millennium later Elba had become a large and thriving commercial population center. That's almost two thousand years before the rise of classical Greece!"

"As I understand it, the find is so significant and so large, they'll be digging there for years."

"Oh yes. The ruins of Elba cover about one hundred forty acres and only a small section has been excavated. It looks like the work will continue for generations. But enough about me, Maggie. How do you want to live your life?"

"Right now, at this moment, I want to finish the work on my doctorate and teach. I must admit I yearn for that academic life you were just downgrading. Then some day, far in the future, I would like to go back to Cambodia, if it's ever possible, and certainly on to China. For now, though, I'm just going to concentrate on preparing myself to work in a profession that will allow me to make use of my many years of living in the East."

"Well, it sounds like you have it all worked out."

"Oh, not really, not at all." I looked out at the passing countryside and was suddenly filled with an overwhelming wave of depression. I felt so rootless, so unattached to anything solid. This feeling had begun to sneak up on me as I watched the easy relationship of Bruce and Mike, his high school friend who owned the auto shop. "I envy you for having always lived in the same place, Bruce. I can't imagine how it would feel to have always known the same people and to have always lived in the same house all your life. Life must seem very stable and secure to you."

Bruce kept his profile to me, his eyes firmly on the road. I could not fully read his expression, but I could see that it was not a happy one. "Bleekston is a comfortable place to live, Maggie, no doubt about it, but being a Vanderleigh is a hindrance rather than a help in forming friendships. I'm just lucky to have Aunt Lizbeth. She's made my life more normal, I guess. Anyway, I think we've helped each other."

"I was really surprised to learn that Lizbeth Keaton was your aunt."

"She mentioned she had seen you before."

"I stopped at the Inn on my way down last week. She was so talkative and friendly until I asked her how to get to the estate, then it was as though a light went out. She became very cold."

"She has a right. She loved my mother; they were very close."

It seemed more proper to ask for clarification now than to ignore that remark. "How did it happen, Bruce? How did your mother die?"

For a moment I thought he was not going to answer me. His voice was choked as he finally said softly, "In a car accident. That's all I know for sure.'' His hands gripped the steering wheel so tightly his knuckles stood up like taut white knots.

I pushed on. ''How would that make Lizbeth so bitter?''

His tortured reply was abrupt and clipped. ''She died in a car accident with another man. Gordon Manchester, Catherine's first husband.'' Shiny beads of perspiration glistened on his forehead and upper lip. He stared straight ahead, eyes glued to the road.

''I see.'' I didn't really, not completely, but it was clear Bruce was upset and I didn't want him to continue talking unless he wanted to.

''Yes, that's the way it looks, but it wasn't true. You see, my father and mother, her name was Anne, were close friends with the Manchesters, Gordon and Catherine. Mother and Gordon were killed in the same car wreck and rumors began circulating soon after their death that they were leaving Bleekston to be together; that they were lovers.''

''Bruce you don't need to tell me any more. I know it hurts—''

He went on, ignoring my words. ''I couldn't believe then that she would leave me without so much as a word, and I can't believe it now. Lizbeth and Mother were very close, more than most sisters usually are. The age difference was so great, it's hard to understand how they could be as close as they were. Lizbeth was only twenty four when mother died; ten years older than I was. Because of their relationship, Lizbeth is certain that Mother would have told her if she were having an affair with Gordon Manchester. She knows without a doubt that mother would have confided in her if she were leaving.'' He took a deep breath, then let it out in an exasperated sigh. ''Anyway, Aunt Lizbeth blames Jonathan and will have nothing to do with anyone named Vanderleigh except me.''

''How can she blame your father?''

''He did nothing to stop the rumors; Lizbeth will never forgive him for that. Then, to top it off, he married Catherine.''

''I guess that history explains Catherine a little bit too.''

His face contorted in disgust. ''Catherine is a nothing. Her only claim to self worth before, was her beauty. She was beautiful, that is a fact. Now that her beauty has vanished into the bottle, she is a total zero. Better yet, she is a minus. She lost her right to zero when she became an obnoxious drunk instead of just a sad one.''

The bitterness with which he spat out his evaluation of Catherine surprised me. It was vehement; I doubt she deserved it. I suddenly didn't feel envious of Bruce anymore. It's nice to have always lived in the same place, among the same people, if it has been a happy life. His was far from that.

''Not long after my mother died, Lizbeth's husband was killed in Vietnam. They had only been married a short time when he was shipped over.''

''She's so attractive, she'll surely remarry.''

''She won't. She and Dirk, her husband, grew up together. They meant everything to each other. She just isn't interested in anybody else. She owns the Inn and she has done well with it. She says she doesn't need to do somebody's dirty laundry to feel fulfilled anymore."

I wasn't as sure of her lack of interest in male companionship. I had seen her frank and open admiration of Martin Ingram. My eyes drifted back to the countryside. The trees were a tipoff that we were nearing the estate, those tall, protective, trees.

"That fellow Ingram seems young to have been a friend of Mat's."

"Yes, I know, but they knew each other in Indochina. He was serving there when he met my father. I didn't know him, but they spent a lot of time together when I was in school in Thailand."

"Are you sure, Maggie? Had Mat ever spoken of him before?"

"What do you mean?"

"There's something about him that doesn't ring true to me. I'm not trying to alarm you, but I just want to caution you not to trust a total stranger. It bothers me, for instance, that he calls you Margaret. Mat always called you Maggie when he talked about you. Mat never called you Margaret once in all the time I knew him. Don't assume he was a friend of your father's unless you know for sure. Certainly don't confide in him as if he were."

I began to feel defensive. "Confide in him—trust in him—about what? He's only been helpful to me. There's no trust involved." I relieved my anger and tension by laughing. "I just don't have any deep, dark, secrets to tell anybody."

"I thought he was helping you to straighten out your father's affairs."

"There's little to do there, and Martin doesn't really help. He expects me to be grown-up and handle everything myself." That remark had spilled out a little more bitterly than I had intended. "I know I should learn; I'll certainly have to some day. I do appreciate your help with the car, though, Bruce. I just didn't know where to start."

"I was glad to help you and I know Mike will do a first rate job. It's hard to get things like that done when you don't know anybody to do it. A car is an expensive machine to turn over to an absolute stranger. I don't blame you for being a little apprehensive about it."

I laughed as we turned into the drive. "I don't think I'll ever fail to be impressed by the way those gates open. I feel so royal, especially since Lillian gave me a transmitter."

"Lillian gave you one? She must really like you! I would expect her to enjoy making it more difficult for someone and raise a big fuss about how she or Nellie has to be around to open the gate all the time."

"Bruce, I don't believe you really feel that way about her. She's only harsh because she feels defensive. She's very shy and it is her protection from the outside world to act like she doesn't want to bother with people, when in fact she is really feeling that they don't want to bother with her."

"In what field did you say you were studying for your Ph.D.? Psychology?" He gave me a sly smile.

"I guess I do deserve that. You certainly should know your own aunt better than I do."

"Not that one. She never really seemed to want me around. I was a boy, and boys can be destructive of houses and knick-knacks. You know how she worships every piece in that house."

"Those aren't exactly your common, run-of-the-mill knick-knacks! There are quite a few very rare pieces there, particularly the jades and porcelains."

"Oh, I know. I've certainly been told enough. When you've been around something all your life, it becomes so familiar you cease to respect it in the same way the outside world would, everybody except Aunt Lillian, that is. Oh, don't pay any attention to me. It is the family joke to kid about Lillian's devotion to everything in that house."

"She sees it as an extension of her father."

He laughed. "There you go again!" He pulled the car into an open bay of the carriage house. "Well, now that you're grounded without your car, I guess you'll have to stay here this weekend."

"Oh, I'd planned to do that anyway."

"Jonathan and I are taking the boat out. Do you like boating?"

"I've never been on a pleasure boat."

"Never?"

"Never in my life. If I was near the water, I was in it. I love to swim. We took an ocean liner over and back once when we had the time, but that's the limit of my boating experience."

"Well, I must introduce you to a new pleasure. We have plenty of sleeping room on the *Bonxie* so we can make a weekend of it."

"Are you sure Jonathan wouldn't mind?"

"Mind? He'd love it! We go out every weekend during the season, like clockwork. Fishing is our excuse, but more often we just enjoy being on the water. Jonathan goes alone when I'm away. He's a true creature of habit.''

"Does Lillian go with you?''

"Never, but with you along we may be able to convince her to give it a try. She loved boating with her father, but she hasn't been out in years. I'm sure you can talk her into it.''

"And Catherine?''

"She won't come. Ask her if you want, but she won't come. She'll stay home with Nellie.''

"Where is the boat docked?''

"Out back.'' He waved his arm in a direction beyond the carriage house.

I looked and saw nothing but trees. "Out back of what?''

"The woods. The estate backs up to the river. We just take the boat out to the bay, then on into the Atlantic Ocean.''

I was delighted, "I can't believe it! I didn't know you were directly on the water!''

"That's because you didn't know Great Grandfather Adam. He would never have built a landlocked house.''

"Let's go see it now.''

"O.K., but go change your shoes; you won't get very far along that rough terrain in those.''

"You're right.'' I looked down at my high heeled wooden bottom sandals. "I'll only take a second.''

"I'll take my luggage in while you're changing.''

Less than ten minutes later, Bruce and I were walking down the rocky path toward the river. "What's in the basket?'' I asked, looking at the wicker basket Bruce was carrying.

"Some refreshment.''

"What kind of refreshment?"

"A loaf of bread, a jug of wine and—"

"Yes, Omar?"

"A piece of English cheddar cheese!"

"That wasn't what you were supposed to say."

He laughed that warm liquid laugh that I liked so much. "Did you want me to recite 'The Rubiyat,' or did you want to know what was in the basket."

"Don't ask."

He laughed again and slung his free arm across my shoulder, not as an expression of intimacy, but in a casual way to gently guide me over the rocky path. "You may well ask why we don't smooth out this path and make an easier walkway. We occasionally ask that too, but we never do it. It would cause more damage to the trees than the path would be worth, if we tried to bring heavy earth moving equipment back here. Then too, if we made a formal and proper walkway back to the water, it wouldn't seem so isolated and we wouldn't have the feeling we were getting away from it all."

Much later, as we continued down the worn path, I could see what looked like water between the trees, and soon it was quite obvious we were coming to the river.

"Oh, Bruce! How absolutely beautiful!" It was certainly the most perfect landscape I had ever seen. The sweeping limbs of lacy green hemlock, beech and cherry birch formed a full-length green curtain right up to the water's edge. The drop to the water was at least ten feet and the banks were covered with mossy rocks, gnarled tree roots, and an occasional low-growing shrub. The boat house siding of split cedar shakes was naturally bleached a silver gray from the sun and salt air. The trim on its large windows was painted white, and flat colonial blue shutters framed each side of the windows. The door was trimmed with heavy brass hardware and painted a matching flat blue.

"Shall we go inside?"

"After that long walk, I wouldn't miss seeing the boathouse!"

He selected a key from his key ring and opened the door. The boathouse consisted of one big lounge room with a huge stone fireplace on the back wall. The decorating was rustic, as was fitting, and the overall impression was one of casual relaxation brushed by a cool breeze from the water.

A large round table surrounded with captain's chairs looked as though it had been lifted from an old English tavern. Two comfortable couches, covered in a cool navy, white, and lime green cotton print, flanked the gray fieldstone fireplace, and occasional chairs in harmonizing patterns were strategically placed over the room to create cozy conversational groupings.

"This looks like a great place to have a party."

"Just what I had in mind. Sit there." Bruce motioned to a chair at the big picture window overlooking the water. He pulled up another chair and placed the basket on a small table between us.

"That was a pretty quick picnic you packed. You must do this all the time."

"I do." He grinned mischievously. "It's what I usually bring when I come out here alone. I packed a little extra for you this time."

We spent the next hour or so drinking, munching, and talking about any subject that popped into our heads. I was relaxed with Bruce now; I no longer felt self-conscious and awkward.

The light was beginning to fade a bit when Bruce stood up. "Hey, I brought you down here to show you the boat. Let's go before it's dark."

He opened the door to the ramp. "We hoist the boat up and store it out of the water during the really cold weather, but when the weather is good, we just secure it to the dock."

Bruce jumped onto the lower ramp and turned to help me down. I felt a warm wave sweep over my body as he grasped my waist and lifted me down to the lower level, holding me hard against him. My hands were on his shoulders and I could feel the muscles of his thighs against mine. I couldn't move; I didn't want to. He looked down at me as I looked up into his eyes. My breathing was quick and shallow in expectation of the kiss I wanted so badly. Then he laughed and turned aside, putting his arm across my shoulders and guiding me along the ramp. He was walking beside me, even touching me, but I felt left out in space, rejected.

I followed him in a daze as he gave me the captain's tour. I knew nothing about boats, but from what I could see, this one was perfect, like a dream. It just wasn't the dream I wanted today.

"Jonathan fell in love with this boat at the boat show a couple of years ago and he just had to have it. It has the classic double cabin layout of V berths forward, a raised salon midship and the master stateroom aft. She's quick for her size. Steering is hydraulic, and it's a very roomy, low maintenance boat. All in all, she's easy to love."

Lucky boat! I tried to shake my mood by telling myself how silly I was to think he would be attracted to me, but I had been so sure that he was. Maybe he doesn't want to rush things; maybe he's shy too. Maybe, just maybe he's in love with someone else and is just entertaining me to be nice. Maybe so. That made more sense than anything else. I kept listening and trying to smile politely in the right places, hoping not to reveal how distracted I was.

Just as the sun was setting, we gathered up the remains of our picnic, closed up the boat house, and made our way back. It was strange how lonely I could feel with Bruce walking at my side. Maybe loneliness was my problem. Could I be trying to create an "instant" relationship to fill the void?

When we returned to the main house, Lillian was in the dining room with Nellie. "Jonathan's working in the library this afternoon. He said to stop by if you wanted to."

"I think I will go talk to him. I've decided to accept his job offer."

"He'll be pleased to hear that, and so am I, Maggie." Her smile was warm again.

Jonathan was leaning over the large oak library table, his papers sorted into several small piles around him. Sunlight spilled through the skylight above, bathing the room in soft light and color. I looked up; no birds or floating faces to be seen today. Were there ever?

"Well, how was your lunch?"

"Nice. The Inn's a good place to eat." I took a

chair at the end of the table.

"I didn't know Mat knew anyone on this side of the ocean anymore. It's been so long!"

"Oh yes, Mr. Ingram's an old friend of Dad's. I just met him a few days ago though."

Jonathan's look became thoughtful. "Maggie, what do you know about him, really?"

Wow, I thought to myself, these Vanderleigh men are really protective. "Not much, I guess." I had to admit. "He works for the government. Treasury. His office is in Manhattan. As to his relationship with my father, I only know what he told me, Dad had never mentioned him."

Jonathan looked as though his mind had drifted to another subject, as though he were thinking of something else. "I don't want to interrupt, I just stopped in to tell you that I'm sorry I was so hesitant to accept your job offer. I'd love to have it, it's perfect for me. I guess my whole world was spinning so rapidly, I was afraid to commit myself to anything for fear I might wobble it."

Jonathan eyed me thoughtfully. For a minute I was afraid he had changed his mind and no longer wanted me for the job. "Well, I can understand how you felt, Maggie, but I'm glad you decided to work with me." He walked toward an upholstered leather chair, motioning me toward the sofa. I was again impressed by the youthful appearance of his body in contrast to his drawn and aged face.

"I'm looking forward to the work and I'd love to get started right away." I sat on the edge of the sofa.

"Relax! Sit back, Maggie! We're not so formal

around here. At least I'm not, Lillian has her airs." I laughed and settled back into the soft cushions. "Well, I'm working on a new series which will attempt to acquaint a broad group of people with the Far East. As I mentioned yesterday, we'll be working on the Tibetan section of the project. It will carry the known history of Tibet up through the Communist Chinese seizure in the late fifties.

"Any student of the Orient will tell you that reliable information on Tibet is hard to come by these days. A few bits have been written about the daily life of today's Tibetans, but little has been said of the condition of the old monasteries or the ancient libraries."

He gestured toward the papers on the table. "Most of these notes are from an earlier, more esoteric, work. This time I plan to pull the subject down from its ivory towers, so to speak, and present it to the man in the street. Everyone's heard a lot about Japan and China since the war, but Tibet is still very much a mystery to most people. The West has become increasingly interested in the Eastern way of life since our relations with the People's Republic of China have started to improve. The Dalai Lama's recent visit also made people realize they knew very little about Eastern thought. His profound and compassionate comments were a surprise to those who expected any religion of the Orient to be unfathomable to the Western mind."

"I think the anxious pace of modern life is causing some Westerners to envy what they perceive as the relative calm of the Eastern people. They want to understand and achieve that inner peace."

"I'm sure that's part of it, Maggie, but the mystery and mysticism of the East excites their imagination too!" He rose and walked toward the library table. "Well, I knew yesterday you'd enjoy working on the project. I'm glad I had the good sense to ask you to join me. Needless to say, we'll have an informal working schedule. Work when you feel like it as long as the work gets done. If the output starts to slide, we'll have to buckle down when we don't feel like it just to get ourselves back on the track."

"Since I don't know how busy I'll be for the first few weeks of the semester, I'll try to get as much done in the next three weeks as I can."

"Good, but you must save some time for pleasure, Maggie, and for relaxing. You should not pressure yourself too much for a while. I'll leave these notes here in case you want to look them over. This notebook is an outline of the entire project and this file covers the section on Tibet." He walked toward the door. "If you want to discuss anything, I'll be in my office in the east wing."

Several hours passed quickly for me as I pored over Jonathan's earlier book and his more recent guidelines. I could learn a lot from this project. Tibet had always held a fascination for me. It had been virtually isolated from the rest of the world for many centuries by its forbidding and protective Himalayas. After giving the world a teasing look at what was to Westerners a mystically tranquil existence, the doors were slammed shut again when the Chinese closed the borders.

My eye caught the large globe in its wooden stand

by the boxed out window. I wonder how much will be left of the Orient I love by the time I'm ready to start teaching the world about it. I imagined a suffocating glob oozing from Russia to China, enveloping it, then seeping slowly over the continent of Asia, spilling into Indochina and edging up against Nepal, India, and Thailand. Where will it all end. Orwell's *1984* seems a haven compared to the stories of barbarism being told by Cambodian refugees: torture, murder, starvation and disease.

Can a system which steals unwilling labor from one to provide for another ever be just? People should be free to give of themselves out of love, to those they love and value. They should never be forced to provide for an anonymous mass of extortionate consumers to whom they owe nothing. Die for the good of the insatiable "all." Those at the top determine who the "all" will be, skimming the cream, and most of the milk, for themselves. Thinking of the wanton destruction of Cambodia and its people made me feel powerless and depressed.

A gentle culture can never afford to lose sight of its own vulnerability. As tempting as it may appear, a passive philosophy does not prepare people to fight for their way of life. Physically fight off external invaders, perhaps, but when the invasion is an acid eating away from within, they will become slaves before they know it.

Unknown to me, my father had tried to prevent what has happened in Cambodia. He and Martin had worked together as members of the Central Intelligence Agency—at least that was what Martin had told me. I felt a chill run down my spine. I was becoming uneasy and I didn't know why. Had I been wrong about Martin?

I began to review the past few days: I remembered that tiring ride home from the church in the heavy rain, running out of gas when I should have had a full tank. I pulled into the puddled driveway of my apartment house, easing past a black motorcycle parked beneath the tree. Then, when I entered my apartment—No! I don't want to think about that again! The next day I had met Martin Ingram for dinner. The train was held up because of a bomb scare on the return trip. When I finally arrived home, my car had been thoroughly searched. I was frightened and convinced someone was harassing me personally and for no reason. I sought refuge with the Vanderleighs. A few days later a motorcycle had passed me at the vegetable stand. I hadn't seen that one, just heard its engine as I talked with Mrs. MacGregor. Then I had seen a familiar looking man on a black motorcycle when I returned to the estate. Martin has a motorcycle! Could that have been him? I tried to call up the memory but it was no use, I had lost it.

I reached for the chain around my neck and fingered the silver medallion—had my Dad really sent Martin his medallion? If not, how did he get it?

Bruce's words echoed: "Don't assume he was a friend of your father's unless you know for sure . . . don't trust a total stranger." Then Jonathan's remark: "I didn't know Mat knew anyone on this side of the Atlantic anymore . . . What do you know about him really?"

I slowly began to take stock of all I really knew

about Martin Ingram and came up holding an empty bag. All I knew was what Martin had told me. Had he told me the truth? Assume for a moment that Martin was responsible for the damage to my apartment, could he have treated me so harshly? The memory of his ice blue eyes, staring coldly at me, came into my mind. Could he really be capable of something like that? But how could he have searched my car? I had just left him in New York! The bomb scare! An anonymous tip! Anyone could have delayed that train! He could have gotten there well ahead of me! But why should he? He knew I had nothing; that I didn't know why anyone would be searching through my things!

There you go, Maggie, letting your imagination run wild again! Just because you don't know, don't invent the answers. But all I knew was what Martin had told me. Had he told me the truth?

My concentration was broken by a hideous and terrifying scream from another part of the house. This one was real, I had no doubt whatsoever. I jumped from my chair and ran up the stairs to the second floor hallway. There I found Catherine writhing on the floor, her eyes wide and frightened. Her arms wildly waved off some grotesque horror visible only to her. She could not see me and did not know I was there. I stood helplessly by, appalled at her condition. Her hair hung in damp limp strands over her bloated face; it looked as though it had not been combed for days, and her nightgown, a high quality design in champagne lace, was wrinkled and stained.

Nellie came running up the back stairs. "Miss

Driscoll, Oh, Miss Driscoll! Don't worry. I'll take care of her, now don't you worry! I didn't want you to know."

"Can't I help? What's the matter? Why is she so frightened?"

"She's seeing monstrous things in her mind. It's the drink. The poor lady is going to kill herself some day, trying to escape her demon." Nellie helped her up, automatically murmuring comforting phrases, and started to walk her back to her room. I reached over to help support her, but stopped still when I saw Lillian charging up the stairs, her face drawn in a furious mask.

"What has she done now? Did she break anything this time? Get her back in there! I don't want her loose in this house when she's like this. She's destructive and ugly. Destructive! Ugly!"

"Oh, Miss Vanderleigh. I'll take care of her. She's a poor sad lady. I'll take care of her. Don't you worry about it." Nellie kept her arms protectively around Catherine.

"She has to leave, Nellie. She must be put away in a home where they can do something for her. We aren't helping her any by keeping her here." Lillian's voice was matter of fact now, no compassion, no anger.

Catherine seemed to come around. "Oh, don't send me away, Lillian . . . I schwear I'll be good . . . Promisch . . . not away!"

Lillian could not camouflage her disgust. A phrase she had used earlier when discussing the house drifted through my mind, "Jaeger's Nest will not absorb anything alien. If it doesn't fit, it stands out as such an eyesore you can't feel at rest until it's eliminated."

"Just get her into her room, Nellie, and stay with her until she's quiet." She walked back down the stairs as Nellie and I helped Catherine through the door.

When we entered her room, I felt I had been magically transported from Jaeger's Nest. This was another world, one of powder blue velvet, lace, and the curved flowing lines of Louis XV French furniture. No natural wood shone anywhere in the room, even the elaborate moldings and carved doors had been painted an antique white.

Catherine fell into the rumpled bed and plunged immediately into an apparent deep and heavy sleep. Her face was relaxed now, still sagging and puffy, but no longer tormented and drawn. I wondered how she could be so miserably unhappy. It seemed to me that this magnificent home and the make-believe world of this room could cushion any hurt. But then, Lillian saw her as an outsider. It was not Catherine's house, it was Lillian's. This was certainly Catherine's room, but I felt sure Lillian made no secret that she disapproved of the decorating scheme.

"She'll be O.K. now, Miss Driscoll. Thank you for helping me with her. Don't ever let her scare you; she wouldn't hurt anybody. When Miss Vanderleigh calls her destructive, she means she falls and knocks over some old knick-knack now and then. Don't be afraid and don't worry. I take good care of her. I've known her since she was a young girl and she's a good person, believe me."

"What happened to her, Nellie? Why is she so unhappy?"

"She was Catherine Manchester before she married Mr. Vanderleigh. The Manchesters were friends of the Vanderleighs when the first Mrs. Vanderleigh was alive. You won't believe it, but that's Catherine's picture hanging there over the bed." She gestured toward an oval framed full length portrait of a beautiful young woman with blond flowing hair and large expressive eyes. "The artist didn't make that up. She was a beauty without equal, in this part of the country anyway."

"If that portrait is any indication, I don't doubt you at all. She was beautiful."

"Many years later, after both Mr. Manchester and Mrs. Vanderleigh had died, she married Mr. Jonathan. She seemed happy to be here at first, then just kept getting worse and worse. You can see that Mr. Jonathan treats her really nice, though. He won't let anybody put her away. He'll take care of her always. I'm sure he will."

"Nellie, the other night—did I scream like that?"

"I don't know, child. I didn't even know about your being taken to the hospital until Miss Vanderleigh told me the next morning. Surprised me. I thought I always heard everything." Catherine moaned as she tried to turn over on her side. Nellie quickly went to help and comfort her. "I'm here, Miss Catherine. Everything will be all right. You keep right on sleeping and try to get a good rest."

Nellie motioned me toward the door and we walked together down the hall. "That was Catherine I heard screaming yesterday, wasn't it Nellie."

"I'm afraid so. I didn't want you or Miss Vanderleigh to know. You saw why; Miss Vanderleigh gets unreasonable."

Once alone in my room, I found I was trembling from the shock of seeing Catherine in such a pathetic and disheveled state. I now knew that the screams I heard were real. The faces—were they real too?

TEN

Bruce was surprised at the ease with which I convinced Lillian to join us on the weekend boat trip, but I was beginning to take Lillian's renaissance for granted. It was a pleasure to watch her act as though she had regained twenty years of her life. I wanted her to become more self confident and search for ways to make her life more satisfying. To get her away from Jaeger's Nest, even for a few hours, could open up new horizons for her.

To overcome her objection that she had nothing to wear, I agreed to join her in a shopping trip to Bleekston. She splurged on a pair of tailored white linen slacks with a matching overblouse; a red, white and blue striped blazer; and a pair of navy deck shoes. Unable to resist the primordial feminine urge for something new to wear, I joined in and bought a navy and white nautical print scarf to perk up my old white duck pants, navy tank top and well worn sneakers.

Contrary to Bruce's prediction, Jonathan did not seem pleased to have us along. Gentleman to the core, however, he did not spoil our fun by acting as though we had trespassed on all male territory. Bruce had been right about one thing; Catherine refused to join in the fun and wouldn't consider the trip for a moment. Since Nellie would be with her, Jonathan was not concerned about leaving her at home for the weekend.

Lillian had set her shoulder length brown hair and combed it in loose flowing waves, a marked improvement over her usual severe style. The softness around her face helped her features seem less sharp and angular. She was not a pretty woman, but I was certain that she had not looked more attractive in the past twenty years than she did today.

Both Bruce and Jonathan were awed by the change in Lillian and I had to laugh at the way they catered to her as if she would break; she loved every minute of it. They carried our cases and the food baskets, were always there to help us over a rough spot along the path to the dock, and lent a hand to help put the food and supplies into the proper compartments on the boat.

Since Lillian had never been aboard and I had been too disturbed to notice more than the broad strokes on my previous tour with Bruce, we looked around together. The salon was large, about twelve feet square, with a fully equipped kitchen that would be the envy of most apartment dwellers, and a lounge area consisting of an L-shaped couch grouped around a white formica party height round table. The plush carpeting was a deep marine blue and the couch was upholstered in a fresh lime green and white geometric print. The master stateroom, again carpeted in blue, repeated the green and white decor of the salon with a bright cotton floral pattern. The V berths were covered in a bold blue and white stripe fabric and topped with throw pillows in lime, white and navy solids.

"Did you notice that Jonathan chose the same colors for the boat as we used in the boat house, Maggie? It looks so clean and cool. I must say I approve."

"It would be hard to imagine anything nicer. I hope you'll be able to join them for trips more often now, Lillian."

"I'd like to, but only when you can come along too! Let's sit on the sun deck and look around. I haven't taken this ride in so long, it will be like a first time for me too."

"Well, you finally decided to join us!" said Bruce in mock surprise as we climbed the steps to the sun deck. He spread his arms wide in a theatrical gesture, "This is the Navesink River, Maggie. Jonathan is touring the shoreline to show it off to you. There, on the north side, is our dock." Absolutely nothing was visible to the eye except a mountain of trees. The house sat so far back from the water nothing could be seen of it at all. It looked as though some primeval forest came right up to the water and stopped. The boathouse and dock gave the only clue that the land was inhabited.

"I used to love this trip with my father," said Lillian. "He would let me ride in the the *Jiddy Hawk* if I promised to sit quietly and enjoy the ride while he had some time to think. Our yacht, *The Skua*, needed a full crew when it set sail, so he used it mainly for business and entertaining. On the *Jiddy Hawk*, though, he was the master and the mate. He'd just relax and enjoy himself."

"Dad kept up the tradition of naming the boats after different members of the Jaeger family of birds, like the Skua and the Jiddy Hawk," explained Bruce. "This new boat is called *The Bonxie*, the popular name for the Great Skua in the Shetland Islands of Scotland. Great Grandfather Adam named the other two boats; Jonathan just followed his lead.

"We don't have those boats anymore." The harping whine returned to Lillian's voice. "Jonathan didn't want to keep a full crew around all the time so he replaced both boats with one about this size called the *Pomarine*, named for another Jaeger. Then last year, he traded the *Pomarine* for this one. The *Bonxie* is a wonderfully modern boat, but the pristine sounds of creaking wood and the thrill of the wind in the sails are what I will always miss." She sighed with exaggerated longing. "I guess I have to admit that one reason I haven't gone boating with Jonathan is that he sold my father's boats."

"Lillian's right, Maggie," said Jonathan, "the *Skua* was truly luxurious, a rare beauty. I hated to sell it. It had enough wood and brass on board to keep everybody busy polishing the year round. I know Grandfather Adam would never have approved of the *Bonxie*; it's a little too modern. It's easy to maintain all right, but cold and sterile beside a sailing ship fashioned of warm teak wood and shiny brass fittings."

"There's where the Montgomerys used to live!"

Lillian sounded excited, her voice was smooth and alive again. "See that big house over there, Maggie? That man was a good friend of my father's. Look at that beautiful stretch of lawn; it goes from the front of the house right down to the water! I always wanted a house like that but Grandfather would never consider taking down some of our trees. He always said that if you wanted to sit on land and stare at the sea, you could feel free to go sit in the boathouse. He spent many hours there, didn't he, Jonathan?"

"Yes, he did love the water, but he wanted the house away from it; he liked to be able to leave it when he wanted to."

"It was as though one side of him preferred the sea, and the other side, the trees, each to the exclusion of the other," said Lillian.

"Perhaps he also knew the destructive mood of the sea; those times when she is better left alone," mused Bruce.

"There's little doubt of that," laughed Jonathan. "He knew her well!"

Compared to the other estates along the riverfront, I could see that the Vanderleigh tract was much higher and the drop from the tree line to the water was considerably steeper, more clifflike. Adam had chosen his haven skillfully.

"Maggie, do you see that point of land jutting out there?" asked Jonathan.

"Over there?" I pointed, "Yes, I see it."

"Oyster Shell Point, one of the most famous oyster beds in early America. The Lenni Lenape Indians, the tribe which owned all of New Jersey before the settlers came, would dig there, shuck the oysters, then throw the shells into a huge heap. Over the years that heap got larger and larger. They'd spike the oysters onto sticks and dry them. A lot of old Indian artifacts have been found around that point."

"Yes, that's where I gained my first archeological experience," laughed Bruce. "I didn't find anything really earthshaking, but I never gave up hope. I learned how much of an optimist I really was; I always expected to make a nationally significant find under the very next rock."

"The oyster industry came to an end when the river became filled with pleasure boats," continued Jonathan. "The boat traffic was so heavy that a river patrol had to be formed to keep order. Some Sunday boaters are worse than Sunday automobile drivers!"

"Dad is an authority on the history of this area," said Bruce.

Jonathan laughed but his face showed pride in Bruce's remark. "Oh, not really a recognized authority, but I do find it interesting. Settlement began in the early seventeenth century and has continued to this day. It is still a fast growing area too. The New Yorkers come in waves and plop their ticky-tacky suburban developments on top of the richest farm land in America."

"Don't start on that subject, Jonathan, you'll ruin our outing," laughed Lillian.

I borrowed Bruce's binoculars and began to sightsee again. In some areas along the south side of the river, every inch of waterfront was filled with small houses and docks. Then further down, large estates owned wide frontages; palatial homes with walls of windows overlooked the water.

"We're entering Sandy Hook Bay, Maggie." Jonathan waved his arm to the left, "That area is called the Highlands. Here, look at this map; it'll show where we're going." He lay the map on the seat beside me. "See that stretch of land there?" He pointed with the index finger of his free hand and held the wheel with the other, "That's Sandy Hook. We'll go up around that jut of land, then on into the Atlantic Ocean, staying on the ocean side of the barrier beach all the way down to Atlantic City. I thought we'd have dinner there this evening and head back home tomorrow. There's a dock right at the restaurant for the boat; it's just like parking a car."

At the mention of eating, I realized that the salty sea air had made me more than ready for Nellie's thick deli-style sandwiches. I brought the picnic basket and a thermos of coffee up from below and passed them around. Nellie had thoughtfully included a piece of Lillian's specialty, a delicious rum-cake, for each of us. Everyone's appetite was hearty as mine and the basket was too soon empty.

"We certainly took care of that in short order," laughed Bruce. "We'll have to lay in a larger supply of stores the next time we invite you two ladies."

"Nellie just didn't realize how hungry we'd be, and neither did I," said Lillian a little defensively.

"Now, now Lillian," chided Jonathan. "You're the guest here. You don't have to feel responsible for the food on the boat. This way you'll have a big appetite when we stop for dinner."

As we passed by a large mansion built into the hillside along the bay, Lillian began to reminisce again. "Look at that big river room, Maggie. I bet it's so wonderfully full of light—and the view! I'll have to show you the ballroom at Jaeger's Nest. It's been shut up for several years now. It's full of light like that. Oh how wonderful it was when Dad was alive! We don't use it though. Jonathan and I don't really live that way; we're just not the type. We're very retiring and then, with the way Catherine is, we can't do that kind of thing anymore."

I noticed a fleeting expression of irritation pass over Jonathan's face, but Lillian kept on talking. "We couldn't open the big part of the house now, even if we wanted to. We can't find household help who will work with Catherine around."

Jonathan could take no more. "Now Lillian, you're being overly harsh and you're talking too much! Has your rum cake loosened your tongue?" He smiled as though he was going to try to remain pleasant and pass off his last comment as a joke, but then he seemed to decide to put a stop to this once and for all. "Maggie is a friend, yes, but Catherine is my wife and I'd rather you made no further comments about her condition or her behavior."

I was a little surprised that Jonathan had come so protectively to Catherine's defense, but Lillian would not be stopped. "Well, it's true, Jonathan. Nellie is very good with Catherine and we're lucky to have her, but there's no one else who'll work for us. We need more people to take care of a big house like ours." Lillian quickly turned toward me. "Oh, don't misunderstand, Maggie. Nellie doesn't have to do the heavy work like the floors or windows; we hire a cleaning service for that. It's just that I love Jaeger's Nest and I would like to see it return to the way it was when Father was alive." The harsh expression returned to her face as she charged forth again: "Jonathan, you really must do something about Catherine. She frightened Maggie the other day."

I was shocked. "Lillian, please! Oh, it was nothing Mr. Vanderleigh."

Jonathan was alarmed. "How did she frighten you, Maggie? What happened?"

"Nothing bad, I—"

Lillian interrupted, "Catherine had another one of her screaming fits; Maggie was nearby and went to her aid, not knowing what was the matter. Nellie came up right away, of course, but something must be done, Jonathan! She's always breaking things in her thrashing about. It's not good for Catherine, and it's not good for us."

Jonathan was adamant. "I don't want to talk about it anymore, Lillian. Not in front of Maggie; not ever again! I'm sure that her breaking things is what really upsets you, isn't it? Ours is a house where people live, Lillian, not a shrine. Catherine is my wife; we will care for her at home. As long as she isn't drinking, she's fine. It's important that we keep the liquor away from her." More to himself than to us, Jonathan asked, "Where does she get it? She seems to be drinking all the time lately. Where does it all come from?"

I was uncomfortable with my involvement in this very personal family discussion and spent most of the remaining afternoon looking at the shoreline through Bruce's binoculars. It was a truly lazy day. I loved the smell of the salt water, and the caress of the sea breezes mixed with the warmth of the sun on my body.

After about two hours in the sun, my skin felt taut and I became a little drowsy. "I'm going below and curl up in a bunk, Lillian. Wake me if you want company." She turned to smile and nod in acknowledgement. It was easy to see she had been crying. Her eyes were red and watery. Was she crying over things she had lost or things she had never had? A little of both, I supposed.

I don't now how long I had been napping when I suddenly awoke, aware that someone was in the room with me. My first reaction was one of uneasiness and fear. My world had churned so much in recent weeks, I wasn't sure where I was when I first opened my eyes. As soon as I focused on the blue and white striped cover of the berth, I realized I had no reason to be afraid. I flipped over in the bunk and gave an audible gasp of surprise when I saw Bruce sitting in the other berth looking at me. I had expected Lillian.

"Well, you finally woke up, sleeping beauty." His voice was low and husky. My eyes must have retained some residue of fear because his look changed from receptive friendliness to one of concern. "What's the matter, Maggie?"

I shook my head, "I'm sorry. I just didn't know where I was for a minute. I was frightened."

"Poor Mag, I shouldn't have bothered you. My father and Lillian were arguing, so I escaped by coming down here."

"I'm okay now. What were they arguing about?"

"Trivia. Their sibling rivalry is continuing after all these years. She was her father's pet; he was his grandfather Adam's only friend, and the twain shall never meet. Grandfather Matthew and Great Grandfather Adam could never get along and now Lillian and Jonathan will never get along. Simple. This particular argument dwelt on how much better things were in the days gone by; how much more of a man Grandfather Matthew was than Dad is. Their usual hang-up."

I shifted on the bunk, suddenly aware that one of my tank top straps had dropped below my shoulder and that my hair was tossed in every crazy direction. When I sleep, I really sleep. Bruce looked at me in a wonderful way and moved over to brush the hair from my face. His hands were gentle as he delicately brushed each strand away. I liked the touch of his hand on my face, it no longer made me uneasy. I longed to feel his lips on mine, to taste the sweetness of him and be held close.

"Poor Mag! Don't worry, I'll help you work everything out." He pulled me toward him, then raised his lips to kiss my forehead. My arms went out to embrace him, to ask for more, but he grasped my hand in a playful tug. "Well, come on now, sleepyhead! Let's go eat. We'll dock any minute and I should help."

I could understand that he had to help with the docking, but I was also beginning to realize that I expected too much from Bruce Vanderleigh. He saw me as a little sister, period; a sister he had to protect and cushion from the blows of life, not as a woman he could love.

He turned to smile as he left the cabin. "Can I depend on you to get up now?"

I tried to sound cheerful. "Oh, yes! I'm starving. I'll be on deck as soon as I run a brush through my hair." I sat on the side of the bunk after he had gone, tears almost reaching the surface. What is the matter with you, Margaret Ann Driscoll? Have you lost all sense of propriety? You practically throw yourself at Bruce Vanderleigh. No wonder he runs away. Enough! Maybe a good meal is what you need to bring you to your senses.

My first impression of the restaurant was a little disappointing. It looked like a run down shack, built by an amateur carpenter, with windows everywhere it was possible to put them. The exterior was of weathered cedar, haphazardly joined. The dock was sturdy, though, and we had no trouble securing the boat and climbing on to the walkway. I grasped the wooden railing out of need rather than form; it was strange to stand on solid ground again. It took me a few minutes to regain my land legs.

Inside, however, the restaurant's nautical decor gave a vastly different impression. The chairs and booths were fashioned from cedar too, but beautifully grained and polished to a high gloss. There were a few tables in the center of the room but most were placed near a window to provide the diners a view of the water and the gliding gulls. The soft background music of the sound system and the smooth dreamlike flight of the gulls would send anyone's mind adrift. Until I saw a gull land on a piling of the bulkhead, I had no idea how large those graceful birds were.

The hostess maneuvered us toward a table for four on the left which overlooked the water but mainly provided a view of the town. Jonathan began to object with uncharacteristic firmness, "We'd prefer a table overlooking the inlet toward the ocean."

"No problem," she smiled appeasingly. "This time of day you can more or less have your choice. It gets pretty hectic later on though."

"Well, since we can have our choice, we'd like that one, Miss." Jonathan pointed toward a round table on the right.

"That's the best seat in the house!" she exclaimed. We followed her over to the table. She readied a seat for Lillian as Jonathan pulled out one for me.

"You sit there, Bruce," directed Jonathan, then he settled down, his eyes going immediately to the inlet. "Good view." He went on to explain, "This view is one reason why I come here and I would just as soon eat elsewhere if I can't have it!"

Bruce quickly interjected, "In addition to the view, Maggie, this place has the best food on the shore. It's one of the few places which still actually boils lobsters instead of splitting and broiling them. Broiling ruins a good lobster, dries it out. They also make a great chowder."

"Why don't you just order for us, Bruce," said Lillian. "We'll place our appetites in your hands." He took her at her word and ordered a fantastic array of seafood: chowder, steamed clams, boiled lobsters, broiled scallops, and a large carafe of the house white wine. The wine was perfect with the excellently prepared food and the waitress made sure our carafe never reached empty until we were finishing the meal.

As the rest of us relaxed, Jonathan seemed to grow more and more restless. His eyes rarely left the water and every new boat entering the channel was thoroughly scrutinized before he took his eyes from it to eat his next bite. We were just finishing the meal when Jonathan's face suddenly brightened and all tension vanished. "There's an old friend of mine! Excuse me, I'll be back shortly. I want to run out and see him for a few minutes."

Bruce laughed as Jonathan was leaving. "This is Dad's big thing. We eat here everytime we come down and he just sits and waits for Al Harmon's fantastic old ship to show. When it does, he acts like a kid who can't wait to see Santa Claus."

"If he feels so strongly about a beautiful old yacht, he should never have sold the *Skua*."

Bruce ignored Lillian's cutting remark. "We might as well relax. Dad usually spends forty-five minutes to an hour visiting with Harmon." The waitress pulled up a cart with a large container of coffee and an array of colorful desserts. "I recommend the cheesecake, Maggie," said Bruce, "It's the thick and cheesey type; the only kind that really deserves the name."

As she prepared a slice for me, I glanced toward the water and saw a small shore boat belonging to Jonathan's friend pull up to the dock. A man in his mid to late fifties welcomed Jonathan aboard. His silver hair shone white against tanned skin. His clothes were distinctive too: well cut cream colored slacks and a dark brown short sleeve tapered shirt; more elegant than was the rule here at the shore. After a few mutual words of small talk, they pulled the boat away from the dock and made their way back to the ship. Even after they had been gone several minutes, I kept seeing the face of that silver haired man. He seemed disturbingly familiar to me, yet there was no way I could know him, none at all. He must remind me of someone from my past. My head began to throb. Oh, not a headache now, I don't want to spoil the dinner!

"Who is he?" I asked Bruce, trying to ignore that pulsating pain at the base of my skull.

"His name is Al Harmon. Dad has known him for years. He lives somewhere along the water and they make it a point to get together for a drink when Dad is down this way. His pride is that magnificent wooden sailing yacht. He restored it to perfect condition and employs a maintenance crew of six, year round, to keep it that way."

"Sounds unbelievable." My curiosity somewhat satisfied, I surrendered my attention to the good cheesecake. "Delicious meal, Bruce. You made a lot of good choices for us." The headache began to fade, leaving only a dull ache as a reminder of its former fury.

"I take care of my girls," he said, reaching his arms out to each side to gently hug us both. Lillian giggled appropriately. "Before we leave I want to take you up to the top floor of this building. There's a great view from there." We climbed the stairs to a small private dining room, now empty.

"Like the captain's bridge," said Lillian as we looked out over the wide expanse of water. From this height you could see an array of small homes packed around man made lagoons, their white roofs reflecting the summer sun. Very few owners of these small seaside lots tried to raise grass; sand or gravel was the rule with an occasional struggling juniper hugging the foundation.

As Bruce was pointing out something to Lillian on the far horizon, I looked down to see Jonathan returning to the dock in the launch with another man, probably a crewman from the yacht. As soon as he was safely on the dock, the crewman left and headed back toward the ship. Jonathan carried a small wrapped package approximately the size of a shoe box. He boarded the *Bonxie* and went below deck. When he returned to the dock, his hands were empty; the package had been left behind.

Jonathan smiled broadly and waved a set of keys when he saw us. "We have a special treat. Al has loaned us his car for a couple of hours to take a tour of the city, then later this evening we're invited to a party on his yacht."

"But we have nothing to wear!"

"It's in a yacht, Lillian! You're dressed perfectly."

I resolved to put my curiosity about Jonathan away and enjoy the party. I couldn't believe he'd be that nervous about a visit with a friend. I'm rarely curious about other people's private affairs, but I found myself wondering what could be inside that neat little package.

ELEVEN

"Perfect timing!" exclaimed Jonathan as we drove up to the deep water dock where we were to meet Harmon's yacht. At least forty people were crowded there watching in childlike fascination as the crew secured this magnificent sailing ship and lowered the ramp. I was relieved to see that we were dressed as sanely as any of the other guests. The women's outfits ranged from satin jeans with tube tops to full challis skirts and soft peasant blouses.

Lillian's eyes became tense and anxious as she watched the party guests board the ship. "It's such a large crowd, Jonathan. Perhaps we should only plan to stay a short time, just to be polite." It was obvious Lillian was not looking forward to this party.

"I thought you missed the old parties at Jaeger's Nest, Lillian. You should enjoy this more than the rest of us," said Jonathan maliciously.

"It's just been a long time since I was around this many people, Jonathan. Please try to understand."

Bruce gave my arm a reassuring squeeze as we stepped onto the ramp. I glanced up and saw

Jonathan's friend with the silver hair staring at me, his expression strangely intense. He smiled, then glanced away as my eyes met his. I was repelled by the sharpness of his hawklike features. His eyes were small and unusually bright; they darted from guest to guest like a predatory bird.

"Glad you could join us, Jonathan. Bruce, Lillian, good to see you both again. Welcome aboard, Miss Driscoll," he said, extending his hands toward me. I consciously exerted self control as he reached for me. I must overcome this fear. I can't always shrink away when people start to touch me in an innocent and friendly way.

"I've heard Bruce and Jonathan talk so much about your unusual ship, Mr. Harmon, I was delighted to finally have an opportunity to see it."

"You said the right thing, Maggie!" laughed Jonathan. "Watch his eyes light up!"

Al Harmon took my arm with a flourish, "Come along, I'll personally show you around. These people are a few of my friends from Atlantic City. I think you'll like them. Some really classy people."

I looked from face to face in the dim light but found little to interest me in this group. They all seemed to be playing the happy game, with no real depth to their facial expressions. This fascinating ship held more interest for me. The rich wood panelling, carved wood moldings and Oriental carpets of the main salon were strikingly unusual selections for shipboard decor. The flowing pattern and soft colors of these rare carpets sharply contrasted with the hardness of the heavily grained wood.

Even in a yacht this luxurious every bit of valuable space was utilized to the fullest. Cabinets were fitted into every available cubic inch, their brass hardware glowing with a mellow patina which gave testimony to their age and usefulness.

"Do you usually have this large a staff?" I asked in amazement as I noticed at least four people beginning to serve drinks and hors d'oeuvres to the guests.

"Oh no, this is a catering service I hired for the party. I picked them up further north along with the band." He raised his hand to signal a waiter to come our way and handed me a glass of champagne from the offered tray. Another waiter appeared bearing an assortment of food. "Have a crab quiche, Maggie. It goes well with the champagne. Here Lillian, you should have one too."

We walked over to a pair of velvet couches. As Harmon sank deeply into the soft cushions, he said, "I've been hearing a lot about your former homeland, Cambodia these days. Unbelievably tragic."

Lillian added, "Tragedy seems an inadequate and theatrical word for what has taken place. Cambodia was a rich and agriculturally self-sufficient land. What has happened is nothing less than horrifying." She sipped the expensive champagne and nibbled on the miniature crab quiche, then wiped her hands and lips delicately with the provided napkin.

"And unjust," contributed Jonathan. The Cambodians have done nothing to deserve such harsh retribution. It makes one ask what use is an organization like the United Nations if not to prevent such an undeserved tragedy. Peaceful Camboida suffers the most for the sins and excesses of it neighbors." Jonathan grabbed another canape from a passing waiter's tray and popped it down in one bite, rinsing with the vintage champagne. "I know you feel personally involved in all this, Maggie, but to consider the problem on an academic level, it is possible to see reasons for the world's delay in aiding these people. The Vietnamese do not want food coming into the country which may be intercepted by the remnants of Pol Pot's forces and provide the strength to enable that tyrant to overtake the country again, not that Vietnam will provide better treatment for their historical enemies, the Cambodians. Thailand cannot accept refugees without becoming embroiled in a conflict which is already spilling over their borders. The domino theory holds that the Southeastern Asian nations will fall to communism one by one. If it is valid, Thailand is surely the next to go. Even some Americans feel they can't be expected to be caretaker to the whole world any longer. Troubles run deep at home and we are suffering nibbling attacks on many fronts. Many Americans want to fold their oceans around them and ignore the affairs of other nations."

I was unable to let these arguments pass without comment. "The issue of three million starving people, destitute and dying through no fault of their own, should transcend politics and outweigh any military advantage." I felt Bruce's hand on my shoulder, his touch was sympathetic, reassuring. I concentrated on the deeply cushioned carpet beneath my feet, unable to meet their eyes as I spoke. "A nation of seven and a half million people is just going to wither away. What has happened there is a grotesque monument to tyranny. It is genocidal, another holocaust." I closed my eyes and shook my head from side to side, trying to focus my mind, trying not to blame them for so blandly discussing Cambodia in this opulent setting. They couldn't be blamed for what has happened there, the burden of guilt is not theirs to bear, but I could not rid myself of that guilt so easily. I was safe and surrounded by wealth while people I knew were dead or dying of starvation.

"Oh I agree, Maggie. Everyone does, really. I was just being academic, I guess; trying to discuss the matter objectively." Jonathan was holding a small piece of sculpture as he talked. It was a crouched human figure of carved wood which he kept turning over and over in his hands. Al watched him intently for a few moments, then laughingly said, "If anything happens to that carving, Jonathan, I'll certainly know where to look for it." Jonathan's face turned scarlet. He returned the carving to its pedestal and walked away to the other side of the salon. Al followed him. I could see them talking excitedly for a few minutes. Jonathan seemed furious, then Al laughed, threw his arm over Jonathan's shoulders and patted him heartily on the back. All seemed well when they returned to our group a short time later.

Al lifted the carving as he sat down near me again. I was uncomfortably aware of his thigh touching mine and shifted slightly to gain separation. Lillian did not miss my movement.

"Look at this piece, Miss Driscoll. Feel the grooves where the blade shaped the wood. Feel the texture of that grain. Just close your eyes and experience the feel. It's an outstanding piece of work."

"I consider the eyes the tool with which one judges a visual work of art, Mr. Harmon, not the nerves on the ends of the fingers—unless of course one is blind," said Lillian in a voice that would be the envy of any schoolmarm.

Al bristled visibly at this rebuke. "Well, that's your problem, Miss Vanderleigh. I use my hands, my ears, even my nose if I want to."

"How vulgar!"

"Don't get on your high horse, Lillian," interjected Jonathan. "You're no expert on sensual experiences of any kind." Lillian's face flushed red. She turned and left the salon, struck speechless by the cruelty of this remark.

"What in the world is the matter with everybody tonight?" I exclaimed as I rose to follow her. I found her leaning against the rail gazing at the shore. "You aren't enjoying this very much are you Lillian?"

"The crowd is a bit more common than I expected, and I've never cared for Al Harmon, not one bit," she said haughtily. Then, letting her guard down, she admitted, "I guess life has just passed me by, Maggie. I don't really enjoy this kind of thing. It's funny, I always thought I would love it!"

"I think we're just tired and a little on edge. It's been a long day."

Bruce joined us. "Hey Maggie, let's dance. There's a great band."

"Oh, Bruce! I was just saying how tired I was! Besides, I don't know how to do these dances."

"Come on silly, I'll teach you."

"Yes, go on Maggie," urged Lillian. "Don't feel you have to nurse my ego. I want you to enjoy yourself."

I gave in. "Okay, I'll try, but keep it simple, Bruce. Remember my inexperience."

"The simplest. Look at this." He illustrated a step which I was able to duplicate easily, then he taught me a couple more. Those few steps enabled me to look like I knew something of what I was doing, and the small crowded dance floor further camouflaged my groping movements.

After several numbers, the beat of the rhythm section and the flashing strobe lights began to make me feel lightheaded. I could feel the beat of the bass throughout my body and became entranced with the periodic focus of the red spotlight on a dancer. The body would fade into the darkness as the face glowed in the eerie red light. The floating faces, this time laughing, seemed lost in the ecstasy of the moment. The beat of the music drew me on.

We danced near a buffet table piled high with food: cold boiled shrimp, crab claws, lobster tails, roast meats, salads and breads. An unbelievably large amount of food for even this many people.

My mind drifted. New faces began to appear in the flashing spot. Each beat of the bass seemed to focus on the figure of a Cambodian child, starving, hopeless. Then finally the spot shone on Al Harmon, whose floating face seemed surrounded by a pink and silver mist, his eyes glowed red like an animal's in the dark. My hands flew to my eyes to stop the vision. I had to get out of here! I left Bruce standing on the dance floor and pushed and shoved my way to the deck. Once there, I ran to the rail. An overpowering nausea overcame me. Several minutes later, my face wet with a cold sweat, I regained control.

The yacht was returning to the pier. I saw a motorcycle silhouetted in the dim streetlight, its lone rider leaning against the dock railing watching the ship. Looking at me. That was Martin Ingram! He was following me! He mounted his cycle and once astride snapped on his helmet, looking at me all the while with what I knew, even in the dim light, was that sarcastic, knowing, smile. I was again overcome, terrified and losing control. I turned to run back inside and crashed straight into Al Harmon.

"Whoa, Maggie!"

"Oh! I'm so sorry, Mr. Harmon!"

"My pleasure, Maggie," he said, locking his arms around my waist and pulling me hard against him. He was a small man, no taller than I, but very strong. I tried to wriggle free from his grasp. His wet mouth pressed against my neck and his quickening breath became deafening in my ear. I froze from fear of him and from the memory of other hands, other sounds of heavy breathing.

"Please don't," I sobbed, turning and twisting, trying to get away, trying to stop his embarrassing advances.

"What are you doing, Harmon?" Bruce's face

was livid with anger. "Let go of her this minute."

Al stepped back, releasing me and holding his arms extended in a mock appeal. "Sorry Bruce. Don't know what came over me!" He laughed and walked away.

As Bruce took me in his arms, I saw Martin's motorcycle turn and pull away from the pier. It's red tail light bobbed up and down as he maneuvered over the rough pavement. I buried my face in Bruce's chest and heaved frightened sobs as he tried in vain to comfort me.

TWELVE

The next morning, back aboard the *Bonxie*, we made our way toward the refuge of the Vanderleigh estate. I frankly didn't care if I never ventured outside those gates again!

"Who's that out on the dock?" asked Lillian as the boathouse came into view.

Bruce reached for his binoculars to take a closer look. "It's Nellie! She's waving a handkerchief or something."

Lillian became alarmed. "Hurry Jonathan! Something's wrong! Oh, I knew I shouldn't have come. Something's happened. I knew it would, I just knew it!"

As we were nearing the dock, Nellie called out, "Oh, Mr. Jonathan! I'm so glad you're back. She's gone! Miss Catherine's gone! I can't find her anywhere, she's just vanished! I've looked for hours." Nellie's face was flushed and her eyes were red and swollen from crying.

"What? Now hold on, Nellie; I'll be there in a second," Jonathan shouted. "Here Bruce, take over. Finish securing the boat." Jonathan jumped to the dock. I followed him, surprising myself with my own agility and amazed at his. "Now, now, Nellie. Calm down. Try to talk calmly. When did you first miss her?"

"This morning. I checked on her in the middle of the night to make sure she was sleeping well. She was in her room then, fast asleep, but when I took her some coffee this morning, she was gone. I can't find her. I've looked everywhere!"

"Did you call anybody?"

"No, Mr. Vanderleigh, I didn't think you'd want me to. I knew you'd be home soon and I felt that you would rather decide if we should call someone."

Jonathan revealed an obvious relief. "That's good, Nellie. I'm sure there's nothing to worry about. You know how she is, she's been missing before. We won't assume that it means anything frightening."

The boat was docked. Bruce helped Lillian ashore where she lost no time joining the conversation about Catherine. "Jonathan, I told you we had to do something about her! Where could she have gone? What is she up to now, I wonder! I tell you Jonathan, this is the last straw. If she has done anything to blemish the family name, if she has let her despicable condition be known to outsiders, this is it, out she goes! You must do something and do it now! You can no longer ignore the harm she can do!"

Jonathan's face was a mask of fury. "Oh for God's sake, Lillian, shut up! I've had enough of your ineffectual emotionalism to last for at least a month! Yes, we will find her. No, we will not institutionalize her and that's final. Now go dust your knick-knacks while we do something effective to find Catherine."

Lillian looked to me for support, but I made sure my face was non-committal. I didn't want to get involved in an argument between these two again. Of course I agreed with Lillian that Catherine needed care, professional medical care, but for her own good, not for the good of the so-called family name. My eyes followed Bruce as he secured the boat; he was staying completely out of this hysteria. When he finished with the boat, he just walked away, heading straight for the house. He didn't like to be drawn into arguments between Jonathan and Lillian either, and since he had no love at all for Catherine, he wanted nothing to do with the entire situation.

I glanced at Nellie; she was still trembling and crying. I went over to comfort her. Of everyone here, she was most concerned with Catherine as a person. "Nellie, we're home now and we'll find her." I saw that the door to the boathouse was open. "Let's go sit down for just a few minutes while you pull yourself together."

Once we sat down, she began to talk. "Miss Driscoll, she wouldn't hurt anything intentionally. Miss Lillian just doesn't understand what it's like to be in a place where people don't want you. She has never liked Miss Catherine. Never. Not even when she was still Catherine Manchester. She was beautiful, too beautiful, and Miss Lillian didn't like her for that reason. Oh, I know it's hard to like a drunk. My husband was a heavy drinker right up till the day he died, but I never stopped loving him. He was sick and just couldn't seem to help himself. Miss Catherine drinks to escape problems she can't seem to cope with anymore."

"Start at the beginning, Nellie. Tell me everything that happened this weekend. Start with the minute we left."

"Well, as I said, this is the first time Miss Lillian had been away for any length of time and Catherine just felt wonderful. She was into everything, looking at everything, happier than I had seen her in a long time. She acted free, sort of, happy and free. I understand that she is still sick, of course, I'm not saying she acted all well and everything, but she did seem happier than I've seen her since she first came here to live."

"Do you mean that in all the years she's been here, she's never felt free to just roam around?" I couldn't believe what she was telling me. "She's never felt that this was her home?"

"Absolutely not! Miss Lillian made that perfectly clear to her when she first came. Miss Lillian wouldn't allow it."

"You mean there were parts of this house she had never seen?"

"Well, I'm sure she had seen anything she wanted to, but Miss Lillian would never let her be, would never let her roam around alone. Catherine particularly loves the ball room, with its big windows and french doors opening onto the terrace. It is a big, bright, empty room and she spent most of yesterday in there just dancing around to the music she played on her portable radio. She was having such a good time! She got exhausted just from dancing by herself."

"Did she stay there all day?"

"No, we had a nice lunch, just the two of us. I fixed it up special and we set a table on the terrace. We had melon, a spinach salad, and some of the carrot cake I made for dinner the other night. You remember, it was so good." She reached toward me pleadingly, "Miss Catherine can be a lot of fun, Miss Driscoll. I know you haven't had a chance to really know her, but she is a very sweet person."

"I know how much you care for her, Nellie. She's lucky for that reason alone. What did she talk about at lunch?"

"Well, after we had laughed and giggled over everything we could think of—don't tell anybody, Miss Driscoll but you should see Miss Catherine imitate Miss Lillian! It was the funniest thing I've seen in years. Don't speak a word of it though; Miss Lillian couldn't stand it if she knew Miss Catherine, of all people, was making fun of her! Anyway, after all that she was feeling a little tired so she went up to her room for a nap while I cleaned the kitchen and washed a few loads of clothes."

"How long did she sleep?"

"Oh, a good three hours, I'd guess. She was up again around five o'clock and she sat out on the terrace for a long time by herself while I watched a movie on television, a really good one with Helmut Dantine. I've always loved his movies."

"Did she stay on the terrace the whole time the movie was on?"

She thought for a minute, "No. No, I think she

went for a walk in the woods. I know she wasn't there when that nice Mr. Ingram called."

"Martin called?"

"Yes, I told him you'd gone on the boat trip with Mr. Jonathan to Atlantic City. He said he'd call again during the week."

Martin had known! He had followed me and was watching me from the dock. I was not seeing things; I knew it was him! My mind drifted as Nellie continued to talk.

"You have to understand, Miss Driscoll, she felt free and I didn't want to let on I was watching her too closely. It would have spoiled everything for her."

"I really do understand, Nellie, go on."

"Well, there's nothing more to tell. We had a light dinner together around seven, then she washed her hair and took a long hot soaking bath. She must have soaked in that tub for an hour! We watched television for a while together, then she went to her room. I checked on her before she went to sleep, then I looked in around two o'clock because I thought I heard a noise. I wasn't sleeping too well; since we were all alone here, I felt responsible for everything. Anyway, she was fine then, but when I went in to wake her up this morning, she was gone."

"What time was that?"

"Just a minute or two after eight, and here it is after four o'clock in the afternoon!"

Through the window of the boathouse I could see Jonathan walking toward us. I pressed Nellie on one point before he came in. "Was she drinking anything, Nellie?"

Her eyes turned from me just a moment, enough to make me feel she was being evasive, "Oh, no, Miss Driscoll."

"Are you sure, Nellie? It's important."

"I don't think so, Miss Driscoll. Well, maybe just a little, but not very much. She wasn't drinking very much because she was acting just fine." I knew now that it was Nellie who would get Catherine a drink when she wanted it.

Jonathan entered the boathouse, his expression one of exasperation. "Well, she's not near the water anywhere. I walked the whole bank area. Let's go on up to the house Nellie. We can start looking from there."

"Yes sir, I'm sorry I got so upset and all."

"Well, it's enough to upset anybody, but she'll turn up soon. She's somewhere on this thirty acres, I'm sure of that."

I was surprised, "I didn't realize the estate was that large."

"Oh yes, it's big and private, or isolated, depending on how you want to view it." We walked slowly back to the house, looking as far as we could see into the woods and calling out to Catherine as we went.

Bruce was leaving as we walked in. "I'll be in town, at the Inn. Don't expect me for dinner." He left without another word as I stood there open mouthed. I was shocked that he would leave without helping us look for Catherine. Jonathan didn't seem to mind, though, and began to divide up the estate for the search. Lillian volunteered to cover the house from top to bottom, including the unused rooms, the carriage house and the other outbuildings. Jonathan, Nellie and I each took a section of the woods: Jonathan chose the one near the road and along the fence; Nellie, the less thickly wooded area around the house; and I took the rear section back to the river.

Ten acres doesn't sound like much for one person to cover until you start doing it step by step. It was still early in the day, however, so I didn't need to worry about having enough light to see by. The terrain wasn't too difficult for walking either, once I got away from the dock path where years of footsteps had caused some erosion. The dense foliage of the tall upper story of trees discouraged a thick shrub growth, but the tree trunks were so thick and numerous I still could not see very far in either direction. Occasionally I would call out, "Catherine, Catherine? It's Maggie Driscoll, Catherine. Can you hear me? Please answer me, Catherine!" I wondered if she were hurt and couldn't come home; or if she were deliberately trying to hide.

As I walked on, I realized I was glad to have some time alone. I needed to think about my feelings for Bruce. Was I so frightened and lonely that I was merely grasping for physical reassurance, someone to hold me close, just anyone? "No!" I spat the words aloud as my skin crawled at the memory of Al Harmon's mauling hands. Bruce helped me then; he saw me as a sister, a friend, and I could benefit from that kind of support too. No more silly schoolgirl crush! I didn't love Bruce, I just wanted to have an effect on somebody; to have someone respond to my presence, to care that I was there. I could accept my relationship with Bruce for what it was and value it.

I heard a sound behind me to my right. I turned quickly and was totally shocked to see Martin Ingram standing not twenty feet away, his expression anxious. He wore a hunter's camouflage outfit which, from a distance, made his body blend into the trees and became virtually invisible. "Martin! What are you doing here?"

His eyes were angry, his fists clenched, "Forget you saw me, Maggie! Forget it! Don't breathe a word to anyone. It's important! I swear by the silver circle." He vanished into the woods, moving toward the water, leaving me standing in shock, alone and afraid.

"You liar! You lying fraud!" I screamed after him. He was gone; he had not heard. The nerve of him! What was he doing here? How dare he try to sway me with that old silver circle gambit again. A horrible thought suddenly crossed my mind: could he have anything to do with Catherine's disappearance? I'd never forgive myself if trouble came to the Vanderleighs through Martin Ingram! I resumed my search, frantic now; I must find her safe!

I had been stumbling through the brush for what seemed like miles when I caught a flash of blue off to the left. "Catherine?" The blue vanished. "Catherine, please wait!" I wished I had been smart enough to ask Nellie what she might be wearing but she probably wouldn't have known. Catherine had left before Nellie came in to wake her. I began to run in the direction I had seen that flash of color. "Catherine?" I realized I was running toward the water again; was it only the water I had seen? I was certainly no woodsman! I could see no indication that anyone had been over this land in the past one hundred years. There was no sign of a disturbance in the rich leaf mulch covering the floor of the woods.

I thought I saw the blue again, through the trees some distance in front of me, and feeling reassured, ran directly toward it once more. It was then I heard a giggle, a childlike laugh coming from behind me. I stopped and turned, "Catherine?" I could see nothing. I turned around slowly in a circle. Nothing. Then again that flash of blue off in the distance. I decided on a new tactic. "Catherine? No games now. I want to talk to you. Come here. Come here to me right now."

I stood my ground and waited. Nothing moved. "I'm leaving now, Catherine. If you want to come to me, come now, or I'm going to go back to the house." Again, nothing stirred, no movement anywhere at all. Not even a bird or an inquisitive squirrel disturbed the unnatural quiet of the surrounding woods. I could hear my own heart beating; this was no time to give in to fear. I must stay in control. In pretended exasperation, I turned to leave, sure of my quarry, sure that she was all right and that she only wanted to play, unaware of any danger.

"Please wait," a small childlike voice called out to me. "Please stay and talk to me."

"Catherine?"

"Yes, it's me. Please stay." She came out from behind a tree then, her large eyes clearer and brighter than I had ever seen them. She wore sneakers, jeans, and a tight fitting tee shirt of a pale sky blue: my flash of blue. Her blond hair was clean and shining from last night's washing. Only her lined and puffy face kept her from looking like a spunky young teenage tomboy, ready for games in the woods.

"We've been so worried, Catherine. We have to go back and let everyone know you're all right."

"You may really be worried, and I know Nellie is, but that's all. No one else cares a bit about me."

"I don't think that's true, Catherine. Jonathan seemed terribly concerned. Let's go find him now." I was concerned about our safety. I felt that Martin had left, but I could not be sure.

Her uncharacteristic raucous laughter echoed through the woods. "Poor little Maggie, don't you see? He isn't interested in me; not this me, not this older, fatter me. He says I disgust him! Jonathan only wants beautiful things."

"Have you been here all the time we've been looking for you?"

She giggled again, "Yes, just here in the woods. I love the trees, Maggie. I never knew I could feel so free. But now I'm beginning to feel lonely. Please be my friend, stay here with me."

I felt the best thing to do would be to give in to her childlike whim for a few minutes; then, after gaining her confidence, I would be able to convince her to return home.

"I'll show you something you've never seen

before, something beautiful and unusual. Will you stay?"

"Okay, Catherine. I'll stay. Thank you for inviting me."

"So you're Bruce's girlfriend!"

"Why do you say that?"

"He's never had one before."

"Oh, Catherine! I'm sure that's not true!"

"It is! He's never had a girl before!"

"Well anyway, I'm just his friend, not his girl."

"Do you want to see it?"

"What?"

"My beautiful thing."

"Yes, of course."

"Give me your hand, I'll show you the way."

We had only walked about a hundred feet when she said, "Here we are."

"I don't see anything."

"You will. Just sit down there," she pointed to the trunk of a fallen tree, "and I'll show you."

I sat, obediently, like a child waiting for the performance to begin.

She dropped to the ground opposite me; then, looking straight at me, so as to miss nothing of my facial expression, she began to lift up leaves from a spot on the ground between us. "Now I want you to close your eyes for just one moment so I can be sure that it is perfect before you see it, okay? Will you do that?"

Again I played the childhood friend. "Yes, Catherine. I'll close my eyes."

I could hear her moving more leaves, spreading them away, creating just the right setting for her play.

"Now open your eyes and look!"

At first I didn't see anything, and then I saw a small group of woodland plants, less than six inches high, absolutely colorless and practically transparent. Each lily shaped flower had one straight stem, straight to the ground, and no leaves. She was right, they were beautiful, and I had never seen anything like them at all. "Oh Catherine! How pretty! What are they? Are they real? They don't even look real!"

She giggled, alive with pleasure now. "I knew you would like them. Yes, they're real. They are called Indian Pipes. My husband, Gordon, taught me about woodland flowers; they were his hobby. The Indian Pipe is a fungus which lives on decaying wood and things like that."

"A fungus? Of course, there's not a trace of green color."

"They have another name you know." Her face abruptly changed, its shadows deepened. "Gordon called them corpses, the corpse plant, their icy white ghost-like appearance earned them that creepy name, I guess."

I shuddered involuntarily, "That sort of spoils their beauty for me."

Her face became animated again, "Don't let it do that! Admit it now, they're the most beautiful fungi you've ever known."

I smiled then, "Why yes, of the fungi I have known, they are by far the prettiest."

"Are you laughing at me?"

"No. I'm just delighted to see you so relaxed. I've never seen you this way."

She quickly began the game again, "And what's the prettiest vegetable you have ever seen?"

"Vegetable? Oh I know! A white eggplant. I saw a white eggplant for the first time the other day. It had just a blush of lilac on the sides. I bought it; it's in my room."

"No it isn't," she giggled. "It's here!" She raised my eggplant aloft in both hands.

"You were in my room?"

"Don't be mad, Maggie. I was everywhere today! I didn't bother anything. I was just afraid of you and I wanted to know you better."

I was shocked! "Afraid of me?"

"I never see people anymore. I was just afraid because you were a stranger. I even sneaked into your room the first night you were here but you were asleep. When I found the eggplant today, I knew you'd be my friend."

"It's yours if you'd like it. It probably won't last much longer though."

"Thank you. It really is pretty. Oh I'm so sorry your boat trip is over. I've been free this weekend for the first time in so long. It felt absolutely wonderful! I've spent all day enjoying the woods. I've covered every inch of them and I've never seen such beautiful trees. It's like a park! Gordon would have loved it here. We visited this estate many times before he died, but we never took the time to walk through the woods."

"You should spend more time out of doors, Catherine. It would be good for you." I was convinced that was true.

"They don't like for me to go out alone."

She looked at me, her eyes straight from a Keene painting. I knew those eyes and that face. "But you do go out, don't you? I've seen you in the woods."

"Yes, sometimes. I sneak out over the roof from a window off my dressing room. I saw you through the library skylight the other night. I went away as soon as I realized I had frightened you."

"Yes, you did, but I wouldn't have been frightened if I'd know it was you."

"Maggie, would you—I mean, sometimes could you just go for walks with me? If you will I'll show you something else."

"Another beautiful plant?"

"Oh no, a beautiful place! A secret place I found today. Will you ask them if you can take me for walks. You won't be sorry, you'll really like my secret place—but you can never tell a soul you've seen it—that's important, Maggie. Never tell!"

Martin's warning echoed in my head, "Don't breathe a word to anyone—it's important." I had to get her home. "I'll ask them, but let's go home now and let everyone know you're safe."

"You promise to take me out again?"

"I promise." I took her hand.

"I believe you, Maggie. Try to be my friend. I'm not pretty anymore, but I'm trying to hold on to what's left of me." Tears formed pools in her eyes and began to roll down her cheeks.

I put my arm around her and gently guided her back to the house. I was certain now that she would benefit from care and I resolved to do everything I could to make sure that she got it. She reminded me of a delicate flower, an ethereal fleeting thing.

THIRTEEN

Jonathan marvelled at how rapidly my work was progressing. The more I studied, the more deeply interested I became in Tibet's fascinating history. Enjoying work must make time pass quickly too. This morning as I finished my final cup of coffee at Nellie's old round oak breakfast table, I realized that this was Friday and I had been here almost two weeks.

"Good morning, Maggie!" said Jonathan as he entered the kitchen. "This is the first morning I've caught you still at breakfast! You've usually eaten and started working away before I even get down."

"I guess I'm running late today. The smell of Nellie's freshly baked bread made me more reluctant to leave the kitchen than usual."

"Oh, you're not late! I'm the one who's off schedule. I have to go into Bleekston today so I'm getting started a little earlier."

"Would you mind if I rode to Bleekston with you? I need to pick up my car. Mike called yesterday and said it was ready."

"No problem at all. I'll be leaving around eleven o'clock, after I do some paperwork in the office. Suppose we meet in the carriage house at eleven?"

"Good, see you then."

I worked until ten thirty, then rushed up to change into a dress and put on some makeup before I met Jonathan in the garage. I had only been sitting in the car for a few minutes when I was alarmed by the movement of a shadow to my left. Before I could react, someone grabbed me from behind. Icy hands covered my eyes. I screamed.

Catherine laughed! "It's only me, Maggie!" She was laughing so hard she could barely talk, "It's only me!" I was shaking. It did no good to be angry with her. She had no reason to think that old trick would frighten me so. "Since you're such a scaredy cat, perhaps I shouldn't tell you what I saw early this morning in the woods."

"A deer?" I wasn't really in the mood for guessing games.

"No, there's nothing scary about that. Guess again."

"Oh, Catherine! I'll never be able to guess. Just tell me."

"A man."

"Who?" The fear began to creep back up my spine, a cold, tight, fear.

"I couldn't see him well enough to tell. He was dressed all in black and wore a white motorcycle helmet. They all look alike in those helmets. I watched him for a long time. He walked down through the woods all the way to the water, then later he came back up to the road again. I heard his motorcycle start up and fade off in the distance." Her eyes became large and pleading, "Please don't tell anybody, Maggie. I want him to come back again so I can watch him. Promise you won't tell! He didn't do anything, just walked through the woods. Promise."

"No . . . No . . . I promise."

She turned quickly, "Here comes Jonathan. I'm leaving. Remember now, don't tell!" She vanished through the rear door.

"Well, Maggie, how prompt you are! I usually have to twiddle my thumbs waiting for the ladies."

"My timing was right for a change. I just got here." Jonathan started the car and backed out of the carriage house. After the luxury of Bruce's car, his ten year old Chevvy was a comfortable old sweater.

"It works, Maggie. I take good care of it, service it regularly, make sure it has everything it needs to stay happy. In return, it has never let me down. I won't trade it until it does."

"I can't blame you for that," I laughed. "I'd like to keep mine forever, too. I hope no one ever decides to rip it apart again; I don't think I want to go through this anymore." As we pulled through the gates, I looked back to make sure they closed behind us. They didn't look as massive or impenetrable today. Obviously, from what Catherine told me this morning and my sighting of Martin the other day, the fence wasn't intimidating enough to keep out determined intruders. My sense of security was becoming a little frayed. "Do you ever have trespassers climb over the fence, Jonathan?"

"Rarely, nothing serious though, kids usually. Why?"

"Just wondering. It looks like such a formidable obstacle, I was curious whether it might merely be a challenge to some people."

"Probably so."

Perhaps that's all it was, a teenage motorcyclist who wanted to enjoy a forbidden walk in the woods and a view of the Navesink. Or Martin.

"By the way, Maggie, that's a pretty pink dress. I haven't seen you wear that one before."

"This is made from Thai silk. Dad bought it for me before we left Thailand. I love the color and the lines are so simple I can wear it anywhere."

"You have good taste in clothes and you wear them well. I'd appreciate it if you'd buy some things for Catherine. She doesn't like to shop and she needs some new clothes."

"I'd love to, Jonathan. I'll look around."

"This is her birthday. We're having a special dinner this evening to cheer her up. Do you think you'd be able to find something for her today?"

"I'm sure I can. I'll pick up my car and then go on to the University to register for my fall courses. There are some shops near the campus. I can also check on the downtown stores when I pick up my mail."

"Has your mail just been piling up at your apartment?"

"Oh, no. I've had the Post Office hold it. I don't know anyone in the apartment building well enough to have them save it for me."

"You're smart to have the Post Office keep it.

Well, as I said, if you could do some shopping for Catherine, I'd appreciate it. I'm sure you would choose nice things for her. I don't care for red or black, her coloring is too delicate. She likes pastels and white looks good if the lines are slimming. She's picked up some weight and I know that's bothering her."

I decided to take advantage of this opening to talk with him about Catherine. "I think she needs professional counselling, Jonathan. I hate to interfere, but I do feel she could benefit from it."

"Do you really, Maggie?" Jonathan seemed genuinely surprised. "Lillian often says that, but I feel she is just being vindictive. I'm sure it's no secret to you that she doesn't care for Catherine. I had felt Catherine was better. She's been spending a lot of time out of doors and doesn't seem to be drinking as much. Maybe she just needs to have some time alone without Lillian harping at her."

"I'm glad you urged her to go out anytime she wanted to, I know it's good for her, but I still think she could benefit from some medical help."

"Perhaps, we'll see. I'll think about it. I want to do what's best for her, of course."

Well I had tried. There was nothing more I could say. We were nearing the center of Bleekston when I asked Jonathan to drop me off at Mike's Auto Upholstery Service. "Thanks for the lift. I'll pick up my car and go on from here."

"You will be back for Catherine's birthday dinner, tonight, won't you?"

"Yes, I'm planning on it."

"Well, here is the money for Catherine's clothes.

This should cover a nice dinner dress and a couple of daytime outfits, shouldn't it?"

"You're generous, Jonathan." He had given me five hundred dollars.

"Keep what you get a secret from her until dinner."

"Will do. I'll be there; nothing will stop me. If my car breaks down, I'll call you to come after me in your trusty old machine here."

"If my trusty machine breaks down, I can always use Bruce's old Harley!" I laughed and waved him on. I wonder what a Harley automobile looks like; I hadn't seen one in the carriage house.

When I saw the first class job Mike had done on my car, I was glad I had accepted Bruce's offer to help; it looked brand new again. Martin may be right when he tells me to depend less on other people, but good workmanship is so rare I could never have picked someone like Mike from the phone book.

A white Porsche was parked in front of the Butternut Inn when I drove by on my way out of Bleekston. Martin's car! He was here! That must have certainly been him that Catherine saw this morning. My body suddenly became so weak I pulled over to the curb and rested my head on the steering wheel. I just couldn't let anything happen to the Vanderleighs because I had introduced that fraud Martin Ingram into their lives! I couldn't put it off any longer, I would have to discuss this with Jonathan. I started the car; just as I pulled away I saw someone walking toward Martin's car. A jaunty gray haired man with a van Dyke beard climbed into that white Porsche and drove away! I laughed out loud. There you go, Maggie! True to form you've let your imagination run away with you again. You silly girl, will you never learn? On your way now, there's much to do and time is ticking by.

The dress shops near the university had nothing Catherine would like; their selection appealed to a younger group. A small boutique a block from the post office turned up two classic outfits. She would love them! One, a soft voile full length dinner dress in a pale aqua, had slimming lines and would look well on Catherine; the second was a street length sheath in a heavily textured cream colored raw silk, with matching fabric buttons and a simple tie belt. Just perfect!

Jonathan hadn't mentioned jewelry, but my eye caught a long rope of natural olive wood beads which would go beautifully with the cream silk. I decided that the beads would be my own gift to Catherine.

After I picked up the mail, I stopped by my apartment to get a few more clothes and have a relaxing cup of tea before heading back to Bleekston. The time away had been good for me; the apartment wasn't such a frightening place any more. I hoped I could fully overcome my fears; I loved this old house so much I would hate to have to move.

There was little mail, mostly monthly utility bills and some advertising circulars. One thick brown envelope was addressed to Dad. I wrote checks to cover the bills so I could mail them on my way out of town, then just sat there staring at that big brown envelope. It would feel so strange to open Dad's mail. It had been postmarked more than two weeks ago and must have arrived right after I left for the Vanderleighs'. The return address was a publisher in Manhattan; it must be about his book on Angkor Wat. I guess I should have contacted them immediately about Dad's death, but I had planned to review his draft to see if I could finish it for him.

I finally ripped the envelope open: a note and some loose slides fell to the floor.

Dear Mat,

Many thanks for the slides. I've studied them and feel sure they'll work well. They are really top notch photographs.

By the way, you must have inadvertently included an undeveloped roll of film in your last package. I thought it was related to the project, so I had it processed. I should have checked with you first, I guess, since these finished slides don't appear related at all. I'm returning them with this letter. I hope you don't mind my having seen them, but now that I have, I'd like to know more. They look very interesting!

Call me when you can and plan to come in soon for lunch and a discussion of the status of your manuscript.

Edward

I took a slide from its container and held it toward the light. Trees. That was an unusual subject for Dad's camera! I didn't want to take the time to drag out the slide projector, so I rummaged through the desk and found my viewer. The first slide was a woodland scene. Others were of the same woods but there was a small building off to the side of the picture that looked somehow familiar to me; it seemed to stick right into the side of a hill. The fourth shot was an inside scene. Oh, of course! The building was the Vanderleigh's boat house; I recognized the interior. The angle of the camera had allowed no water to show in the two exterior views.

There were two totally blank slides and the rest seemed to have been taken in some museum. These must be the ones Dad's editor, Edward, was interested in knowing more about. The art pieces were not from the same time period or geographical location, but seemed to make up a broad based collection. Even from these poor shots I could see they were magnificent pieces. Could Dad have visited some private collector? The quality of the slides puzzled me, though. Dad had always taken pride in his photography and these transparencies were nowhere near the usually high standards he demanded of his work.

The next slide in the viewer jolted me to full awareness: it looked like a Tibetan prayer wheel! From what the monk had said, this could be one of their pieces. I quickly ran through the remaining slides. Another shot resembled a prayer wheel and a third could be a Wheel of the Law.

I didn't recognize any more of the works, but I would love to see this collection. A stucco relief panel looked as though it may have been done during the Cambodian Rouluous period of the late ninth century; the same period the Angkor Wat complex was being constructed. The intricate background of the panel was clearly inspired by a woodcarving tradition.

I ran the slides of the Tibetan objects back through the viewer. I was certain of my identification! One was a Wheel of the Law, made of silver; I had no doubt about it.

The deep rich patina of the silver and the work of a master silversmith made it stand out as an irreplacable piece. The slide of the prayer wheel was not a good one, the second view was only slightly better. It was difficult to do more than identify the object, the detail was not clear. I couldn't, of course, be certain that these were the missing pieces; the only way I would know that was to visit the temple and have the monk look at the slides. I decided to make a quick trip by the temple before I returned to the Vanderleigh estate and in less than two hours was parked in front of the beautiful little building so alien to its surroundings.

As though he knew I was coming, the monk met me outside the main entrance. "Miss Driscoll, so soon! It's nice for you to come again."

I nodded acceptance of his pleasant greeting and smiled in return. "I hope it's more than a friendly visit. I've found some slides I'd like you to see. Do you have some time to look at them now?"

"Of course." He reached for the viewer.

"These transparencies were taken by my father before his death. Do you recognize anything?" I showed him how to press the button to light the slide.

He held the viewer up to his eyes. "Our Wheel of

the Law!" His face beamed with pleasure. The delight was diminished somewhat, however, when he realized I only had the slide, not the object itself. "Where were these taken?"

"I don't know. I think Dad took them after he talked to you and died before he could have them processed. I just received the processed slides." I placed another slide in the viewer. "Is this the prayer wheel?"

"I have no doubt, these are our pieces. Please, how did you get the pictures?"

I explained how the slides had been returned by Dad's editor. "But I don't want to sound hopeful about their recovery; I have no idea where Dad took these pictures. I can only assume they were taken shortly before he died, since he wouldn't have been aware of the missing Wheel of the Law and the prayer wheel before he talked to you."

"Well, from these pictures it is clear they are in the hands of someone who knows their importance and value. I feel better about their safety now. They will make their way back to our people some day, of that I am certain. Thank you, Miss Driscoll, you've relieved my mind about them."

I could not share that relief. "Did a man named Martin Ingram stop by to see you?"

"Yes, last week. A most impressive person; I like him very much and I'm glad you told him about our problem. He didn't expect to learn anything quickly, but he assured me he would do all he could to help us. He was most interested in our temple and our collection of Tibetan, Russian and Mongolian artifacts."

Again I felt a pang of regret that I had involved someone else with Martin Ingram. I hoped no further misfortune would come to them because of my poor judgement. We chatted a while longer and then I left for Jaeger's Nest, promising to let him know the minute I learned anything more about the pieces.

When I reached the Vanderleigh's, Lillian was in a total state of frustration. She had prepared an elaborate dinner for Catherine's birthday celebration and no one could find the guest of honor. "She never appreciates anything. I told her we were planning a party for her. She acted appropriately delighted and then went dancing off like a woodland nymph! No one has seen her since. Oh, where is she? It would be so like her not to come. She vanishes at the drop of a hat now; we don't know where she is half the time. Why can't she keep to a schedule like everybody else? Can't she understand that she inconveniences other people when she tells them she will come and then doesn't bother to show up."

"I'll look for her again, Miss Vanderleigh." Nellie was busy straightening the lace tablecloth and its pink liner. She had arranged a floral spray of pink miniature roses, baby's breath and pink candles. "I'm sure the time just slipped away from her. She loves parties and was really looking forward to this one."

"You're always making excuses for her, Nellie. I'm sure she didn't even think about this party at all."

"That's not true, Miss Vanderleigh!" protested Nellie with uncharacteristic rebellion. "Just this morning she told me it was her birthday, and that Jonathan had said you were planning a special dinner. In that wistful little voice of hers she assured me she would behave all day; she didn't want to do anything to spoil her birthday dinner."

"Wistful little voice is an understatement!" Lillian was becoming a shrew.

I felt it was a good time to make my exit. "I'll run upstairs and get dressed, Lillian. I'll be back in a few minutes." As soon as I shut the door to my room, I flopped on the bed exhausted. I was glad to be away from Lillian's hysterics. I tried to fathom the meaning of Dad's slides. One thing was clear, the Tibetan pieces had been found and they weren't too far away. Dad wouldn't have had an opportunity to go much further than New York or Philadelphia during the time he had learned those pieces were stolen and his accident. It was becoming apparent that I had to talk to someone about them. Not the Vanderleighs, I didn't want to endanger them; they've done too much for me already. And not Martin, I wouldn't be that stupid again! "Old school friend of your Dad's," Oh! How gullible I had been! And how lonely. I drew up into a ball on the bed, fists clenched, eyes closed, writhing in embarrassment. I guess loneliness causes people to misjudge others sometimes. You dream up qualities the real person lacks and hang them on his empty soul like ornaments on a straggly Christmas tree.

As much as I would have liked to escape in sleep, I had to get dressed. All Lillian needed was another tardy guest and her day would be a total disaster! I decided to wear a plain chiffon wrap style blouse with my long black skirt, and dress it up a bit with my rope of cherry amber beads. After a quick cool shower and fresh makeup, I was more receptive to a gay celebration and felt a lot more relaxed when I joined the others below.

Catherine still had not returned, but Lillian had changed to a taupe crepe sheath. Its severe lines and drab color were reminiscent of the late forties, so I was sure it was another of the dresses her father had bought her. There aren't many people who can wear the same clothes thirty years later and still have them fit. She was certainly lucky in that respect.

"Here she comes, Miss Vanderleigh!" Nellie breathed a vocal sigh of relief as Catherine walked toward the back entry. "I'll have her dressed and down in no time at all." She gently guided a surprisingly docile Catherine up the back steps as Jonathan decended the front stairs elegantly attired in a black tuxedo.

"Catherine will be down in a minute, Jonathan. She was a little late getting back from her visit with the woodland wildlife tonight," explained Lillian in a voice dripping with bitter sarcasm.

"Well, people are allowed to be late for their own party, Lillian. It's more or less expected. You've spread a pretty fancy table for us, though, a thing of beauty!" He turned to me, "And how did the shopping go, Maggie?"

"Very well. I think you'll be pleased with my choices. I've wrapped them and can bring them down now if you'd like."

"Yes, let's do. We'll get her to open them directly after dinner."

I turned to go and rammed straight into Bruce. "Oh, I'm sorry!" I stepped back and stared unbelievingly at his purposefully informal clothes: blue jeans and a sleeveless tee shirt. He flashed a sarcastic grin as he performed a mock curtsy. "I don't believe you, Bruce!" I left him staring after me as I ran up the stairs.

As I returned to the dining room, Catherine was also on her way back. Nellie had done wonders with her hair. It was brushed back into soft curls and secured with a wreath of silk flowers which blended perfectly with the pale lavender of her gown. She walked slowly, sadly.

"Wait, Catherine. I'd like to walk with you." She turned and looked at me with dull eyes, showing little response to me and none to the gaily wrapped packages I carried at my side. "Birthdays aren't all that bad," I chided, touching her hand and trying to elicit a smile as we walked into the dining room. No luck. She walked in head down, looking at no one in the room.

It was a dreadful dinner. Catherine was completely unresponsive. Soon Jonathan stopped trying and we began to talk in a strained way about totally unimportant things. Lillian's disappointment at the reception of her elegant dinner was evident and growing.

Nellie brought in a big tray. "No silly cake for you, Miss Vanderleigh has made your favorite: chocolate mousse." Catherine looked up and tried to smile at Nellie, but quickly lapsed back into her morose expression. I really hated to put her, and the rest of us, through the opening of the gifts. In this mood it would be no fun for anyone.

Jonathan wanted the whole show, though, and as coffee was served, he lifted the first big box from the floor and passed it over to her. "From me, my dear. May you wear it in good health." I had wrapped the full length voille in a fancy bright red and white polka dot paper and tied it with a big red bow. It was the gayest thing I had seen all evening. She opened the package slowly. A hint of pleasure lifted the corners of her eyes as she saw the soft color of the dress, but her reply was only a stiffly polite, "Thank you, Jonathan."

Jonathan became more subdued and it was with a solemn face that he wordlessly handed her the second large box, the cream colored street length sheath. When she opened the box, I knew she was pleased. She caressed the nubby texture of the raw silk and held the matching fabric belt to her cheek to fully sense its feel. She glanced at me then, as though she knew I had picked it for her, and smiled a wan smile as she closed the lid of the box.

"These are from me, Catherine. Happy Birthday." I handed her a small box, wrapped in hot pink paper. "They match the dress." She opened the box and lifted the rope of olive wood beads. She ran them through her fingers, pleased with their color and fascinated at the unique pattern of the wood grain.

As if to quickly catch Catherine in a good mood, Lillian placed a small carton, wrapped in lace patterned paper and tied with a pink ribbon, on the table in front of her. "I had Nellie pick this up as a gift from me. I hope you appreciate it."

Catherine carefully untied the bow, sat the box on the table and slowly unfolded the embossed paper. As she lifted the lid of the carton, a look of terror crossed her face. "You knew!" She screamed shrilly as she rose in her seat and glared hard at Lillian. "All the time you knew!" She turned and ran up the stairs, slamming the door to her room with a blast that reverberated throughout the house. Nellie was right behind her.

Lillian remained frozen in her seat, a look of horror and confusion on her face. "Knew what?" she asked. "Knew what? It was just a bottle of perfume!"

FOURTEEN

Nellie returned a short time later, shaking her head sadly. "I don't know what happened. She won't talk. She just sits there and stares into space."

Jonathan rose from his seat, his expression angry. "I'll stay with her, Nellie. You can finish up here."

Throughout dinner Bruce had viewed the unfolding scene with cynical amusement. When the final curtain fell with Jonathan's exit, he turned to me, laughing. "This is a bit much! Join me in a walk, Maggie, if you can bear to miss a chapter of Catherine's old fashioned melodrama."

My mind was reeling with what had just happened. I wanted to get away too. "Just a short one?"

"A short one. I promise."

As we walked through the woods toward the river, I asked, "Why do you hate Catherine so, Bruce?" I could hold it no longer; I had to speak up.

"I don't hate her, I just have no appreciation for that delicate little girl act of hers. To me she's a nothing. I shouldn't let myself get roped into silly things like birthday dinners anyway. The only reason Lillian had that celebration was because you were here; no one has noticed Catherine's birthday in the past five years."

"What do you think was wrong with her?"

"I haven't the vaguest idea. Those little screaming fits lost their impact on me years ago."

"I guess I just feel sorry for her."

"Well save it! She doesn't deserve it."

In my view, Catherine would benefit from some support and understanding, but I could see Bruce was adamant in his opinion and nothing I could say would make him act differently toward her.

We leaned on the dock's railing, looking at the lights across the river. Bruce held me close in the protective curve of his body. His arm encircled me, but his mind was somewhere else. I could almost feel the tension and anxiety emanating from him.

As I watched the play of the lights on the rippling water, I was reminded of the time I had seen Martin Ingram from Al Harmon's yacht. I could see those hard cold eyes as clearly as if he were here right now. Iron tentacles clutched my spine and I shuddered.

"Hey! What's the matter, Maggie?"

"Just tired, I guess. Let's go back to the house." I didn't feel safe outside the Jaeger's Nest.

"That's right, I promised you a short one. You wouldn't mind walking back without me, would you? I just don't want to face that soap opera any more tonight."

"Of course not. See you tomorrow, Bruce." I left

him standing on the dock and walked back alone.

Later, as I curled up in the guestroom's leather chair, I found I could not concentrate on the book I was trying to read. My eyes had just moved over a full page and I didn't remember a word of it. Did I feel guilty for leaving Bruce alone on the dock? He had been so helpful and supportive of me and now, when he was obviously disturbed about something, I had left him to handle it alone without a second thought. He wouldn't have done that to me.

Remembering his casual dress, I quickly slipped into a pair of white duck pants and a pink tank top, pulled on a pair of sneakers, then went down the stairs and out the back. Once away from the lighted house, I began to feel frightened again and kept up a constant conversation with myself all the way to the boathouse. "Actually, Dad, I would much rather be able to see. The dark can hold peace for some people and evil for others."

"Bruce?" I didn't see him anywhere on the dock. "Bruce?" No answer. I tried the boathouse door and found it locked. As I walked back toward the path, I heard the rustle and crackle of leaves as though someone had taken a step. I stopped still, afraid even to breathe. Surely it was a squirrel. No, there it was again, undoubtedly a step, a definite movement in the woods near the rear of the boat house. "Bruce is that you?" No sound. No noise at all. I was really frightened now. I could feel that someone was nearby in the woods; every part of me was aware of it, instinctively. Someone was standing quietly nearby, just watching me; I knew it! From the recesses of my memory came the chilling sound of heavy breathing and the touch of brutal hands. I turned and ran, half stumbling, half running up the path to the house. All external sounds were drowned out by my own gasps for breath.

Fright does definite things to your body. Your lungs won't expand to hold enough air so you breathe faster. Too fast. Your mouth becomes dry and your throat even drier.

As I neared the house, I realized all the outside lights had been turned off. The only illumination was the bright full moon. I ran up the steps and onto the back terrace. The door was locked! No lights were visible in any rooms on the back side of the house. Control yourself, Maggie. Don't be foolish and disturb everybody just because you think you're locked out. I started toward the front door. As I rounded the corner, I heard the controlled and muffled sound of a powerful engine running at only a small fraction of its capability. Someone was slowly guiding a motorcycle toward me! The man from the boat house! I ducked into the shadows of the shrubbery as he moved past me and onto the gravel, then watched as the motorcycle's rear red light bobbed up and down, bouncing over the rough driveway. Once it was gone, I shuddered, half in fear, half in relief. Who could that be?

I waited for several minutes, then tried the front entrance. It too had been locked. The house had shut me out. I looked up to see if any room remained lighted. As I stared at the windows I became entranced with the vision of an old ghost ship, sailing through eons of time, its aged captain never allowed the release of death but forced to sail on and on through eternity. Lillian's words echoed: "The Jaeger's Nest will not absorb anything alien." Well, Adam Vanderleigh, captain of Jaeger's Nest, are you rejecting me? The vision slowly faded from my mind.

"Maggie? Is that you standing out there?" Lillian was unlocking the front door. "Why didn't you ring, for goodness sake! I thought you had gone to bed and I locked all the doors for the night."

"Oh Lillian! I'm so glad you're still awake! I had started to go to bed, but I decided I wanted to talk to Bruce a little longer so I went back down to the dock—"

"I heard the motorcycle leave and I wondered whether it was Jonathan or Bruce. Did you notice? One of them is always taking a midnight spin on that wretched thing."

For a moment I stood dumb. Finally I answered, "I wasn't sure who it was. I didn't know—Bruce wasn't at the dock when I went back to find him, but I had no idea it might be him on the motorcycle."

"Oh yes, he likes to ride it at night, particularly when he's mad at the world. Well, I guess it doesn't matter which one it was, they both have keys. Are you coming in now?"

"Definitely! I don't want to stay out one minute longer."

Later that night as I lay awake in the dark, I tried to laugh at myself. Well, Maggie of the infinite imagination, would you really suspect Bruce? Surely not him! One good thing, the Jaeger's Nest decided to keep you around for a while. This fortress is secure; the phantom searcher will not find you here.

Then a vision of the young and beautiful Catherine floated through my mind. She did not feel safe at Jaeger's Nest; far from it! She was a tortured and miserable soul.

I was up bright and early the next day, "How's Catherine this morning, Nellie?" I poured some coffee and took a muffin from the warmer on the sideboard.

She shook her head sadly, "No better, Miss Driscoll. She just stares off into space and won't talk to anybody. I've never seen Mr. Vanderleigh as mad at her as he was last night. She just looked at him with meanness in her eyes and wouldn't say anything about what was bothering her. I don't know what's going to become of that girl if she doesn't straighten up."

"Is she still in her room?"

"I think she went out to the woods again. She was being real quiet to keep me from hearing her, but I'm sure she tiptoed down the back steps about ten minutes ago. I didn't say anything to her because she was obviously avoiding me. I swear I don't know what's gotten into her, she doesn't seem the least bit sorry for the way she acted and you know as well as I do that she's not usually like that!"

"Yes, I know. Well, if she won't talk to you, I know she doesn't want to see me either, so I'll leave her alone. I have a lot of work to do in the library this morning."

As I worked on Jonathan's notes, I came across a handwritten entry: "Newark Museum, Newark,

N.J.—one of the world's most impressive collections of Tibetan art—Collection begun early 1900's when Dr. Shelton, American missionary, met museum's curator on a ship returning from Far East. Dr. Shelton was returning to U.S. to obtain medical supplies by selling Tibetan art works. Through the luck of their meeting, the museum was able to purchase nearly 500 objects."

I quickly grabbed the phone and dialed 411. "Information? I'd like the number of the Newark Museum, please. Thank you." I dialed. "Who is the museum curator for the Tibetan collection? May I speak with her? Thank you . . . Hello, Miss Jerard, I'm Margaret Driscoll. May I have an appointment to see you today? . . . Yes, it is in reference to some stolen articles taken from a Tibetan temple and some evidence I have that may help me locate the missing pieces . . . I have some transparencies taken of an unknown collection which includes the missing Tibetan objects . . . I would appreciate any help you could give me in identifying the collection . . . Yes, thank you. I'll be there at two thirty this afternoon."

Jonathan stopped at the door of the library just as I hung up the phone. "Good morning, Maggie. At it already, I see."

"Yes, and it looks like I'll be here most of the morning."

"I just wanted to borrow a few pages from these notes, I'll return them later. I'm very pleased with your work, Maggie. You're doing a nice job."

"Thanks, Jonathan. I'm enjoying it."

I spent the morning revising Jonathan's outline.

When I finally finished, I realized I must dress and leave immediately if I was going to make it to Newark in time for my appointment. Lillian was walking through the foyer as I came down the stairs. "Sorry to give you such short notice, Lillian, but I'm visiting the Newark Museum today and will probably miss dinner this evening."

She laughed resignedly, "After last night's debacle, I don't know if we'll ever serve dinner here again! Maybe by the time you get back we'll have figured out what's the matter with Catherine."

"If not, I'll try to talk with her to see if there's any way I can help her. I'm sure she wasn't drinking last night, Lillian, if that's any consolation."

"I guess it should be, but somehow it doesn't help to know that. Jonathan is becoming convinced, finally, that something has to be done. Well, go on now, Maggie, enjoy yourself and don't worry about us."

The questions raised by Dad's slides kept swirling through my mind as I drove out the estate gates and turned onto the main road. Where had he taken those pictures? Some scenes were unquestionably views of the beech woods and boathouse on the Vanderleigh estate. In a way, that did make sense; once in a great while Dad did photograph a scene he found particularly interesting or appealing. The bothersome thing was that these shots were poorly focused, a little over exposed and awkwardly angled. The boathouse was not photographed from its most attractive view, but from its back side; its beauty was ignored. The colonial blue door with its shiny brass knocker and the matching blue shutters were not even included in the picture. Dad never took such casual snapshots, he was a professional. If he truly did take those pictures, then he merely wanted to record them quickly and had no time for thoughts or lighting or composition. But why would he have been in such a hurry to photograph the boathouse?

Another bothersome thing was the importance of these Tibetan articles to Dad. Of course I knew he would consider it an obligation to help locate them but I had to admit that finding them seemed to loom larger than that. Why did he mail the unprocessed film to his editor? Something more had to have been driving him! Where did he see all those pieces? A museum? Could a museum have purchased the Tibetan articles unknowingly? I glanced at my watch and realized that I needed to speed up or I would be late for my appointment.

I was nearing the outskirts of Bleekston when I looked in my rear view mirror and saw a black motorcycle beginning to pass me. I don't know what warned me, objectively I only saw a motorcycle with a white helmeted rider, but I was immediately frightened of that machine. It was as though some evil vibrations projected from the rider to me and I became filled with fear. I veered to the right to get out of his way and give him an unimpeded path, but he kept coming straight at me! In a panic I turned to look at him but could see nothing of his face; it was hidden by the dark tinted shield of his helmet. The car spun out of my control as it hit the soft shoulder. I screamed as it plunged through the thick underbrush and crashed to a stop in a shallow drainage ditch running along the side of the road.

I was unsure how much time passed as I sat dazed in my car. I stared at the green leaves of the shrubs pressed against my windshield and watched with total concentration as a little brown grasshopper danced across my hood, treating my car as a perfectly natural part of his environment.

To my left, a hand reached for the door handle. I screamed again and lunged in terror in an attempt to get out the other door. It was stuck; I couldn't open it! I shoved the full weight of my body against it in frustration.

"Hold it! It's okay, little lady. I'm here to help you. Are you all right?" The hand reached in to pull me from the car. I backed away, not wanting to be touched, to escape from any contact.

I could see his face now. He was confused and obviously exasperated with me. "Look lady! I'm Pete Forester. I live down the road on my farm. Now let me help you."

I began to calm down and edged toward him on the seat. "I'm sorry. I'm still a little shaky. A motorcycle just ran me off the road—I guess it's only fair to say that I let him run me off. If I'd only had the presence of mind to resist him, he'd be the one in the ditch now instead of me. No motorcycle is a match for any car."

"I thought he acted peculiar. I was coming from the other direction and saw him keep going when you left the road. He didn't bother to stop or even look back!"

"You did see him? Did you see that he just kept coming at me? It didn't make any sense. I was so shocked and surprised that I lost control of the car."

He held the door open as I tried to climb out. My hands were still trembling, but as far as I could tell, I was uninjured and all in one piece. He took my arm and helped me avoid the ditch. "Careful now. If I were you, Miss, I'd be sure to see a doctor just to make certain that you're okay. Sometimes in the shock of the moment you can be unaware of the damage done to your body."

"No, I'm all right. I really feel sure that nothing's wrong." I began to inspect my car. "This poor car has been through so much lately, I wonder how much it will cost to fix it up this time.

"I think you only have some small dents and scratches. Nothing major. Nothing that will affect its performance."

"I think I'll try to get it back on the road."

"Well, Miss, there is one thing I am sure of, you're stuck. You managed to run right into a pretty muddy ditch. Let me turn my truck around and I'll use my winch to pull you out."

I watched as he expertly attached the chain to my bumper and then maneuvered his truck into the best possible position to pull my car up from the muck. Within ten minutes from the time he started, Pete had my car back on the road. If you overlooked the thick coating of mud on the lower part, it didn't look so bad at all. The front window on the passenger side had been cracked by the brush, but that was the worst damage. The front right fender had a small dent and the paint was a little scratched up, but as Pete said, nothing major.

"See, it won't take much to make it like new. If you need a witness to what happened, you be sure to let me know, I'd be glad to tell them about it. Young kids these days have no sense of responsibility or obligation. No sense at all is the way I look at it! Why, he could have killed you if it had happened on another part of this road! Not long ago a man was killed near here when he went over and there was nothing to stop him. I didn't see that accident, I just heard about it. Driscoll I think his name was."

I gasped aloud, "On this road? It happened on this very same road?"

"Yes, quite a way's back, where there's a steep drop off to the right side. It was a sharp drop down, some trees, but not much underbrush. No one saw it happen and they never did find out why he ran off the road. He wasn't from around here either. Folks who live here know this road is dangerous. Lots of bad accidents have happened on it, mostly involving out of towners."

I just stood there staring at him, my mind numbed by what he had just told me. Had a motorcycle rider killed my father? Had he killed him like he just tried to kill me? Mr. Forester stopped talking and looked at me intensely, "Are you sure you're okay, Miss?"

I was trembling again, worse than before. I didn't want to hear him describe Dad's death any further. "Yes, I'm sure." A thought thrust itself into my consciousness. "Mr. Forester, you mentioned that the motorcycle rider who ran me off the road was a kid. Did you recognize him?"

"No, can't say as I did, really. Out here the kids ride motorcycles all the time and they all look alike to me, the kids as well as the motorcycles.''

Martin could hardly qualify as a kid; could Bruce? I guess to Pete Forester, a man of sixty plus, they both could. ''Mr. Forester, I don't know how to thank you for just being here at the right time. What would I have done without you? You're the first lucky thing that's happened to me in a long time!''

He laughed, ''Well, if I'm the best luck you've got, cheer up. Things can only get better from here!'' He wrote out his address and phone number for me in case I needed him as a witness, then watched me drive on my way. Another guardian angel, just when I needed one. If it weren't for him, I'd still be solidly stuck in that mud!

The remainder of the trip to Newark was blessedly uneventful. Turnpike traffic was light, and I was able to avoid most of the downtown traffic congestion. I pulled into a parking garage, turned my car over to the attendant for a claim check and began walking the remaining two blocks to the museum.

I heard a noise; my senses quickened and again I felt afraid. Someone came running up behind me, then shoved me hard against the nearby building. I fell to the ground in a daze, but conscious. He jerked my bag from my hand. I looked up and saw my own reflection on a dark convex mirror directly above me. I fainted then; my world went totally black.

I came to when I heard an engine start a few feet from me. I opened my eyes and ducked as something came flying toward my face. My hands automatically went toward my head for protection, but not quickly enough. It hit, its sharp edge biting into my cheek. My handbag! I grabbed it quickly, then looked up to see a flash of chrome, a glistening white helmet, and a man dressed in black riding away. I held onto the building for support and rose to my feet. I was trembling uncontrollably, but otherwise seemed unhurt: just a scrape on one knee and some nicks on my hands. The small cut on my cheek was bleeding, but nothing was broken.

I began to cry, not out of fear, but out of frustration. I sat on the sidewalk again, my back against the building, crying big jerking sobs. An aged couple walked by, taking small steps and looking in every direction but mine. They probably think I'm on drugs or alcohol, or maybe just plain crazy: "What is this younger generation coming to!"

Suddenly I was dry. No more tears would come. I opened my handbag to fix my face and realized immediately what had been taken: Dad's slides! I emptied my bag bottom up onto the sidewalk. The package of slides was not there. It was gone! The tears began to flow again. Moans, groans and a furious raging feeling soared through me. "What is this? Who are you?" I screamed. "Is that all you wanted? What could those slides mean to you?" My angry screams seemed to echo off the concrete.

I shoved everything back into my bag and tried to stand up. I must get to that museum. Maybe there was still some way they could help me, even without the slides. I staggered along the sidewalk clutching the buildings for support. I had to get help. I couldn't handle this alone anymore. There's nothing I can tell myself that will make me straighten my back and enter the ring for another round. I have no more fight left; I've taken all I can take!

The ridiculousness of my thoughts came echoing back at me. Here I was, basically unharmed, merely frightened. My friends in Cambodia, if they were still alive and not in the three million already killed, faced horrible things every day: starvation, disease, and violent death. Their normal day is much more difficult than anything I will probably ever have to encounter in my entire life. I have no right to fold up; I must keep fighting.

Dad took those pictures for a reason I did not understand, but he felt they were important. I must keep going. I am alone; there's no one to help me. I must start where Dad left off and find the answers.

FIFTEEN

"I'm Margaret Driscoll. I had a two thirty appointment with Miss Jerard. I know I'm very late, but I would appreciate seeing her if at all possible."

The young receptionist looked up at me with large dark eyes. "I don't believe she's in her office now; if you'll have a seat, I'll try to locate her." She vanished down a corridor, her clogs clacking loudly as she went. I began to rehearse how I would ask Miss Jerard for her help. I had gotten no further than trying to explain the missing slides when the receptionist returned. "Come this way, please." She took me into an empty office. "Wait here. She's tied up right now but will be with you in just a moment."

"Thank you." I sank into the soft vinyl chair as she left, closing the door behind her. Alone again, I tried to concentrate. How could I begin to tell someone this confused story?

The books in a cabinet on the other side of the room caught my attention. I rose to look over the titles; what a collection of references on Oriental artifacts! If only I still had those slides! I heard the door open and turned to greet Miss Jerard. The face I saw made my knees go weak!

Martin's hand was still on the door knob when I turned around. That sarcastic and knowing smile taunted me. I backed against the wall, certain my eyes showed every nuance of the fear I felt.

"Margaret! What is it? What's the matter?" His color drained, his face went white. "Tell me what in the world has happened? You're late! Are you all right? Tell me what has happened to you!"

I must regain control. I had to appear calm; weakness would be my downfall. A thin veneer of composure veiled my fear. "What are you doing here?" With effort I kept my voice flat and hard.

He looked at me strangely; his answer was guarded. "Miss Jerard called me. I had talked with her several days ago about the Tibetan articles stolen from the temple. She contacted me immediately after she talked with you. Why didn't you call me, Margaret?"

He was the picture of innocence. His brown hair and lightly tanned skin blended with the flat woven texture of the beige linen jacket and created a clean, crisp, masculine image. Fraud! His self control was beyond belief! I would never win a war of wits with this man. "Why are you doing this to me, Martin? You have what you want now. Just go away and leave me alone! There's nothing more you can take from me."

"What the devil are you talking about, Maggie?" His voice was sharp and angry.

My thoughts spun in confusion as I saw the genuine dismay in his face. The dam broke then, I lost all semblance of control and burst into tears. I felt so alone and frightened. Martin took me in his arms and held me close against him. I could feel the woven texture of his coat against my cheek and the protective cradling of his hand at the nape of my neck. The sobbing slowed as I began to realize that it was anxiety for me, not anger, which had made his voice sound harsh.

His hand touched my chin and lifted my face toward his. There was pain in his eyes I had never seen before. He moaned and crushed me to him, closing his lips over mine. A liquid warmth spread through me and I floated in a soft down-filled world. Those fumblings with Bruce belong on a lower plane. This was what it meant to want someone, to desire to be touched. This was a need I had never known.

He looked down at me, his eyes full of tenderness. My expression must have asked too much, for he suddenly seemed wary. He knew now that my feelings went further than simple gratitude from the comforted to the comforter. I made some comment about mussing up his jacket with my makeup and turned aside, keeping my eyes low because they were red and swollen from crying. Martin led me to a chair near the desk. He seemed completely composed again and I knew my moment with him had passed. I would never forget it.

"Margaret, tell me what happened, now. What has upset you so?" Back to "Margaret" again, no longer "Maggie" as before.

I forced myself to put my feelings for him away

until I was better able to deal with them; tucked away, but not repressed. "I need to ask you a few questions, Martin. Please tell me the truth." He nodded, his expression guarded. "First, was that you I saw on the pier the other night?"

His eyes dropped and he turned his face from me. His voice was hoarse as he answered, "Yes. I saw Harmon manhandle you and your white knight Bruce Vanderleigh come to the rescue."

"And the next day, in the woods of the Vanderleigh estate, why were you there?"

"I can't tell you that, believe me, Margaret, I can't. Not yet."

My fear came creeping back. In an unsteady voice I asked, "And did you also run me off the road this afternoon?"

"Maggie!" For once his voice betrayed his emotion, he was alarmed. His control was quickly regained, however, and the look he gave me was withering. "What do you think?"

I did not answer right away. Put in his position, I felt sure my reaction would have been similar. It was obvious to me now that I had mistakenly suspected Martin, but if not Martin, who? Bruce? Surely not. I was back where I began. "I'm sorry, Martin, but given everything that has happened, I had to ask."

"You told Miss Jerard you had some evidence which may help locate the Tibetan articles." His tone was businesslike. I deserved it.

"Well, to start at the beginning, I've learned that Dad found the Tibetan pieces before he died."

"How do you know?"

"His editor returned some slides Dad had

mistakenly submitted with those for his book, included were shots of the objects taken from the Tibetan temple."

"Are you sure, Maggie?"

"I stopped by the temple late yesterday afternoon to verify it. There's no doubt. There were also pictures of several more items which he photographed at the same time, but I couldn't identify any of the other pieces. I don't know where he shot those slides; there's no clue. It looks like an exhibit room in some museum. That's why I came here."

"Mat wouldn't mistakenly send those slides to his publisher, he must have done it deliberately."

"His editor, Edward McIntyre, didn't seem to think so; he assumed it was an error, although he did say he was very interested in knowing more about the pieces."

"I need to see those slides. Where are they now?"

"They were just stolen from me, not two blocks from here, by a man dressed in black clothes, a white helmet, and riding a motorcycle." I shivered as I remembered that helmet and my own face, drawn in terror, reflected in its shield.

"I see," said Martin quietly. "I understand now. You thought I had done that too."

I nodded, sorry now. "He's been following me everywhere for weeks, how else would he have known about the slides? He tore up my apartment, then my car, looking for that film; then almost killed me today by running me off the road near Bleekston. I honestly can't believe the trouble he has caused me for something I knew nothing about until yesterday. He knew who I was and exactly what I was carrying. He was after that one insignificant packet in my purse."

"He also knows where those pictures were taken and what they represent. Tell me everything you can remember about them, Margaret."

"They were not good shots, which puzzles me because Dad was an excellent photographer. In addition to the Tibetan antiques there were some beautiful jade pieces, the most delicate and perfect ones I have ever seen. They were so outstanding in those poor pictures, I would love to see the real things."

"Is there anything else you can remember?"

"Some archeological pieces, one even looked Cambodian."

"Could you identify anything specifically, any piece you had known about before you saw the slides?"

I shook my head, "No. The only other thing I can remember right now is the Vanderleigh boathouse and a couple of pictures of the beech woods on the estate, but they were not related to the art works."

"Can you remember anything more about this man who just robbed you?"

"Nothing really. As I said, I thought it was you. Pete, the farmer who helped me get my car back on the road, thought he was young. His body was slim, and he moved quickly and confidently like an athlete." I would not mention Bruce. I had been wrong once before about Martin.

"And the motorcycle?"

"I don't know what kind, I don't know anything about them, they've always scared me. It was just black, the same color as the one which ran me off the road. Martin, I learned today that Dad's accident happened right on that same road. They never found out what caused him to go over the edge."

He said nothing for a moment, then spoke softly, "Well, Margaret, like the silver circle, you have another legacy you didn't anticipate. You've become a part of this because Mat was somehow involved."

"Involved? How?"

"If you've been reading the papers at all lately, you must be aware of the tremendous increase in art thefts during the last decade. Public buildings, libraries, museums and churches can't leave any old or valuable piece on their walls or in an unprotected display anymore. The appetite of this new breed of art thief is enormous. Your father was involved because he cared about art and he cared about the world and its history. A civilization's art is an expression of its values, its view of life. He felt that no nation's treasures should be plundered to grace the living room of some rich collector, one often unaware of the history behind the piece. Your father cared deeply about such things, Margaret. He was involved in the world and involved in life."

"You feel Dad may have discovered a cache of stolen art before his death?"

"It looks that way."

"Do you think my father's death was an accident?"

My words hung on the air; I felt suspended in time. When he finally spoke, Martin's eyes evaded mine. "Was his death accidental, Maggie? I don't know. With everything that has happened to you,

I'm beginning to doubt that it was. Mat and I discussed the problem of art thefts in a general way the last time we talked. He was going to work with me and we planned to talk further when I got back from my trip. It looks as though he stumbled onto something while I was away, something unexpected."

I was suddenly very tired, battered, emotionally beaten. "Oh, what does it matter anymore! My Dad is dead, the slides are gone. I don't want to think about it anymore! I just want to go to school, get my doctorate, then teach. I want no interference, and I want to be left alone. I'm sick of it—sick of this jungle!"

"Snap out of it, Margaret! You're acting like a child!" His voice was scolding in its tone. "This is real; it is the world." He had no pity for me. He was a hard rock. Hard, immovable, stiff and unyielding. How he and my Dad could ever have been friends I didn't know.

Martin was not my father, however, and I was far from being his little girl! I was repelled by that vision of myself. Bruce was the one who was fatherly; he saw me only as someone to protect and nurture. I didn't want that from a man. I wanted to be respected and loved for what I was, not for what I wasn't. "I'm sorry, Martin. I've done it again."

"Margaret, you've had some pretty nasty knocks." He put his hand over mine, "The problem is, the world can't stop to give you time to heal."

Suddenly the man on the motorcycle didn't matter anymore, nor did the slides. They were the past. I loved Martin Ingram. I knew now that I must be strong enough for him to love me.

SIXTEEN

I drove back to Bleekston in a daze. I felt absolutely wretched; never had my ego been so bruised. I replayed my conversation with Martin. Recognition of the problem is the first step in solving it, they say, but I didn't know where to begin step one and one-half. I knew I was in love with Martin Ingram and had never loved Bruce at all. I had responded to Bruce's helpfulness in the moments I needed someone to lean on, but need is not love.

My hysterical outburst to Martin echoed back at me: "I didn't ask for any of this . . . I don't want to think about it anymore . . . I just want to be left alone!" Then Martin's unvarnished reply played crescendo, "You cannot hide your head in the sand . . . The world can't stop to give you time to heal." He was so right! Why had it been so hard for me to see that he was right? After today he would never again see me as anything but a silly and frightened child. Why hadn't I realized how wonderful he was? I had seen him as a friend of Dad's, certainly a handsome friend, but nothing more. All I had wanted was his help and advice. I tried to use him as a father substitute and he quite rightly rebelled at that. Now that I could clearly see how I had acted, I was embarrassed.

So here I am with no one again! Why do I have to lose everyone I love? There you go, Maggie, right on cue, feeling sorry for yourself. I wanted to reach out to Martin for warmth, for a response of concern. I wanted to know that I mattered to him in some way; that the world would seem incomplete if I ceased to exist.

At the end of a tiring drive, I pushed the button of my transmitter and turned in at the gates to the Vanderleigh estate. Safe again! I swerved to avoid hitting a cute little chipmunk bouncing across the drive, its cheek pouches filled and overflowing. These protected woods were just teeming with life.

There in the middle of it all sat Catherine, resting in the curve of a huge beech trunk. I pulled over and stopped. She didn't appear to notice me at first, then her eyes turned toward me as I walked in her direction. Although she did not seem to be drinking, she looked terrible: her hair was uncombed, her clothes wrinkled and stained. "Good afternoon, Catherine. You've certainly found a quiet place to sit. May I join you?"

"Sure," her body shifted slightly, just as if she were on a couch, indicating that I should sit down. Her voice was dull, lifeless. As an afterthought, as though she wanted to try to make me feel welcome, she added, "There's plenty of room under this big old tree."

After I was seated, with my legs stretched out like hers, she turned to me, her eyes big and brimming with tears. "I want you to know that I love the dresses, Maggie. I can guess that you picked them out. Although I didn't act like it at dinner, I do like them very much, really."

I had gotten my opening. "I'm glad. I thought they'd look terrific on you. You look so sad today, Catherine; can I help in any way?" As I reached out to touch her arm, her tears began to flow.

"I don't know, Maggie. I know you think I'm crazy and I know I've given you plenty of reason to feel that way, but I don't think anybody can help me now."

I was puzzled by this hopeless attitude. "Try me, Catherine. I'll do my best."

"I know that, but it's too late. I've thrown my life away."

"Too late for what?"

"Gordon is gone and nothing can bring him back. It's too late."

"That was a long time ago. Your wounds will heal with time. It just seems to be taking longer for you, but the healing will come." My words sounded empty to me; I hoped they were true.

"You don't understand, Maggie, I know what happened now! It's all clear. I knew Gordon loved me, I knew it! Oh, Maggie, I want to show you. You have to see so you will know that I didn't make it up, that I'm not crazy. But you must never tell, for both our sakes. It must remain our secret."

"Of course, Catherine, it will be our secret." I wasn't really humoring her now. I was mystified at this change in her. I had to know what she was talking about. No longer merely the little girl lost and sad, she was now the little girl who had lost all hope and was totally defeated. Her eyes no longer held that look of injured innocence; it was now the look of bitter loss, of hopelessness, resigned to a life of sorrow. "Now, please try to tell me what has happened."

"I can't tell you; I can only show you. I want you to see. I want you to understand. Will you come with me?"

"Let me take my car to the house first and let Lillian know I'm back."

Her eyes grew wide with fright. "No! They must not know. Come with me now, you can't go back!"

"I have to get the car out of the drive, Catherine; there's no room for anybody to get by. Come ride to the garage with me, then we'll walk back together. I won't say anything to anybody." Once we had parked the car, she took my hand and, again like a child, led me through the woods. This was a section of the estate I had not seen and, though much the same as the other woods in terms of tree varieties, it was of a more uneven terrain. She dropped my hand and ran ahead, hurrying now, her bare feet expertly making their way toward her goal.

Up ahead a small building came into view. It was like a gazebo, only there was no wide expanse to gaze upon. I guess it was really just a pretty place to rest in the woods. She stood there against one of the fluted columns, waiting for me. Again I felt touched by her waiflike appearance. "I haven't seen this building before. How long has it been here?"

"Since the beginning. Grandfather Adam Vanderleigh built it as his personal summerhouse. No one else was allowed here until he died. It was his private place to think and be alone. Now I know why."

She took my hand again, "Come, I'll show you." She led me to the center of the small building. There a huge round stone slab mounted on a pedestal served as a table. The pedestal itself was three to four feet in diameter; the slab was nearer seven. She stood by the table and began to push the slab aside. It looked so heavy I was amazed she could move it. "It's the way he built it," she explained. "There's a lot of gears underneath which let it move easily." When she had pivoted the slab aside, a staircase was exposed, stone steps, and a stone wall enclosing the stairwell. I hesitated to follow her. "Don't worry, Maggie. I've been down here many times. There's nothing to be afraid of. The steps are safe." She pulled a candle from her pocket, lighted it, and held it above her head to light the way. "Come on Maggie, I want you to see." I followed her then, holding to the wall for support. How eerie everything looked in that dim candlelight.

"How did you ever find this place?"

"I was lying on the rock slab table watching the animals play in the woods. As I got up to leave, I stumbled and fell against the slab and was surprised that it moved. I kept pushing and when the stairs were revealed I just walked on down. I wasn't afraid; I had nothing to lose."

At the base of the stairwell was a large ship's wheel. She turned it to the right and I could hear the table closing over us. I felt a moment of panic. We would be trapped. She looked at me with understanding for what I was feeling and tried to reassure me in her childlike way. "It's okay, Maggie. I know how to open it too." Now I was the child and she was the leader.

She walked ahead of me, talking all the time, until we came to the end of the corridor. There it appeared to stop, as though we had taken the wrong turn in a maze. Another small ship's wheel was mounted on the wall; she turned it. I was amazed to see the slab at the end of the corridor shift aside, leaving a three foot passage way into a dark room. My eyes caught reflections and shapes in the candlelight, but nothing identifiable. She made her way directly to a large trunk in the corner and sat down beside it.

"Here, Maggie, hold the candle while I open this." I took the candle, my eyes admiring the beautifully carved teak wood and the heavy brass hardware of the chest. "This is what I want to show you. It belonged to my husband, Gordon Manchester." She gently lifted a leather briefcase from the chest.

I was shocked at her calm revelation. "How did it get here?"

"I don't know for sure, I can only guess. I do know that it was put here after his death. He wouldn't have left it here by choice." She opened the case very carefully, treating it as though it were fragile. "This was inside," she showed me a gift box of an expensive popular perfume. A card was attached: "to my dearest wife on her birthday." She read the printed portion of the card, a standard but loving verse, and said in a soft voice, "Here Maggie, I just can't read anymore. You go ahead."

The handwriting was barely legible, but legible nonetheless. "Catherine: I'm giving you this as we enjoy your birthday dinner, darling. You've made me a very happy man in the few years we've had together. I look forward to our future ones confident that they will be even more rewarding and happy than those seemingly perfect ones of our past. Gordon."

Her eyes were filled with shining tears. "You see, Maggie, he wasn't leaving me! It was my birthday dinner! He never came home. He was killed in a highway accident with Anne Vanderleigh. He was not leaving me. The rumors were not true. See Maggie, he did love me after all!"

"That's why the perfume upset you so! It's the same fragrance! I don't think Lillian knew."

"I'm not so sure, Maggie, not that sure at all. Here read this one too." She handed me a small envelope of an expensive creamy vellum. A simple "Gordon" was written on its face. I turned it over and saw the embossed AV. "Anne Vanderleigh," I whispered aloud.

"Go ahead, Maggie, read it."

I opened the envelope, the initials AV were repeated on the stationery inside, "Gordon, you and Catherine have been our friends for years. I hate to impose on that friendship, but I must. I need your help. I am leaving Jonathan and need you to drive Bruce and me to the City. There is little time to explain now, but please say you will. If you can come, just drive up to the gate after your last class, ring and I'll open it. We'll leave as soon as you arrive. I'm counting on you, Gordon, it's so very important. Anne"

"You see, Maggie, they were not leaving to be together! Gordon was mine as I always knew he was. I could not believe that I had been so mistaken about our love. In my weaker moments, yes, I felt rejected and deserted, but in my rational moments I knew it made no sense."

I raised the candle and looked into the bottom of the chest. Something else was there: a small navy duffle bag. "Have you opened this, Catherine?" I asked as I pulled it out and placed it on the floor between us.

"No, I hadn't seen it. I found Gordon's case yesterday before my birthday dinner and I haven't looked at anything else since then."

I zipped open the soft and yielding canvas bag and found some boy's clothes, assorted toilet articles, and another letter. This one was addressed to Lizbeth, the envelope unsealed: I opened it and read aloud: "Lizbeth, Just a note to let you know that I have left Jonathan. By the time you return from your trip and read this, Bruce and I will have been away for several days. It was unexpected but urgent and necessary.

"Jonathan is a madman, Lizbeth. I don't want to say anything more right now, but I will fill you in on everything as soon as I know we are safe. Gordon Manchester was kind enough to take us to the City and to drop this note by your apartment. Don't try to call me and do not let Jonathan know that you have heard from me. I will get in touch with you. Love till later, Anne."

Lizbeth had never gotten this letter and Bruce was not in the car when they had the accident. "I don't understand," I said aloud.

"I don't know the whole story, Maggie, but I feel better now that you've seen this too. I don't feel so alone and afraid." She reached out for my hand. "There's more to see. Bring the candle and come on."

"Old Adam built this place in such fantastically intricate detail, you'd think he would have wired it for electricity too. Oh, I'm kidding! I know it was originally built before electricity."

"But there are lights down here, he must have put them in later. For some reason, though, the control panel is way at the back of the room." She led me cautiously through a maze of shadows and shapes. After we had walked to the end of what must be a huge room, she flicked a switch and flooded the room with light.

I was struck dumb, I could not speak. Row after row and case after case was set around the room: Jewels, sculpture, antique artifacts, and priceless archeological treasures. In one display case, brightly lighted against rich blue velvet, sat a silver Wheel of the Law and a Tibetan prayer wheel. I felt the tears start. "Oh, no," I said aloud. "How long have you known about this room, Catherine?"

"I found it when you went on your boat trip, but I only found Gordon's case yesterday. It took me a while to look at everything. I'm just now starting to open things to see what's inside. I never expected to find anything except more jewels or carvings in that heavy wooden chest."

The room was filled with works from all periods and all nations, but my biased eyes caught the Orient's treasures first. In the center of the room was a rosewood chair, an Eighteenth Century Chinese piece. Its carvings were primarily the key pattern and the Chinese symbol for long life. The deep natural patina of the richly grained rosewood made this utilitarian piece one of the most appealing in the room. Its place of honor seemed chosen so that the hoarder of these magnificent works could sit here to gaze upon them. I carefully sat down in the chair, then lifted my eyes to the wall it faced. A magnificent Aubusson Chinoiserie tapestry, also from the Eighteenth Century was in my direct line of sight. It was a superbly executed work, even the glare of the spotlights revealed its perfect condition.

On a pedestal at the side of the tapestry, also under its own spotlight, stood the most beautiful piece I had ever seen. I was sure it wasn't the most monetarily valuable item here, but to me it was a treasure in itself. It was a jadeite vessel of the Ch'ien Lung period, only a foot or so high, with a cover attached by a movable linked chain. The entire piece, including the vessel, its cover, and its chain, had been carved from a single piece of jadeite. Its coloration ranged from milky white, through blue to green and then to more earthy tones. The intricate and complex carvings were of birds, flowers and intertwining leafy vines. The spotlight increased the beauty of this piece by emphasizing its translucence.

More jadeite carvings, each beautiful, but to me a

little less striking, sat on a nearby rosewood table. When you've seen perfection, even another perfect piece seems a little less outstanding. A white jade incense burner of the Ch'ing Dynasty, carved in the form of a pogota with handles of carved dragons and fish, was the largest piece. Sitting nearby was another delicate Ch'ien Lung incense burner of lavender jadeite.

A carved teak chest, this one smaller than the first and more elaborately trimmed with brass inlays and hardware, rested at the base of the tapestry. I opened the lid and gasped as I saw an exquisite jewel studded sheathed dagger. "Oh, let me see that!" exclaimed Catherine looking over my shoulder. "How beautiful! The gold alone is worth a fortune and the jewels—do you think they're real?"

"I'm sure they are!" I laughed. "Nothing in this room could be less than genuine."

She held the knife above her head and slowly turned around. "Look at these things, Maggie, just look at all these things! They've been here for years with no one to appreciate them. No one ever comes down here."

If only that were true, I thought, knowing that my father had stood in this very spot shortly before his death.

SEVENTEEN

"Maggie, look! Would you just look at this pendant?" Catherine lifted a teardrop ruby, the size of a baby's fist, by its heavy golden chain and fastened it around her neck. It promptly settled lumplike in the cleavage of her ample bosom. "Do I look like a bejeweled pagan queen?" She began to dance around, holding the unsheathed jeweled dagger over her head and twirling in childish delight.

I gave a mock curtsy. "Madame is the picture of elegance in her rubies, faded tee shirt, jeans and dirty bare feet."

We both laughed then, louder than the remark deserved. It was a tension release for both of us. She continued her dance, pausing occasionally to mimic the pose of the life size Asparas in the stone plaque at the far end of the room. That plaque could have come from no other place than Cambodia's Angkor Wat. The dancer's serene face and delicately posed hands stood out against an intricate background reminiscent of a highly detailed wood carving.

My mind reeled at the implications of this treasure

hoard. What did it all mean? I could waste no more time; I had to call Martin. "Catherine, let's leave now and come back later. I have to make an important phone call."

"I'll let you out, Maggie. I'm going to stay here a while longer."

I gasped as the huge stone plaque shook slightly, as though the dancer was breaking free of her centuries old pose. "What is behind that wall, Catherine?"

"Nothing, why?" We heard a definite sound of movement as the dancer shuddered again. Catherine's eyes enlarged in fear. "What could that be?"

A panel of the stone wall began to slide aside, revealing another entrance to this room with what looked like a tunnel beyond. We both stood frozen as Jonathan came into full view. He stared at us unbelievingly. His face became a caricature of rage as he glared at Catherine, his eyes steaming. "Remove that pendant at once, you cow! You're no longer fit to wear that perfect gem."

Catherine made a slight movement toward me. Gone was her lost waif look; she met Jonathan's eyes without fear, her shoulders thrust back, her spine straight—a picture of defiance. I felt less courageous by far; my knees were quivering. I had never seen Jonathan or any other human being act this way and had no idea what to expect next.

He strode toward us angrily gestureng with tightly clenched fists. "You've no right to be here, either of you! This room is mine; its secret is mine. No one is to know of it, do you hear? No one!" He stood like an avenging angel of death, dressed all in black. His feet were set wide and his eyes smoldered with hate as he cursed these trespassers onto his private playground. The previous impression I'd had of Jonathan's mild, almost passive manner and his polite civilized way of dealing with life's petty problems went flying away. He looked the personification of evil. His face, already lean and angular, was drawn by rage into an elongated triangle.

He ranted on, "I half suspected someone had been here but I couldn't really believe it! Things didn't seem just right. This vault is mine as it was my grandfather's before me. I deserved it, I earned it. You merely stumbled upon an interesting treasure chest! I have cared for it for decades, since I first learned of its existence." He began to strut around the room and his voice took on a cocky lilt. "Not even my father knew of it. To him, Adam was a used up old man who did nothing but tell boring tales of the sea." His arms swept the room in a wide arc. "This was my grandfather's legacy to me. I am Adam Vanderleigh's heir; his biological heir, his intellectual heir. He was the Jaeger, this is his nest. He sailed the seas and brought back precious things, excellent works of art from the world's oldest cultures. He came here to roost and to die, nothing more. I earned my inheritance by being his friend, by listening to the adventure stories of a lonely and bitter old man."

He seemed to calm a bit and began to walk more slowly around the room, gently touching a statue here, or a vessel there, talking all the while. "We shared a love of beauty for its own sake. We worshipped a beauty man seldom achieves and which must be protected or it will be destroyed by valueless vandals. In this room he kept the things he valued most. He protected and shielded his collection from the eyes of those who would destroy it. I have added a piece from time to time, but it is still ours, Adam's and mine, not for the eyes of outsiders. Everything is perfect in this room; from this flawless gem to that magnificent tapestry. Nothing in this small world lacks perfection."

His eyes fully focused on us once more. "How did you get in here? How did you find this place?" His voice was sharp, harsh, no longer that of a cloyingly polite gentleman. His eyes fell on the slightly ajar entry panel to the summerhouse. "That way? I never use that! How could you have known?" He shoved the panel shut with a resounding crash.

We remained still and silent, not daring to anger this obviously insane man.

His eyes narrowed as he raised his head slightly, seeming to look down on us from a superior position. An ominous tone crept into his voice, "Gordon and Anne saw this room before they died; your father found it too, Maggie. He followed me here, an underhanded maneuver! It is an unlucky place to have been, and I'm sorry you came. I cannot let you leave knowing of its existence." He stood there glaring at us, pondering his next move. A chill ran through me; a queasy feeling of fear grabbed the base of my neck and a paralyzing numbness began to spread over my body. I shivered to shake it off, I had to keep alert.

Suddenly, I could see nothing but his slim body

dressed all in black. "It was you!" The fear and frustration bottled for days within me erupted with a vengeance. I could keep silent no longer. "It was you! You're the one! You killed my father! You destroyed my apartment, my car, and horribly, sickeningly, frightened me; all this while pretending to be my friend. Today you tried to kill me by running me off the road! Why? All for this?" My arms swept the room. "How am I a threat to this? You are insane, Jonathan Vanderleigh, insane!"

He seemed to gain strength from my emotional outburst. "Your father planned to tell the world of my secret. Poor Mat, he felt I could be convinced of the error of my ways. I learned too late that he had taken photographs when he found this room. I couldn't find the film but I knew you had it. It could have ruined everything! I even drugged you in an attempt to get you to talk, then Al Harmon gave you one shot too many and I had to rush you to the hospital."

My stomach turned. Drugged me! I hadn't lost control of my mind! That's why Al Harmon looked so familiar; he was the inquisitor!

"Ah yes, Maggie, you looked shocked. I deal with some very tough people in this business; there's no room for sentiment. I finally got the pictures back when I heard you calling that museum. I had to stop you, don't you see? They would have taken everything! Mat had no right, and you had no right, this room is mine!"

Catherine broke in then, her voice strong. "And Gordon? What did he ever do to you? You were his friend."

"Friend, hah!" Jonathan spit the words. "My wife Anne went to him for help when she discovered my secret. She wanted to leave and take my son. Gordon was going to help them—help them to leave me! He tried to tell me that I was a traitor to my profession. As if history were my profession. This is my love, this and this alone. This is my profession! But they didn't get away; I stopped them. They had no right to destroy me. None! I arranged their accident and then when the world assumed they were lovers, leaving to be together, I didn't deny it. The world is always ready to believe a story like that."

"And my father, did you so coldly murder him too?"

Jonathan winced. "Mat was my friend, but he wouldn't listen to reason. He had an accident—an accident off the drop. It happens all the time; tourists are always misjudging that road."

"Edged over by your motorcycle, no doubt!" I heard my voice, much calmer than I felt, demand more answers. "Why? These are beautiful things, but how can knowledge that they exist be so deadly?"

"Yes, Jonathan, why?" asked Catherine. "Is it money—the money these pieces will bring?"

Again his eyes became flaming pits. "Money? Never! These pieces are not for sale; not now, not ever. For the art! Look around you, cow! Have you ever seen such magnificence? This is mine and only mine and it will last forever!" He paused for a moment, his arms outstretched, and gazed lovingly upon his hoard. "We have collected art from all over the world, masterpieces unappreciated by their caretakers. Often they had hung in musty old buildings for decades, barely noticed, if at all. We find people who want to protect and appreciate them. Such people exist all over the world, wealthy people who will pay any price for authentic pieces whether the sale is legitimate or not.

"Once in a great while, I find a piece for my collection, and I take it. See this small Greek head? Absolute perfection! Remember hearing that it was taken from that small museum in France? It is mine now. Mine! I just received it on our boat trip; I had been waiting so long! It's where it belongs now. Al Harmon gets the pieces and I, sometimes with Bruce's help, authenticate and store them until we find a buyer."

"Bruce knows about all this?"

His voice was scornful. "Of course not! He thinks he helps me validate pieces for museums. He knows nothing and never will. He is his mother's son; biologically mine, yes, but emotionally and intellectually hers."

I was relieved to know Bruce was not involved, that he was my friend.

Jonathan walked toward Catherine and reached for the pendant around her neck. She did not flinch, but stood her ground, unafraid. "You've changed, Catherine."

"Gordon loved me, Jonathan. I know that now. Our life together was not a lie. I was loved by him and I loved him, totally."

"I loved you. I took care of you even though you never loved me."

"Guilt, somehow, Jonathan, not love. You have

no idea what love, human love, is all about."

"Love of beauty—you were beautiful Catherine, absolutely and perfectly beautiful. I had to have you for my own." He continued to hold the pendant, gently kneading it with his thumb. "But human beauty never lasts, not like this stone." He shook his head in an insane, frustrated way. "I'll hate to kill you. I don't like to kill anything, but I have to protect what is mine."

Her eyes held his, unwavering. "You killed my reason for living a long time ago."

A shout came from behind us. "The killing is over! There will be no more killing!" We turned toward the voice in unison. Lillian stood in the entrance, her eyes alive with fury. "Enough Jonathan. Never again!"

"You knew?" His face was momentarily frozen in shock.

"I always knew about Anne and Gordon. I've even tried to forget what you must have done to that gentle man, Dr. Driscoll, but it's over Jonathan. This is the end. There will be no more killing."

"Why did you help me by keeping quiet about your suspicions?" He was incredulous.

"Help you? You worm! Never! You incompetent and weakwilled blot on your father's name! I did nothing for you. I must protect my father and his house. You will not destroy all that he built in the name of your precious trinkets."

Jonathan seemed to visibly shrink before her wrath.

"You knew Gordon's briefcase was here," said Catherine matter of factly. "That's how you knew I would like that perfume."

"I didn't mean to torment you, Catherine, not that time."

Jonathan's voice raised to an inhuman pitch. "You knew about this room?"

Lillian laughed. "Of course!" Her look was one of scorn. "Do you really believe you could carry on like you have for the past forty years and keep me unaware of it? You and that silly old grandfather of ours—a perfect pair of imbeciles! But it is over now; finished!"

"You'll not destroy this; it is my life!" He grasped a Saracen sword from its mounting on the wall and turned toward her, his arm raised to strike. She backed away, her crossed arms ineffectually raised as a shield.

Catherine suddenly jerked her hands from behind her and with a cry of rage struck him on his back. She turned away, and then I saw the golden glint of the ruby encrusted dagger protruding from his upper back. He gasped, fell forward and looked up at her in alarm, unbelievingly. All the while he had been raving, she had been holding the dagger, waiting for her chance to strike. When it came, she did not hesitate.

He momentarily writhed in excruciating pain, then lost consciousness. Lillian screamed. "Is he dead? Oh my God! Is he dead?" Catherine retreated to a corner of the room, her hands covering her face.

"I don't know, Lillian," I said leaning over Jonathan trying hard not to fear him as though he were a wounded animal which might lash out again. "I don't think so. Go call a doctor. I'll stay here with him and Catherine."

"Yes, yes, I'll go, Maggie. I despise him, but I don't want him to die like that."

After she left, I sat down near Catherine. I hated Jonathan too, for causing my father's death. But could I have killed him? Was Catherine stronger than I would ever be? I looked at her now, crouched in her corner, clenched fists covering her eyes.

It was less than a month since my father stood in this room. I could feel his awe and dismay as he looked on this pillage. I could see him rushing to photograph some key pieces. He must have slipped the unprocessed film into an envelope prepared for his editor, then mailed it in the roadside box, thinking Edward would have them if anything happened and that he would be curious enough to seek the truth. His mistake came when he tried to talk to Jonathan. Anne was right, the man is insane.

I knew now why Dad reacted so strongly to the taking of art and antiquities from improverished nations. I had read the draft of his manuscript on Angkor Wat. Words from the dedication page rang in my ears as I looked around this room: "I dedicate this work to the people of Cambodia. They must never forget the greatness they can achieve. If the ruins are leveled or destroyed in the conflict, it is important that they value their past with pride."

Jonathan's leg jerked, involuntary and he moaned. Catherine began to cry. Through her sobs, I heard footsteps near the door. Could Lillian have already returned? I got up and stepped back toward the opening, not knowing who to expect. The face that met mine was certainly not Lillian's.

EIGHTEEN

"Holy—This can't be real!" Al Harmon stared in open mouthed astonishment at the splendor of the room. "So this is old Vanderleigh's private collection! I would never have believed it!" In the unrealistically bright light of the vault I was struck once more by the dramatic appearance of this man. That hard angular face was unchanged, no softness about it at all, and the mouth was still thin and harsh. His shining silver hair shone brilliantly, contrasting too sharply with his darkly tanned skin. The result was theatrical, bordering on the grotesque.

"So what happened here? What happened to him?" he asked, walking toward Jonathan. His look was idle curiosity, no pity or compassion for this man purported to be his friend. He avoided touching Jonathan, as though he were protecting his blue linen pants and soft white kidskin loafers from some disagreeable stain. As he leaned closer for a better look, I glimpsed the slight movement of several gold chains in the curly chest hair exposed by his low buttoned navy silk shirt. That glint of gold polished off his narcissistic appearance. "I asked how this happened," he demanded again, his voice sharp now, like a courtroom inquisitor.

"It was an accident," I mumbled in a barely audible reply, feeling defensive, frightened and unsure of what to expect from this callous dandy.

"An accident!" He laughed. "A bejewelled golden dagger plunged deep into a man's back by accident? Highly unlikely young lady! You'd better think of another story. That one just won't wash!"

He began to walk slowly around the room, touching several gold items as though he wanted to assure himself that what he saw was real, not a dreamer's vision. His tanned hand softly caressed the hanging Aubusson tapestry in such an awed way that I felt sure he was yielding it one of the highest compliments he would ever pay a work of art.

"Al? Is that you?" Jonathan stirred painfully and turned unfocused eyes toward his friend. He licked small bubbles of blood tinged saliva from his dry lips as he tried to say more.

"It's okay, Jon," soothed the silverhaired hawk, without even turning around to look at Jonathan. "I'm here now. Everything's going to be all right." He lifted a Faberge jeweled box toward the light, watching the stones shine and sparkle as he turned it slowly in his hand.

Jonathan tried to push himself up on one arm to look at him. "Al, you don't un—understand. I need your help to move my collection. It's on—only a matter of time before other people come. I'll p-p-pay anything if you'll just take it on your ship!"

"Sure Jon, sure. Just rest easy, I'll get the boys in

here now and have them start loading up."

Jonathan lowered himself to the floor again. "Tell them to be careful, Al. I can never sell anything, not even one small piece of this, bu—but I'll more than repay you for your help."

"Sure, Jon. Just lie there and try to relax, now." He called from the door, "Rick, you wait in here. Jed, bring the men, all of them, immediately! Tell them to bring all the blankets they can carry. We have a quick loading job to do." An armed man, tall, thin and slightly balding, stepped in and stood by the door. He relaxed his arms across his chest, cocking a revolver at the ready in his right hand.

Al walked toward Catherine. She curled up into an even tighter ball, her arms hugging her knees as though she wanted to disappear, her head kept down to avoid his eyes. She visibly shrank further into the corner with each step he took toward her. She cried out as he grabbed her by the arm and pulled her roughly toward him. "Please!" She seemed to beg him to be more gentle as she looked at him with eyes full of fear. He understood and put his hands to her throat. He began to stroke her neck in a terrifyingly gentle way as he stared directly into her eyes. The look of fear melted from her face and one of absolute loathing took its place.

"You were so quiet over there in that corner we barely knew you were in the room—and look at what you were hiding!" He grasped the chain of the ruby and pulled it quickly, snapping the clasp. Catherine shuddered partly in pain, and partly in relief as he turned from her. She fell to the floor sobbing and rubbing the back of her neck.

He opened the lid of a small gold chest, revealing a diamond, certainly the largest I have ever seen, snuggled into a base of royal blue velvet. He shoved the ruby pendant into the chest with the diamond, closed the lid and thrust the box under his arm. He continued around the room, choosing small valuable pieces he could easily carry.

Jonathan stirred again, his eyes stared wildly around the room, then focused on me. His face was grossly contorted with pain. "Maggie, I tried to make it up to you. I tried to take care of you. I gave you a job, took you into my home—even though I suspected you were working with that Interpol man. I was going to take care of you forever! I hadn't wanted—Mat was my friend; why couldn't he understand?" I felt nothing. There was not one word I could say. He tried to move once more. I made no effort to help him. "Where's Al?"

"Your friend is gathering up your best pieces, Jonathan. I don't know whether he's helping you, or whether he's just helping himself to your priceless collection. If you manage to come through this all right, you'll just avoid the responsibility of your actions one more time."

"You're wrong, Maggie, so wrong about me. It was my responsibility to my heritage. It was what I had to do; what I was born to do. I had no choice."

"No material thing is worth the price you've put on this collection, Jonathan. Three lives have been lost and now two more will undoubtedly follow, Catherine's and mine. Perhaps your own will make it six, Jonathan. Nothing, absolutely nothing, is worth that price!"

Footsteps sounded in the tunnel again. This time it was an army; at least ten men entered the room carrying several blankets each. They too stopped briefly to stare at the riches displayed in the room. "Get a move on, men. Carry all you can to the ship. Use blankets and protect the things as much as you can. Carry them carefully," he looked toward Jonathan, "very carefully. We can't take the time to pack anything, but nothing must be damaged, nothing at all." I watched with a kind of perverse satisfaction as the men, not quite as carefully as they should, gathered up piece after piece of the priceless hoard and carried it through the tunnel. Jonathan's eyes darted wildly from brute to brute; the perspiration poured from his face. His gasps for air became labored as the seconds passed.

Al held one side of the tapestry as one of his men held the other and a third loosened the catches on the wall. I knew from the look in Al's eyes that Jonathan would never own these things again, certainly not that tapestry. He helped roll the ancient handiwork and watched as two men hoisted it to their shoulders. In the midst of all this activity my mind recalled colorful visions of pirates and their booty from my childhood adventure stories. These men didn't need a golden earring through one ear or a patch over a mangled eye to appear villainous; even I would know better than to cross any one of them.

Al continued to direct his men with the loading. "Forget that heavy stone plaque," he said, indicating the Asparas on the wall near the door. "It's too heavy and will take up too much room." I watched in amazement as piece after piece of the hideous hoard vanished from the space it had occupied for decades.

They opened the large carved teak trunk and, after searching the briefcase and the duffle bag, threw them to the floor. Catherine ran to retrieve Gordon's case. "Rick, get her on board now," Al said, pointing to Catherine. Rick kicked the briefcase back into a corner and reached for her. She did not fight, but moved with surprising docility toward the door. I could hear the soft padding of her bare feet mingling with the hard leather of Rick's boots as they vanished into the tunnel.

As the last piece was being carried away, Al came toward me with an oily smile. "Well, well, I do believe it's your turn now." He grabbed my arm and pulled me toward the door. There was no way to fight back now, and no Bruce to come to the rescue.

"What about Jonathan?" I asked, trying to delay. "He'll need to be carried on a stretcher."

"Well, you see, Maggie, he loved this room so much, we're going to lock it up and leave him here; no one will know about it for centuries. When and if they do find his bones, they will think he was merely placed in some kind of fancy burial pit."

Jonathan screamed in fear, "No, Al! No! Don't leave me! Take me, please! I must—I must protect my collection!"

"You have no more collection, Vanderleigh. What I take is mine! Consider that knife in your back a gift from me." He shoved me toward the tunnel. "Move on!" he said roughly. Jonathan's terrified screams followed us. I knew his imagination was presenting horrible visions to him, but I also knew Lillian would find him there. If he lived until then, he would probably fare better than either Catherine or I from this ordeal.

Once through the tunnel, we reached another room, the storeroom. It was empty now except for three or four large packing cases in one corner and a black motorcycle near the exit. "There's Vanderleigh's old Harley! Imagine a grown man fooling around like that!" Al laughed.

So that was the Harley. The white helmet with its tinted shield hung harmlessly over the handlebars.

Al quickly found a way to close off the panel to the vault. "Once you know something exists, the answer seems obvious. During the many years I've come to this storeroom to load and unload pieces, I never suspected a roomful of treasures could be behind that wall. I guess I just figured old Jonathan kept the few things he had at his house." Al malevolently shoved the sliding panel closed with a jolting force. "May you rest in peace, Jonathan Vanderleigh!" We walked through another door. I was amazed to see that we were now inside the boat house. Once closed, there was no indication that a panel to the left of the fireplace had ever been moved. "We have no more time to waste. Let's get on that ship and get out of here!"

In the brief period we were on the dock, I could see nothing but the quiet landscape of lush foliaged trees and rippling water. Where was Lillian? How would she even know what had happened to us? I reached to my neck, broke the chain holding my silver medallion, and let it fall. I looked back as we boarded the ship and saw it shining on the wooden dock.

Once we were on his luxurious sailing yacht, Al shoved me into a small cabin where I found Catherine curled up on the bed. When I sat down beside her, she looked up at me with dull eyes staring from a bruised and tear stained face. "That man is a sadistic beast, Maggie. I don't care for my own life, but I don't think either of us will get out of this alive. They are certain to kill us and no one even knows where we are."

"You're probably right, Catherine, but I'm not ready to fold up just yet. Can you swim if we need to?"

"It's been a long time, Maggie, but I'm willing to try." She laughed bitterly. "Anything from here on has to be up."

I lay back on the bunk exhausted from the emotional strain. I wondered how much strength I would be able to muster myself in case we did get a chance to swim for it. Well, there was no one to depend on now. It was entirely up to me. Catherine would barely be able to help herself.

In this cabin we could not hear a sound from above, only the piercing screams of the gulls and the breaking of the waves against the hull as it cut through the water. To onlookers on the river's bank we would appear to be on a pleasure cruise. Just a wealthy boatowner taking a few friends out to sea on his wood-masted sailing yacht. I could be sure of one thing, though, anyone who saw this ship would be sure to remember it. Sailing yachts this large and luxurious cannot be commonplace anywhere, even on the Navesink.

I sat up on the bunk and I looked out the brass rimmed window. I could see the river bank easily. It didn't seem very far away at all, perhaps a mile or so. I felt sure we had a better chance of surviving in the water than if we stayed on this boat.

"Where do you think they're taking us, Maggie?" asked Catherine, her eyes becoming alert again as though the moment's rest had restored some of her strength.

"If they plan to take us back to land at all, I imagine it will be where he docks this ship."

The door of the cabin opened abruptly and Al entered the room. I sat up quickly, but Catherine again avoided his eyes and curled into the corner of the bunk. He looked at her and laughed. I'll never forget that cruel sound, not loud, but menacing in its tone.

"Well girls, we'd like you to feel right at home here, for a little while anyway. I don't want to hold out any false hopes for your safety, though, for as soon as we get through the channel and into the ocean, we'll wave goodbye to you. No one else knew of Jonathan's secret hoard, I know that for a fact, so once you're gone, we're home free."

I closed my eyes. I could visualize myself blindfolded in a maze with many false openings. I kept running from one opening to the next trying to find a way out, trying to find an answer. My vision was interrupted by a voice; its sentence half over before I realized that the voice was my own. I had said, "I'm surprised you left behind such a valuable part of the treasure of Jaeger's Nest."

"What did you say? We took everything of significant value that we could carry!"

"Don't you realize what was missing? I'm sure you must have helped Jonathan get it."

Al looked at me, his eyes narrowed suspiciously. "Get what? I didn't miss anything."

"Did he ever get pieces for his collection through other sources? Oh, that's a silly question! I guess he must have since you don't seem to know about it."

"Why are you so certain I don't? You haven't even told me what it is."

"Did you check those crates in the storeroom?" He momentarily looked struck dumb, then quickly recovered. I knew then that he had not, and had assumed that they wouldn't be in the storeroom if their contents were of great value. "If you had known, you wouldn't have left the crate. It was extremely valuable."

"That's impossible. I know everything that goes on in this business. There's nothing he could have gotten I wouldn't have heard about."

"Well, I guess I don't know how he got it. Maybe it isn't even authentic after all, but Jonathan certainly seemed to think it was. He considered those pieces a valuable addition to his collection."

He continued to eye me suspiciously, his jaws tight, his eyes intense. "What was it, this valuable thing; what's it supposed to be?"

"I have to admit I didn't get to see it. He had just received it and it was still in the packing crate in the storeroom. He just said it was a chest filled with gold ornaments, some jewel encrusted."

"I don't know anything about it," he said haughtily. "It must not be of any significance." He shifted his gaze from me to the window as though whatever he could see on the riverbank was much more interesting than anything I had to reveal.

I sat quietly, saying nothing.

He suddenly turned toward me, those hawkish eyes flashing anger. "There's absolutely no truth to what you say. There's no way he could have gotten anything like that without my hearing about it!"

"From Tillya Tepe." The name rolled off my tongue as though I said it every day of my life.

"Tillya who?"

"Tillya Tepe. From Afghanistan. A new archeological find."

"Archeological?" His face showed shock. I knew I had hit an exposed nerve.

"Oh, I see! He mainly worked with you on art pieces. This was an archeological dig, a very important one. The work in these pieces is reported to show that the area was influenced by many cultures, Indian, Mongolian, even Roman."

"Skip the history! I don't know anything about all that!"

"It was a Russian dig."

"I said forget the his—say, how could Jonathan get it if it was under Russian protection?"

"He was very secretive about it. He wouldn't tell me how it was accomplished. He just told me that they didn't know it was missing yet. He called it his greatest triumph." Al looked directly at me—through me would better describe it. My back felt as though it had been grasped by millions of icy tentacles. I had to make him believe me or we would surely die. He had to turn back toward the estate again.

There was no sound in the cabin. Catherine seemed frozen in silence. Nothing moved. The only sound was the rhythmic creaking of the wooden mast and the sound of the water hitting the wooden hull of the ship. My chest was aflame with pain, crying for much more air than I could quietly give it. I had to keep my breathing shallow. I couldn't afford to make one sound which would betray me. My story had to work. He had to believe me!

He stared at me with half a smile, half a smirk, his eyes unwavering from my face. "Tell me about the pieces, Maggie."

The words poured out. "As I said, I didn't see them. Jonathan said they were almost pure gold, at least seventy per cent . . . the Soviets feel it may be equivalent to Tutankhamun's treasure."

He laughed then, that cruel menacing laugh which made my flesh creep with dread. "You're lying, Maggie."

"How could it possibly make any difference? Why should I bother to lie? You're going to kill us anyway; nothing I've told you would affect that! I was just surprised to see that you left the crate behind."

He rose from the bed and walked toward the door, then turned to look at me once more. I tried to think of anything, anything other than my fear that he would know I was lying.

"Nice try, girl. Nice try, but it won't do you or your weepy friend there any good."

NINETEEN

He left, closing the door firmly behind him. I sat on the bunk in a hopeless daze. I had failed. I dropped my head to the pillow, wanting to bury my face and cry like a frightened child, but I was spent; the tears refused to come. I moved my hand to cover Catherine's and whispered, "I'm so sorry. It just didn't work. He didn't believe me." She quietly gave my fingers a reassuring squeeze, then looked up and pressed her index finger to her lips in the age old "Sh-h-h" sign. Her eyes shifted toward the door as she tried to signal that Al might still be listening. I nodded silently that I understood, but I was certain that no one could hear our whispers over the sounds of the ship and the sea.

Catherine raised to her knees and looked out the small brass rimmed window over her bunk. She clasped her arms tightly around her legs and rested her chin on her knees. It was so like her to assume that childish pose, but there had been nothing childlike about her attack on Jonathan. That was adult and straight from the jungle. She had acted, though, and that was more than I could say I had done. She drew strength from the depths of the rage and fury she had felt at learning Jonathan had killed Gordon, leaving her to believe the lie that her husband had deserted her for Anne. Now she had spent that energy of hate and was a child again. Her face suddenly came alive. Without making a sound, she grabbed my arm and forcefully pulled me to the window. In a restrained, but joyous whisper, she said, "He's turning, Maggie! He's turning the ship around! You did it!"

She was right. We could tell by the banks and the relation to the other boats on the river that the ship was making a wide arc now and would soon be turned back toward Jaeger's Nest. "We have to find a way to get off this ship and swim to shore as soon as we're close enough to try it."

"I know you're right, Maggie. I just don't know if I'm that strong a swimmer. It's been so long and I've so abused this tired old body of mine."

"I guess you could say I'm more afraid not to try it, Catherine."

"Are you sure you can swim that well? It's further than it looks to the bank and I'm not at all sure how strong the current is, or which direction it's flowing, or anything. . . ." She was frightened. Her hands were curled into tight little fists. "Oh, Maggie, I'm not afraid to die, not afraid at all—as long as it doesn't hurt!"

I put my arm around her shoulder to help relieve some of her fear. "You won't die, Catherine, and neither will I. You must admit you've never heard me brag about my ability to do anything before, but if there's one thing in this world I know I can do, it's swim! It just doesn't matter about current, or direction of flow, I can do it. I'm perfectly at home in the water. I've been swimming since I learned to crawl! Now, are you game?" She shook her heard from side to side, not really saying no, just showing how hopeless she felt. We sat on the bunk and watched silently as the boat continued its turn in the river. I just couldn't believe it had worked. I couldn't believe he had fallen for my story of the Afghanistan treasure. There was such an archelogical dig, of course; Bruce had told me about it, but as far as I knew Jonathan had no knowledge of it at all and he certainly didn't have the pieces.

Without realizing it, I had been unconsciously running my fingers over the heavy brass rim of the window. I suddenly became aware of the window as an opening, not just a clear thing to look through. "Catherine! This opens onto the deck. If we could get out through here, maybe we could make it over the side before they caught us. We'd certainly have to move fast though!"

She laughed bitterly. "Not me, Maggie. You, maybe, but not me. It's been over five years since I could have wriggled through that small space." She was right, of course, I might be able to make it, but it would be a tight squeeze for her. In fact I had to admit there was no way she could make it through at all. We'd have to find another way.

Catherine inched toward the door and quietly tried the knob. It revolved easily in her hand. She cracked the door just enough to make sure there was nothing holding it, then turned to make sure I had seen that it opened. I felt a little silly. "It hadn't occurred to me to try the door, I was so certain he had locked it!"

"I listened for the click as he left, but none came. He's pretty sure of himself I guess."

I would never underestimate her again. "Sure that we can't leave, you mean. I hope we prove him wrong. I wonder what our chances are of just walking out that door and diving over the side?" The expression in Catherine's eyes as she visualized herself doing just that action made it clear to me that she might well freeze and be unable to hit the water when our chance did come. "We can't hesitate, Catherine. We have to dive out as far from the boat as possible and keep under for as long as our lungs will allow. We'll have to swim underwater away from the boat and toward the shore."

"I'm really afraid, Maggie. I can't deny that, but I'll try. I do feel you should go first, though. You have a better chance of making it than I do."

"It might not work that way, Catherine. Whenever our chance comes, we have to take it quickly, no matter who must go first. We'll both make it that way!" I tried to smile reassuringly. "You'll just have to dive in and swim toward the bank, staying under water as long as you possibly can. Once we get some distance between us and the ship, I can help you make it in."

"At least the light will be in our favor." She was trying to be positive. "The sun's setting now. It will be harder to see anything in the water at dusk."

We both jumped like a shot when the door opened suddenly behind us. We turned to find Al standing in the doorway, one hand on the knob, the other braced against the jamb. "Well ladies, I'm glad to see you've decided to relax and enjoy the trip."

Catherine's reply was bitter. "Under different circumstances, I think we'd enjoy it more."

"Unfortunately true." His tone became more forceful, "I want you both topside now—let's just say I'd like the pleasure of your company." I realized company was not what he had in mind, but once on deck I knew we would have a better chance to get away. I glanced at Catherine. She nodded imperceptibly as though she too had thought of this.

Anyone who valued art would have looked at the jumble of pieces piled into the main salon of the ship with dismay. "You aren't treating these works with the respect they deserve."

His grin was menacing. "Time was of the essence, as you well know." He unrolled the tapestry on the floor. There wasn't enough space to open it completely, but its magnificence was undeniable. "What do you know about this piece?" He again touched the beautiful handiwork carefully, almost lovingly. I could not understand how someone could value this outstanding work of art so highly, yet consider human life with so little regard.

"I have little knowledge of Western art; my education was in the Far East. It's Aubusson, Eighteenth Century, but I don't know its history."

He gently began to roll it up again. "Well, no matter. I know experts in all fields. By the way, I'm sure you can see that we're going back to get those pieces you told me about." He turned sharply toward me. His eyes were flaming probes, glowing as though hot coals burned at their depths. "Time is running short so I want you to tell me exactly which crate it's in. One of my men will go in alone to get it."

My mind was racing. I was grasping for time to think, but the forcefulness of his eyes had thrown my thoughts into disarray and I felt confused. "No! I mean two should go! From what Jonathan said, it's too heavy for one."

He waved his arm in an impatient gesture. "All right, two. Now which crate?"

I tried to concentrate on the big empty room. "It's one of those crates in the corner of the storeroom. I don't know which one. As I said, I never saw the collection; Jonathan just told me it was there. Since he referred to it as a chest of gold ornaments, I assumed it would be in one crate. You might want to check all of them just to make sure you have it all." My legs were shaking from the tension. I pushed my heels hard against the floor to gain control.

He dropped his eyes from me in a gesture of annoyance and concentrated on rolling up the tapestry. My heart was pounding wildly in my ears. Have I ruined everything? Did he see through me this time? Those horrible, horrible little eyes!

Catherine reached over and touched my arm, then turned to look at the water. She mumbled something in a low and barely discernible whisper. I turned too, trying to figure out what she had said. I could see nothing but a few boats near the bank. What was the name of Jonathan's boat? A funny name, the *Bonxie*—Bonxie! That's what she had said! After a few moments I felt in control again. I rose to my feet and walked slowly toward the door of the saloon. "The sunset is beautiful. You don't mind if we watch from the deck do you?"

He replied impatiently, resenting that his attention was distracted from the ruby pendant he had ripped from Catherine's neck. "Just stay away from the rail and out of the way of the crew. Oh, one thing, ladies, I brought you up so you would be visible in case we ran into trouble. Hostages are a form of insurance in my business. Any indication of trouble and we'll tie you both to the railing."

We walked out on the deck. "Are you sure that's the *Bonxie*, Catherine?"

"I'm sure. I've seen it in the distance from the woods." Her voice was stronger; she was obviously feeling more confident now.

"Well, that settles it, we'll have to hit the water. I was hoping we could wait until we were closer to the estate, but that's too much of a risk now. If he recognized it too, he'll turn the ship around, tie us up, and we'll lose our chance. The *Bonxie* is no match for this one in a race."

We stood close together, drawing strength from each other. There were other boats on the water, of course, but for us the *Bonxie* was the only one that mattered. From the corner of my eye I saw Al walking toward us from the main salon of the ship. I moved quickly, placing my body in his path. "Run, Catherine, now!" I was surprised to see her respond immediately and take a running jump over the rail. I turned and shoved Al in the chest with all my strength. He fell backward, tripping on Jonathan's large carved teak trunk. There was no time to lose. Now was the time, there would not be another.

I felt a moment of elation as I dove clear of the ship. An indescribable shock went through my body as I hit the cold water. It was much colder than I had expected, but I was free. Free of the fear which had dominated my mind for the last several hours. I knew I could make it. The streets of these urban jungles may turn me into an incompetent piece of quivering jelly, but this was one element in which I was confident I could function like few other people in the world.

I stayed under for as long as my lungs could take it, slowly expelling the air as I went. My arms and legs stretched and pulled, thrusting me rapidly through the water. My body, crying for air, seemed to take over and say, I can't hold out any longer, surface! Surface or I'll have to give up! I finally rose, broke through, gasped a lungful of air and immediately went back down, still swimming toward the shore. I hadn't seen Catherine; I hadn't seen anything really. Surely she had made it away from the ship. I knew she would be okay if she just stuck to our plan of staying under and heading straight for the river bank.

Just as I broke the water again, rising for another breath of air, I heard a popping noise. Something hit the side of my head with a tremendous force and everything went black. I felt as though I were slowly floating into a big black whirlpool. I must stay awake! Stay awake! If you go to sleep, you'll go right into the whirlpool and never wake up again!

TWENTY

Clear sparkling water swirled around my body. I felt exhilarated and in perfect control. A soft, hauntingly beautiful, melody began to play in the distance; it seemed to call my soul. I was suddenly bathed in a shimmering silver spotlight and my body began to flow with the music in precision water ballet strokes. The water liberated me, a carefree spirit unhampered by gravity. I could move in this pale blue liquid the way I'd always dreamed of floating freely in the air.

It fascinated me that I could also rise above the swirling pool and critique my own performance. I silently applauded the perfect execution of a difficult series of strokes. At the finale, I raised my arms and smiled a tribute to my enraptured audience, then dove to the bottom alone. As I resurfaced to begin the next number, a lone male swimmer approached; then two more, one male, one female, began to move in rapid synchronized strokes toward us. The music for this next number was much faster, more forceful and exciting than the score for my earlier solo.

I realized that the lone male swimmer was Martin Ingram. I was not surprised, but smiled happily, knowing that in this world of dreams, wonderful things can happen. I was struck by the beauty of his strong masculine body; long powerful arms, broad shoulders narrowing to slim hips, and muscular thighs. We met in a choreographed embrace, then swam briefly in a flowing duet of fluid backstrokes, sidestrokes and turns. We then performed an intricate series of moves with fantastic precision, our bodies worked well together, perfect fit, perfect timing. I found it hard to keep in mind that this was merely a theatrical performance and that Martin was only acting his role. The music and my response to him were so overwhelming that I felt compelled to hold myself in constant check lest I reveal my desire and ruin the performance.

The other two swimmers moved in closer now, taking our hands to form a circle. A strikingly beautiful, but very pale, woman took my left hand and then the man took my right. I smiled at the lady feeling overcome with a warmth and love I didn't understand, then turned to acknowledge the other performer and was overjoyed to find that it was my father. He looked at me with understanding and sympathy, then seemed to say, "We'll have this one dance together, then we must go. You and Martin must be on your way too, but we will at least share this one brief moment." The spotlight shone brightly, illuminating only our circle and casting the rest of the pool in darkness. Our intertwined bodies moved round and round in the dance of the silver medallion.

The music stopped abruptly and the water began to drain away. I became anxious, dreading the next step. "Dad, I don't want it to end. Don't go, not now. Please stay just one more moment. I must talk. There are some things I need to know. Please—" Martin began to pull me away. I reached out to hold my father but the distance between us had become too great. Dad embraced the pretty pale lady and they both smiled and waved as Martin drew me further and further away. The water continued to drain, the level became lower and lower. I broke from Martin and began to swim back to my father and mother. I became lost in the dark. They were gone and Martin had not followed me. I was alone.

Maneuvering became increasingly difficult. I made all the motions of swimming, but seemed to get nowhere. It was as though I was no longer in water but immersed in some soft, enveloping, substance. I must surface to breathe. I must interrupt this dream dance to reach the surface for air. I've lost all sense of direction. Where can I break through? My arms and legs were flailing in the gelatinous substance, but I was making no progress. My arm caught something. I couldn't break away. I must surface. I must have air. "Let me go!"

"Maggie, please Maggie! You're okay." Martin had found me!

"But I must have air." I fought him still.

"No, Maggie, you're all right. You're no longer in danger." His voice sounded strained, almost frantic.

A strange voice said, "She thinks she's swimming underwater. She's afraid to breathe."

"Dad?"

"You're not in the water. Now breathe!" It was Bruce.

I shook my head back and forth. "No, must reach the surface!"

"Breathe!" Martin's voice was commanding. A sharp slap stung my cheek. I began to cry, then breathed.

"Oh, Maggie!" I was suddenly in Martin's arms. He held me tightly, protectively. I smiled at him, then closed my eyes and began to drift off again. I could hear muffled voices, first close to me then further away. Martin held my arm, anchoring me to the present. He seemed to be talking to someone else. "Got her just in time . . . while to get her bearings . . . no permanent damage. Bullet impact . . . slight concussion . . . did not penetrate skull."

". . . might have drowned." The other voice broke in: Lizbeth.

"Swam like a fish . . . would have been the ultimate . . . I threw her to those human sharks . . . could have gotten her killed . . . thankful I got there in time. . . ."

I wanted to say something. This drifting sensation was terrible—people discussing me and I can't talk back to them. Phrases, bits and pieces of conversations kept flowing through my mind. I finally found my voice. "What . . . what happened? Why am I here? Where am I?"

Martin asked, "How much can you remember?"

I lay quietly, my head sunk into the soft down pillow, and tried to keep my eyes focused on Martin. I tried to remember coming back to the estate. I let my mind drift, purposely this time. I could see the gates opening in that magical way. I was in my car on the drive. Catherine was sitting beneath a big tree. We walked hand in hand into a cave. I saw jewels, a dagger, Jonathan all in black, Al's silver hair, the ship

. . . Catherine! I spoke, "Where is Catherine?"

Martin looked certain now that I would recover. "She's in the next room, very badly wounded, but showing a surprising will to live. She was shot three times and lost a lot of blood, but Bruce was able to get her out of the water."

"Bruce? He saved Catherine!"

"After you jumped, Harmon saw the Coast Guard closing in from one side and us coming in from the other."

"Coast Guard! I hadn't seen them!"

"Harmon tried to kill you both. Catherine was hit when she surfaced too soon after going in; she could do little to save herself. You were under water most of the time and harder for them to see, but you did manage to get a head wound. The Coast Guard took Harmon and his crew, I went for you, Bruce headed for Catherine, and Lillian stayed on board to guide the *Bonxie*."

"Lillian piloted the *Bonxie?"* I laughed visualizing that.

"After reacting like a mother jaeger to the raid on her nest, all claws and fury, she's watched over you like a gentle mother hen. Nellie's taken full charge of Catherine. It's been pretty hectic around here!"

"Who called you? How did you know to come?"

"Right after you left the museum, I rounded up Mat's editor about those slides. He not only remembered them, he had made prints! I recognized some of the pieces as stolen items known to Interpol and was on my way to the Vanderleigh's to see what more I could learn. When I stopped off at Lizbeth's to call you, I found Bruce there on the phone with

Lillian. She called him right after she had reached the doctor for Jonathan. Bruce and I left immediately. By the time we got there, Lillian had seen Al's ship load up and leave. She had alerted the Coast Guard and was on the *Bonxie* ready to go when we reached the dock. The doctor was too late for Jonathan, but it was a good thing he was there for Catherine. She probably wouldn't have made it if he hadn't been at the dock when we got back. The rest you know about, except that I have something to return to you. If I hadn't known you were in danger before, I certainly knew it when I found this." He held my silver medallion in his hand.

"I had no idea you were within fifty miles, but it was the only thing I had time to do."

I melted again as he looked down at me. "I'm so sorry, Maggie. I encouraged you to go to the Vanderleigh's because I felt you would be safe there, and safe is what I wanted you to be. When I learned Jonathan knew Al Harmon, a known art criminal, I became alarmed. That is why I was in the woods that day. I had searched the estate house for art works while Mrs. Morgan looked for Catherine. I found nothing to make me suspect Vanderleigh. I just didn't know there were so many sharks in the pool. I'll never forgive myself for what you had to go through." He diverted his eyes to our clasped hands. "I couldn't cope with the death of Mat's daughter on my conscience."

My heart died a little at that remark, but I couldn't let go now. I pushed on. "Only because I'm Mat's daughter?" He looked up. My eyes met his with all the strength I could gather. I would not waver. I would not weaken. There would be no doubt in his mind how I felt about him as a man.

First his eyes, then his whole face broke into the most joyful expression I had ever seen. "A little more complicated than that, I'm afraid."

"You! Afraid?" I tried to laugh to show some of the joy I was feeling, but my heart was beating too fast and too loud. I was sure he would hear it. He reached toward me to touch my face. I pulled his hand to my lips, still keeping contact with his laughing eyes. "I'll get better more quickly if you'll come here just a moment."

He leaned over me, his lips touching mine in a teasing, tantalizing way, touching lightly, leaving briefly, then touching lightly again. "I'm not that fragile!" I put my arms around his neck and pulled him closer to me. His kiss became stronger then, searching, demanding.

After a delicious moment he pulled away, then looked down at me. He put his finger softly to my lips. "I insist that you sleep now. When I know for certain that you're rested and fully conscious, we'll pick up this discussion again. I'm not turning my heart over to an incoherent woman who could say something now she may well regret later."

"I won't change, Martin.'

Three months later, during the University's Thanksgiving holiday, Martin held my hand as we waved goodbye to the Vanderleighs and Lizbeth. It was a small wedding, beneath the shelter of the beeches, but more beautiful than I'd ever dreamed it would be. Bruce was best man and Lillian beamed as my maid of honor. Catherine and Nellie cried enough for a whole roomful of people, then everyone showered us with rice as we made our way to Martin's white Porsche.

As we started down the drive, I looked back to wave a final time. My attention was distracted by the movement of a large light colored bird on the roof of the library. He seemed to stand on the tips of his claws and flap both wings. Was he also waving goodbye? Then, briefly, Jaeger's Nest became enshrouded in mist and the old sailing ship obscured the house from view. The vision quickly faded and I saw Lillian, Catherine, and Nellie smiling and waving again. The bird was nowhere to be seen. Oh Maggie of the infinite imagination, will your illusions never cease?

Those magical gates opened for me one more time as I left this fairyland world, much more a woman than when I came. We had all changed, except Martin, and I wouldn't have wanted him any other way.

Bruce was leaving for the Middle East, deeply shocked to learn that Jonathan had killed his mother, but somehow comforted to know that she had not planned to leave him that day. Perhaps he could allow himself to trust and love once the pain had eased.

When she returned from a leisurely world tour, Lillian planned to donate Jaeger's Nest as an art museum and park, provided she could be its director, of course. She had returned the stolen pieces to their owners, including those belonging to the Tibetan temple, and planned to display Adam's remaining treasures in the ball room. The rest of the house would remain the way it always had been since the death of her father. I had felt she would find happiness if she became involved in the world outside Jaeger's Nest, but she found a better way: she invited the world in.

Catherine had opened a small plant and flower shop in Bleekston, called the "Forget-Me-Not-Greenery." She didn't drink anymore—life had become too valuable to her; she didn't want to blur the edges. Nellie worked in the "Greenery" and they shared a small house in the village.

As we rode down the highway, I saw Pete on his tractor, plowing his field. Martin blew the horn and Pete turned to wave as we drove by. Dozens of sea gulls followed in the tractor's wake, swooping periodically to the ground, then flying back up into the air, just as though they were following a fishing boat at sea.

"What are the gulls doing?" I asked.

"The tractor turns the earth, exposing the worms and grubs. The gulls are not as vicious as the jaeger, but they're much more adaptable. They're survivors—they'll soar and glide until they find a way."

"Their screeching always sounds like they're laughing at Man."

"They may well be. Perhaps he doesn't soar enough to satisfy them."

"One more stop before we go home, Martin. I have to say goodbye in a small churchyard."

"From both of us," he said, pulling me closer.